ALWAYS GRAY IN WINTER

BY MARK J. ENGELS

ISBN 978-1-945247-19-4

ALWAYS GRAY IN WINTER

Copyright © 2017 by Mark J. Engels

First Edition, 2017. All rights reserved.

A Thurston Howl Publications Book
Published by Thurston Howl Publications
thurstonhowlpublications.com
Knoxville, TN

jonathan.thurstonhowlpub@gmail.com

Edited by C.L. Methvin
Cover artist: Bone

Printed in the United States of America
10 9 8 7 6 5 4 3 2 1

To my wife: thank you for putting up with me on this emotional roller coaster ride, also known as my creative journey.

To my son: seek your heart's desire, pursue it with everything in you, get back up when you stumble and fall, stay the course until you get where you want to go. I will always believe in you, believe that you too can Do the Hard Thing.

ACKNOWLEDGEMENTS

IT TAKES A VILLAGE TO RAISE A child, so the saying goes. I'm grateful to the community that inspired, supported and encouraged me to bring my "book baby" to term:

Sione Aeschliman	Christ Jesus	Kaelan Rhiwiol
Angela Carina Barry	Stephanie Komasin	Stacy Ricco
C. R. Benson	Judi Lauren	Nate Rotunno
Jason Beymer	Edith Lalonde	Elizabeth Roderick
David & Andrew Block	Jeffrey Layton	John Silah
Brett A. Brooks	Laura Lee	Jordan Skiff
Tami Croft	Alison Luff	Gregory Patrick Smith
Daniel DeFrisco	Katie Mauthe	Daniel Snyder
Amber R. Duell	Tone Milazzo	James Stryker
Amanda Elg	Leslie Miller	Alexandria Sturtz
Penna Fischer	Mike Morrey	Tanna Tan
Almighty God	Sheryl Nantus	Stopher Thomas
Kerri-Leigh Grady	Christopher Nugent	Wesley J. Thomas
M. Crane Hana	Alan Odekirk	Deanna Vaughan
Michelle Hazen	Matt Parmentier	William Alan Webb
Jodi Herlick	Frank Pita	Kristopher Wilson
Sherry Howard	Rachel Rainey	Ken Wolfe

Support from my fellow Allied Authors of Wisconsin members throughout this process has been especially appreciated:

Marilyn Auer	John D. Haefele	Tom Ramirez
Bill Binder	Alexia Lamont	Roberta Bard Ruby
Jody Wallace-Binder	Maureen Mertens	David Michael Williams
Jack Byrne	Fern Ramirez	Stephanie Williams

This book has come a long way since my manuscript first landed in my publisher's slush pile. For that we all have the dedicated and talented crew from Thurston Howl Publications to thank:

Tabs Abernathy	C. L. Methvin	Sherayah Witcher
Sendokidu Adomi	Jonathan Thurston	

To all of these and my new friends among the Furry Writer's Guild, I have only one thing to say:

Thank you.

CHAPTER ONE

THE SPEED AND PRECISION OF the two combatants surpassed even the human race's best martial artists and white arms experts. Time escaped Mawro's notice while he stared up at the flat-panel display above his head, rolling footage from the recent fight on a continuous loop. With a growl he leaned back in his rickety roller chair and tugged at the sides of his goatee with his thumb and forefinger. His stomach gurgled as his mind winnowed down the list of possible explanations for this spectacle. The probable ones no longer seemed so far-fetched.

He followed his operative's movements to and fro beneath the port's artificial daylight. Hana executed one technique after another, monolid eyes trained on her target while her jet-black hair bobbed about. Her fur-covered hands moved so fast that their surveillance equipment managed to capture only an orange-and-white blur. Black stripes on her exposed forearms left artifacts behind, resembling speed lines following Hong Kong Phooey from the Saturday morning cartoons of his childhood. With neither misstep nor hesitation, the young woman landed every strike exactly where he expected. Exactly as he had taught her.

But Mawro found the likeness of Hana's opponent captivating and chilling both at the same time. The other woman's digital camo uniform pattern confirmed what their Revolutionary Guard contact had barked out over their comm link before Mawro cut the connection. She resembled dozens of US Navy sailors guarding the beachhead marking the start of Coalition supply lines into Afghanistan—violating Irani sovereignty all the while. To that extent he agreed with the smug bastard, handpicked from among the Ayatollah's staunchest zealots sent straight from Tehran to "advise" them. But no one had been able to account for the silver-gray fur covering the woman head-to-toe and the long white ruffs lining her neck on either side.

An instant after her utility cap flew off a pair of long, slender ears poked forth from her disheveled, rusty blonde mop. Mawro paused the video and chewed on one knuckle, not wanting to believe what he was seeing. The unmistakable black tufts at her eartips, however, dispelled any hopes of reasonable doubt.

The chair creaked under Mawro's weight while he pushed away from his workstation and got to his feet. He jammed his hands into the pockets of his field uniform trousers and shuffled over to the portraits of a smiling Kim Il-sung and Kim Jong-il bracketing his compartment window. The sun had begun its ascent over the Gulf of Oman's brilliant blue-green waters beyond where the ship's ensign whipped in the wind above the stern.

He glanced up behind him at the clock above the cabin door and scratched at the curly hair above his graying temples. Hardly an hour had passed since their operation had begun. He would have never conceived he and Hana might encounter one of his own kind in such a godforsaken place like Chah Bahar. But now he had. An American at that, half a world away from her home.

Biting at his lip, Mawro returned to his console. The interloper's remarkable physique served as a conduit for raw, unbridled fighting talent. Being her mother's daughter, he would have expected nothing less. He magnified her cat-like face with a flurry of keystrokes and gazed into the slits at the center of her eyes. Past the focused resolve there, he saw the things he had hoped he would never see.

Anger. Pain. Forlornness.

Mawro reached over to one corner of his desk and picked up the small frame containing a battered and weathered family picture. A father and mother stood toe to toe in the center. He sported a bald pate and an orange goatee, beaming toward the photographer with his hands clasped behind his wife's waist. She smiled up at her husband, her arms thrown around his neck. Platinum blonde hair spilled down to the middle of her back. The couple's two teenage children stood next to them, one to a side. On the left, a lean and lanky boy with curly red hair flashed a toothy grin. On the right, a short and wiry wisp of a girl whose red-and-gold hair trailed down each shoulder in a long, thick pigtail. The camera captured her glaring upward, trying to blow her bangs out of her eyes.

By force of will he gazed up at the frozen image on his console. He puffed out his cheeks as he studied the woman's hair, the same color as the girl's from the photo. *Forgive me, Pawly. Who knew we would ever come to this?*

The sound of the door opening gave him a start before the characteristic tinkling of Hana's earrings announced her arrival. "Say Chief Park you meet when I aboard come?"

"Yes, thank you. No witnesses save for . . . her?"

"*Ne, apa!*" Hana replied in her native Korean as she closed the cabin door. Mawro cocked an eyebrow, and her fur-covered ears drew back alongside her head. "As you requesting," she said in Polish, acknowledging his silent reprimand.

She was a mess. Blood stained the orange and white fur on her muzzle and forearms. Hana's battle dress uniform, similar to his own but darker, was patched with dirt. The hand-to-hand melee, explosion and insertion team's hasty retreat left her normally neat and tidy bob sticking out every which way like black straw. She appeared to have come straight from the ship's hold after her crew berthed their go-fast boat. Exactly as he had asked.

Mawro stared at the floor. "How is the captain?"

"Medics on he working. Tough one is. I expect he fine! Brilliant plan, *ne?*"

"NO! If you had both kept to the plan, the Americans would have never spotted you. Didn't I say to leave the theater as soon as you released the gas?" Hana's black-and-white striped tail drooped while Mawro breathed deep. "Look, I know the old man pulled rank after *she* showed up and you had to improvise. But goading the Iranians into detonating the shape charge was a damn fool thing to do, and you know it!"

"But me live to—"

Mawro pulled her into a bear hug and ran his fingers through the fur on the back of her neck. "The Affliction has already taken our families from us, Hana-*ttanim*," he said, staring over her shoulder toward his desktop and the photograph lying face up in its frame. "I couldn't bear to lose you too."

Hana laid her head on his shoulder and hugged him back. "We should check on our comrade," he said after a long moment. "Maybe you should freshen up before we—"

"*Dongji!*" came a man's voice the instant before the compartment door burst open. Hana and Mawro turned to where the away team's boatswain leaned against the jamb, gasping for air. "*Blaznikova-sangjwa! Blaznikova-sangjwa!*"

Her dark-brown eyes went wide an instant before Hana bolted from the cabin. The two men followed, led by her panicked cries reverberating off the passageway walls.

Mawro pushed his way through the bulkhead door. He brought a hand to his eyes for a moment until they adjusted to the harsh glare from the sodium vapor lamps above. The medics' equipment had been strewn about the ship's hold in their frantic bid to stabilize their patient's condition.

He snorted. The old fool had really done it this time.

The medics raced about, working on Blaznikov lying unconscious on the gurney nearby. Their worrisome stink was thick enough to taste. The man's lynx-like face was similar to that of the sailor from the video, but the fur hanging down the sides of his neck was far scragglier. His final instructions before the explosion played over and over in Mawro's mind.

Harm not the Children of Affliction!

Hana stood a respectful distance away near one of the bulkheads and chewed on a chin-length tendril of her hair. She hung her head and sniffled after he walked up and began to rub her shoulders. Grotesque gurgling sounds emanating from the medics' charge punctuated the noisy cadence of their instruments.

"Commander!"

He glanced up and caught sight of the ship's surgeon waving him over. With a pat on Hana's back, he requested she stay put for he would be right back. She nodded. "Blunt force trauma severe to internal organs," he pieced together from the stocky Russian's broken Polish. "Estimate Captain's survival below ten percent."

Mawro stared down at the deckplates beneath his feet. Hana's gambit enabled her and Blaznikov to escape capture, but the blast had taken an enormous toll on his body. The crew aboard *Pe Gae Bong* monitoring their scrubbed offensive reported he had been at the epicenter. His mental calculations led him quickly to believe the shock wave would prove more than his kinsman's aged body could bear, ailuranthrope or not.

The shrill tone from the flatlined ECG snapped Mawro back to the present. Hana grabbed the first medic within her reach and began cursing at him in her mother tongue. Blood trickled down the front of the man's jumpsuit as she sunk her claws deeper into his shoulders with every word. Her native dialect was difficult to follow when she spoke quickly, though he understood enough. If he and his fellow medics failed to revive their leader, she would add them to the body count. Each and every one.

By most gruesome means.

Mawro exchanged looks with the surgeon and approached her side. "Drop him!"

Hana turned and glared at him a moment before her arms went limp. The frightened medic pulled free from her grasp and scampered off. Tears streamed down the sides of her face, leaving damp trails in her cheek fur resembling another pair of stripes. "But Kindred, *apa!* How we Kindred find do?"

He took her in his arms. "I . . . I don't know," he whispered into her ear.

The Russian man drew a hand across his neck to order his medics to stand down. They killed power to the ECG unit and packed up their crash cart. An eerie silence permeated the ship's hold like a damp chill. It was over.

Blaznikov's eyes stared lifeless up at the overhead until the surgeon drew the bed sheet over his fur-covered face. He and one of the medics rolled the gurney into the passageway while the weight of the old man's burden settled upon Mawro's shoulders. The survival of his clan—of his entire race—was now his responsibility.

And his alone.

He could research those dimensions of their Affliction the old man would have never allowed. He could step boldly forward onto a world stage, confident any link to his tumultuous past had died with Blaznikov. The old man had spooked generations of their clansmen into isolation, aided and abetted by the reclusive regime bankrolling their entire operation. No longer would Mawro avoid scrutiny's white hot light like a cockroach scurrying for cover to avoid being crushed underfoot. Nor could he. The Americans would surely seek them out, intent on settling the score.

And Pawly will be with them!

One corner of his mouth slowly turned upward. Now he saw the path by which he could set his clan's course right. By which he could set *everything* right.

He hardened his gaze at the medics and nodded toward the bulkhead door. With ashen faces they made a hasty exit, leaving Mawro and Hana alone in the hold.

CHAPTER TWO

Pawly balanced herself atop the fire escape handrail and stared up into the night sky. The Transamerica Pyramid towered over the thick fog bank enveloping the vacant warehouses and run-down tenements stretching out around her in every direction. She glanced out over the harbor after a ship somewhere out in the soup blew its foghorn. Though radar, GPS, and dynamic positioning instruments had long made their use unnecessary, she knew first hand ship captains from the Great Lakes to the Gulf of Oman were sticklers for tradition. Likewise among her own family of seafarers, especially at Christmastime.

She twiddled at the tuft of fur atop one ear and took in the sight of the Crown Jewel shining brilliantly atop the Pyramid, a grim reminder of the half continent separating her and her loved ones. This year's rapidly approaching holiday marked the first time since Navy boot camp they would have been able to celebrate together like normal people. Lenny had been anxious to meet her family, staunch Blackhawks fans all, surely to talk up his beloved Bruins. Though grateful having been spared any drama after Boston thrashed Chicago in the Stanley Cup playoffs this past summer, her heart ached at the thought of missing them all this Christmas. And for untold more to come.

An approaching vehicle's rumbling engine helped squelch her dark thoughts. Pawly looked down to the alleyway beneath her feet to find a black late-model muscle car rolling toward a sharp corner between two buildings. She tugged at the strap of her bracer covering her watch and set her jaw. Right on time.

The driver stopped short of the turn and killed the lights. Sobs of the girls tied up in the back seat echoed upwards as the driver and his passenger climbed out. One manhandled the girls out of the car while the other yanked a massive cooler free from behind his seat with a grunt. It landed on its side, spilling ice cubes and soda cans all over the pavement at his feet. The man pulled the cooler's false bottom free and tossed one of the sawed-off shotguns to his partner. One by one, the girls emerged from the back seat blindfolded, gagged, and bound. Their captors forced the three of them to sit down on the car's rear bumper dressed in only halter tops, hot pants and stiletto heels. Their long black hair had been pulled into fat pigtails draped behind each shoulder, none could have been a day over fifteen. And they were shivering.

Her fangs bit into the fur below her lower lip. Pawly fell forward and thrust out her legs against the railing. Claws sprouted forth from the tips of her fingers with a flick of each wrist. She dove toward the car and yowled to goad the driver into turning her way. Her claws sank into the skin above the bridge of his nose as she slid across the car's hood on her butt. With a grunt she yanked her hand free, tearing both of the man's eyes free from their sockets. He screamed and crumpled to the pavement, cradling his ruined face, weapon all but forgotten. His partner whirled around with his shotgun in one hand, leaving his chest wide open. Before reaching the wall, Pawly raked the toe claws on both feet across the man's abdomen. She pushed off with her legs and landed past the front bumper. When she spun around, the wide-eyed man stood before her, trembling as he stuffed his entrails back inside him with both hands. Pawly responded to his horrified whimper with but a shrug before he collapsed.

She reached into her pocket and pulled forth a rust-colored handkerchief. Pawly darted her eyes from one dying man to the other to ensure their weapons lay well outside of their reach. Wiping their blood from her fingers and claws, she cocked her head to listen. Only the soft sobbing of the terrified girls, still seated on the car's bumper, remained once their death throes subsided.

Pawly stuffed the handkerchief back into her pocket and stepped over to the girl nearest her. She drew one claw across the rope binding the first girl's wrists together, tearing it neatly in two. Likewise, she cut through the cloth holding the gag in the girl's mouth. After wrapping the teen's trembling wrist in a piece of the tattered fabric, Pawly gently guided her toward the alley entrance. "No, no. Not yet," she said in Korean as the girl reached up toward the blindfold tied behind her head. "Can't risk anyone seeing what I look like if I'm to help more kids like you."

The girl nodded and said nothing while Pawly removed her companion's bindings and gags. "You three take one another's hands and follow me," she continued in a firm tone and lined the girls up shoulder-to-shoulder next to the alley wall, careful not to let any part of her fur brush against their bare skin. "When I tell you, pull off your blindfolds and run as fast as you can away from the car toward the street. Turn right and go two blocks until you see a big neon cross on the left above a shelter for runaways and battered women. Someone who speaks your language will get you a shower, a hot meal and a place to sleep. You'll be safe there until the staffers can get you back to your—"

"What the fuck? We had a deal!"

"Yeah, bring back those girls!"

Pawly whirled around and saw another pair of thugs running toward them from up the alley through the fog, each toting a shotgun. She glanced down at her watch and swore. Rival gang's mooks arriving for their pickup just *had* to be early, didn't they?

The men raised their shotguns and took aim at Pawly. She glimpsed her reflection in the car's rear window and turned back toward the deserted street beyond the alley. Though the fog had grown thicker as the night drew on, it didn't camouflage the gray-and-white fur covering her face and hands nearly as much as she would have liked. But there was no time left.

"Now run! And don't look back!"

Pawly turned and broke into a sprint. She leapt for the fire escape an instant before the first shotgun blast. Two more followed, eliciting screams from the teens as they ran. But each pinged harmlessly off metal and brick behind the spot Pawly had occupied an instant before. In three bounds she was on top of them. She dove for the pavement with arm outstretched to catch one of the thugs in his neck. Gritting her teeth, she rolled through her rough landing and jumped back up to find the man thrashing about on the now-slippery concrete all around him. He grabbed at his neck with both hands to staunch a torrent of blood gushing from where his Adam's apple had been.

The second man let go of his shotgun and raised his trembling hands in front of him. Pawly closed the distance between them in a heartbeat's time and kicked the weapon beneath a nearby dumpster. She pursed her lips and fixed him with a searing glare while he dropped to his knees, begging for his life in both Korean and English. "I don't play around," she whispered in kind. "Especially not with rats like you."

Pawly slashed upwards and flipped the man head over heels into the trash cans behind him. With a pained shriek he clutched his now useless arm to his chest. Blood from gashes cut clean to the bone quickly stained his white shirt red. She stepped calmly over to him and hauled him up by the knot in his tie, bringing his nose to within an inch of her muzzle. A smile spread across her face after glancing down at a dark area growing around the groin of the man's light-colored khakis.

She snarled and bore her fangs. "You chose to pimp little girls," she said in even tones, brandishing the claws on her free hand beside his face where she knew he could see them. "Now I'll choose which part of you to slice off and cram down your . . ."

Fssst!

Her ears pricked up as she glanced around, trying to pinpoint from where the familiar sound had come. *Thirty yards away—no, twenty-five—shit! He's within range already!*

Her brain barely registered the shrill hiss approaching before instinct took over. Pawly dropped to all fours and pulled the man's body over hers the instant before the fleshy *thwack*. The man moaned and clutched at the blaze orange fletchings of a tranquilizer dart sticking out of his back, unable to reach them.

The muscles in her neck tensed. She knew the company he kept would have used bullets if he had been their intended target. Someone wanted her. Alive.

She tossed him into the side of a dumpster and ran. After nearly a year, hostiles from Chah Bahar had at last tracked her down. Pawly had dreaded this very moment since stepping aboard the train at Union Station. Would she ever be able to return to Chicago and her family without fearing for their safety? And would she—*could* she—ever tell Lenny the truth about them? The truth about her?

Catch me if you can, motherfuckers!

She sprang atop a trash compactor after another brightly colored tranquilizer whizzed past her ear. It struck the utility pole behind her as she landed in a wide stance.

That's two.

The tip of her short tail swished back and forth while she scanned the rooftops. Pawly lunged to her right and glimpsed another dart fly over her shoulder.

Three!

She executed a tuck and roll and coiled into a crouch. With a grunt she jumped for the rungs of the fire escape ladder stowed overhead. It couldn't end like this. Not before she saw Lenny again. Not before he *knew*.

One hand over the other, she made her way along, eyes focused on the roofline opposite her. Perhaps her pursuers had done her a favor by tracking her down. She had run to protect her family, run to protect that idiot Lenny from himself. Forcing herself to satiate her bloodlust month in and month out had done little to make her longing for him every moment in between any less unbearable. But now she would fight, fight them head-on. She wouldn't have to run anymore.

Fssst!

Pawly grinned. With the shooter's second adjustment of his weapon's firing pressure, she could now confirm both bearing and range. Only twenty yards away . . .

There!

She made out a trace of movement in the murky darkness. Though the fog would have surely obscured the shooter's ducking behind the parapet high above the alley opposite her from a normal human, it was all she needed. By muscle memory developed from years of her mother's punishing instruction, she swung up onto the landing and launched herself toward the next flight. On the other side of the alley.

Pawly shot out her legs as she drew near the fire escape and pushed off. She flew back in the direction she had jumped from, now two stories higher. Over her shoulder she glimpsed a hooded man stand and take aim. She slapped the bottom of the platform with her hands to thrust herself downward, landing on all fours on the grating below. A dart lodged itself into the wooden window casing above.

Four down. She sniffed at the air, recognizing a familiar stink. *Worry. One to go, I'll bet!*

She hopped atop the third story railing with an indulgent chuckle and leapt across the alley. Body tight to the building beneath the shooter's position, her wannabe captor would have to lean over the edge to sight her in. That would take time, more than she planned to give him. This would end. Now.

Pawly took hold of the railing and twirled her body upward to close the gap between them. The weathered metal creaked in response to her acrobatics before it failed spectacularly with a tinny *ping*. She cursed and catapulted herself away from the wall with her legs. Forty feet above ground and losing altitude fast. Along with her confidence.

"Everyone around you will die, Pawlina," boomed Blaznikov's mocking voice in her mind. It had done so every day since her and Lenny's detachment was torn to shreds. "Just like when you—"

A sharp pain accompanied the explosion from her memory while the sniper's dart bored into the base of her neck. Pawly bit her lip to stifle a squeal and reached out toward a downspout an instant too late. She slammed headlong into the brick wall and tumbled like a rag doll to the concrete below. Cats fled in all directions from the stand of trash cans she upended, screeching in anger at having had their late-night snack so rudely interrupted.

With a long groan she propped herself up to one knee. The damned streetlight at the end of the alley taunted her, spinning no matter how much she squinted.

No! Gotta keep moving! Mom, Tommy . . . Lenny . . .

Her arms hung from her torso as if made of lead. Gravity soon won out, and Pawly collapsed into a pile of refuse face first. She turned her head and smirked toward the hissing cat closest to her. "Thorry ta crath yer party, cuth," she said before passing out.

CHAPTER THREE

TOP CLICKED OFF HIS SIDEARM'S safety and plucked a pebble from the chest pocket of his fatigues. He tossed it toward where the dark-haired man lay slumped up against the alleyway wall, chin to his chest. The pebble skittered across the pavement and bounced off the man's thigh. No response. Nothing.

He slid his night-vision goggles onto his forehead and crouched. Careful to step toe first, Top approached, inspecting for movement as he drew close— any movement at all. Observing none, he slid his forearm up underneath the man's chin and jabbed a finger toward the man's neck to check his pulse. His hand plunged into the flesh beneath the man's jaw with a sickening *schlorp*.

Top started. His elbow drew up beneath the man's chin and lifted his head, allowing him to glimpse the guy's face. Or, rather, what was left of it. He glanced down around the crook of his arm toward the man's chest. Skin and muscle sliced clean off the bone dangled from his pectoral tendons.

With a gulp he stood and trotted over to their car. He holstered his weapon and drew out a trash bag from a pouch on his web belt. After shaking the bag open, Top thrust his left hand inside and carefully worked off his blood-soaked fingerless glove through the plastic with his right. Once finished, he unzipped another pouch and pulled out a packet of antiseptic wipes. He opened the car door and knelt down to rest his elbows on the seat while he tore open the wipes and began to dab at the blood on his fingers. Several times he held his hand up to the car's dome light until his brown skin no longer showed any trace of the man's blood. Once satisfied he was no longer in imminent danger from bloodborne pathogens, he dropped the wipes into the bag and stuffed it back into his pouch.

Top finished his inspection by giving the car a quick walk-around. On the pavement between the alley wall and the right front tire, he found the man's partner lying face down in a puddle of his own blood. He tapped at what appeared to be a freshly-made salami with the toe of his boot, as if it were tied up in string and ready to hang behind a deli counter. That's when he realized the slick steaming mass lying beside the man's body was his colon.

He shook his head and sighed, his breath forming a cloud in the chilly air. No amount of SEAL training could have prepared anyone for carnage like this. But the gruesome sights he and his fellow sailors had seen charging ashore at Chah Bahar had done just that. Like everyone who had survived that horrible night, those were memories he would just as soon as forget.

Dear God, Pawly—what the hell have you become? Or was this your true nature all along?

Top trotted up the alley, certain Pawly had neutralized the remaining punks in similar fashion. He had heard their panicked screams crescendo and die out one after another from his rooftop perch. Stepping over the body of the man whose throat had been torn out confirmed his suspicions. Had Pawly been raging even as he drew a bead on her? Would he have shared this guy's fate if his last remaining dart had missed its mark?

A smile came to his face as he approached where the final man lay with his back on the pavement. No blood, nothing torn open, nothing missing. Pawly's family would certainly want to know more about what she'd been doing in the months since she ran off. If he lived, this punk might be easily swayed to furnish details. But his face fell as he turned the man over on his stomach. Hopes of a successful interrogation evaporated upon seeing the tranquilizer dart sticking out of the man's shoulder. Jabbing his finger into the skin above the man's carotid artery confirmed what Top already knew.

Able to do no more for the man, he pulled the dart from his back. Top glanced up and found another one sticking out of a utility pole about fifteen feet away. Both he tucked into the small tin canister full of tissue paper clipped to his web belt. Making his way toward the street, he came upon one more lying half underneath an overfilled dumpster.

Beyond lay Pawly, face down atop a trash heap. After tugging the dart from the base of her neck and stowing it, Top wrapped a handful of her uniform around his fist. With a grunt he pulled her free and gently laid her down on the concrete. He knelt beside her to search for a pulse within the thick white fur along either side of her neck. In a moment he found one, rapid and weak.

Top reached around behind for a pouch on the back of his web belt and fished out a little glass bottle filled with clear liquid. After giving it a good shake, he reached into his pouch for a syringe and held the needle cover with his teeth. He stuck its rubber bung and drew the plunger about three-quarters back, emptying the bottle just under halfway. With Pawly's sleeve rolled almost up to her shoulder, he felt along her light gray pelt to the middle of her bicep. He injected her in the center of a dark spot there and stuck the needle back into its cap. Then he poked the needle back in his pouch, peeked at the chronometer on his wrist and checked her pulse once more.

A smile spread across his face as he smoothed her rusty blonde bangs away from her eyes, much longer than he remembered them. Pawly's heart rate was slowing and gaining in strength. She would be fine, at least until his teammates got their hands on her.

"Cat Box, Big Top," he said quietly into the boom mic sprouting downward from his earpiece. "Copy?"

"Big Top, Cat Box, go ahead," came a man's voice in reply.

"Found our lost kitten. Ate up all the mice between the two of us, though."

Silence.

"Cat Box, do you copy?"

"Er, a-firm, Big Top. Retrieve as many darts as possible, especially those coming into contact with secondary subjects. Brain trust believes coroner'll rule cause of death from heroin overdose given the formulation of tranqulizer we used."

Top supposed Chinatown had been spooked enough by the spate of 'Slashing Tiger' incidents in the weeks prior. He scanned the alley above his head and spied the orange fletchings on the last dart sticking out of a wooden window casing. Leaving it behind was risky, but so was dwelling here too long. Besides, he would have sworn it was just another old survey marker had he not known better. A leftover from yet another stalled attempt to repurpose the run-down warehouses all around them.

Their boss would be grateful nevertheless. No 'dead civilian' issues would hang around their necks. Not this time, at least. "Done. Head toward Pier 9 and turn right on Powell as soon as you exit the Broadway Tunnel. Go south a block or so. You'll see us."

"Be advised, Big Top, our rig can negotiate alleyways."

"Negative, Cat Box, no need. I carried men twice as heavy four times as far back in theater. And I want us on the other side of the Central Valley by the time SFPD gets Forensics over here."

"Yeah, suppose we can't shovel the chum overboard for the sharks like before."

"Roger that, Cat Box, so we'll just lie low and wait for you at the curb. Big Top out."

Top scooped up Pawly's limp form into his arms and got to his feet in one smooth motion. "C'mon, sailor. Let's find you some fair winds and following seas for a change."

The doors of the subway car hissed shut after Dory exited the train. The string of silver cars glided away to reveal the sun inching upwards into a blood red sky. He drew forth a pair of sunglasses from a pocket inside his trench coat and placed them on the bridge of his nose. Clouds had greeted him as he peered through the curtains of his hotel room window three hours ago, his first hint of a pre-Christmas snow bearing down on Washington. Now he walked along the deserted platform toward the turnstiles, enjoying the beautiful winter's sunrise.

Through the leafless trees Dory caught sight of the American flag flying at half-staff over the Robert E. Lee Memorial. A sudden chill made him shudder, though he knew air temperature had little to do with it. He poked at the black wireless headset situated in his right ear, fully aware he would be in no shape to tend to business following his visit.

"Call Top."

The simulated female voice repeated his command, and the phone began to ring. "Yes sir?" the man answered in a gravelly baritone.

"I can speak freely as no one is around."

"Sorry, sir, can't say the same," Top said over voices in the background. "We stopped to fuel up and get us some breakfast."

Dory grunted and scratched at the closely-cropped hair above his ear. "You were scheduled to leave the Bay Area over four hours ago. Have you made it to the state line yet?"

"Just. At a truck stop just outside Reno now. Fog was pretty heavy through the Valley, so we had to take it slow."

He swallowed his lips. "How is she?"

"Sleeping like a kitten, sir, no pun intended. I'm told she'll be, uhm . . . *comfortable* until we make Des Moines at least."

A hurried glance at his wristwatch confirmed she had been under for nearly five hours already. According to the mission itinerary that he insisted everyone memorize, she would remain so for another twenty-four as least. "Have there been any complications?"

"Excuse me a moment." The sound of boots clopping across the floor punctuated the muffle of voices until a bell dinged. "Sorry, sir, wanted to put in my food order before I stepped outside," Top said above the low rumble of diesel engines. "Wanted to take all due precaution discussing Agency business, you know. And no, sir, nothing outside of parameters that we're aware of. But we'll keep watching her close even after her 'medication' wears off."

Dory couldn't help but chuckle. His longtime friend-cum-subordinate could always be counted on to follow protocol. "No worries, Commander, though this is a personal call. I have utmost confidence in you and your team, but I—"

"But you wanted to know she was safe, just the same. Right?"

He blew out his breath and pulled at the skin below his chin with his thumb and forefinger, still tender from his morning shave. "You know me too well. Though maybe I *do* worry too much."

"I suppose that's your job, sir. But I'm surprised you aren't worried more about that former Agency guy at Homeland Security sniffing around our brain trust. Interservice rivalry is the last thing we need right now."

"*El Toro* is smart, dedicated and as bull-headed as his call sign suggests. Which makes him delightfully predictable, I might add," Dory said and hefted the strap of his travel bag higher on his shoulder. "All traits that ought to prove useful soon enough."

"I know, I know—'keep friends close and enemies closer'. Still sounds to me like you're letting the camel get his nose in under the tent, sir."

"A calculated risk. We will draw attention to ourselves if we keep avoiding him. Though I did want to mention I made some calls after reading today's morning brief from DHS." Dory's face spread into a wicked grin. "Imminent staffing changes in Chicago are about to make things a lot more, shall we say, interesting."

"Sir, I *really* hate it when you say things like that."

Dory laughed. "Now who's worrying too much? Go grab your grub, sailor. Greasy eggs and bacon taste best when they're hot."

"Aye, Cap'n, that they do. So, when shall we rendezvous?"

"I have to meet the Director and brief the Joint Chiefs before I head to National for my flight. Red sky this morning, so plans might change if the snow blows in before then. I'll text you when I touch down at O'Hare so we can . . ."

Dory raised his voice to be heard over the jet engines screaming overhead to no avail. He followed the plane with his eyes until it disappeared behind the craggy brown treeline beyond the rows of tombstones.

"Sir, are you at Arlington?"

So the penny drops, eh, Topper my boy?

"Yeah. I . . .I wanted Barry to hear from me first that his little girl is coming home. He would . . . he would want to—"

"I know, sir, I'd do the same. Please, pay my respects. Will await your text."

The line went dead.

Dory removed his earpiece and tucked it into the pocket of his trench coat. He strode through the Memorial Gate, shoulders squared. As he walked he couldn't help but notice how quiet the park was, though being early morning on a weekday during winter probably had much to do with it. Suited him quite fine that, gatekeeper aside, he had seen no one else since stepping off the train.

The sights and sounds of birds twittering among the barren trees along the path did little to ward off the sad and bitter memories. He steeled his mind for the coming battle versus his own emotions, one he was destined to lose.

Just like every other time he came here.

CHAPTER FOUR

ONE ADVANTAGE TO WORKING at night was getting a jump on the rest of the world. Top enjoyed his "beer thirty" rolling around before most people even woke up. He had passed the morning shift opening up the travel plaza's small deli on his way to the diner and after breakfast dropped in to restock their A-rations. Limiting their stops to fuel only would help make up some time.

He stacked the dozen freshly-made hoagies two high on a shelf inside the rig's small refrigerator. With a whistle Top pulled plastic containers full of antipasto pasta and couscous salad from a cardboard box jammed between their small dinette table and the back of one of its vinyl-covered bench seats. Taking a hoagie and a Coke back out after stowing the rest gave him just enough room to close the door.

Top stepped over to where Tommy sat behind his console and plunked the sandwich and soda down next to him. "Oh! Thanks, skipper," the younger man said as he adjusted his rimless glasses.

The big RV lumbered forward out of the parking lot while Top crossed his arms and leaned atop a server cabinet. "You're not foolin' anyone with this workaholic routine, you know. Just because we're on a tight schedule doesn't mean you can't take time to roll in and out of the places we stop," he replied while eyeing the back of Tommy's wheelchair.

"It's okay, really." Tommy popped open his soda and tore into the sandwich. "Stuie asked me to get some footage of the eclipse for her science class," he said between bites.

"Don't play coy, shipmate. Stepped out onto the ramp beside the restaurant to take a call from Dory shortly after I headed inside. Sure looked like you had Pawly's vitals up on your screens to me."

Tommy looked down at the floor between his feet and rubbed at his wavy auburn hair with his free hand. "I . . . I just wanted to make sure she's—"

"Look, spacing out while I was extracting her was bad enough. I need you to stay frosty until we reach Chicago in case one of Blaznikov's people tries to tail us. Keep your mind on your job and let the rest of us do ours. Deal?"

Tommy set down the sandwich on his console and scratched at his chest through his muscle shirt.

"Stow it with the hand-wringing. Your sister'll be just fine," Top said after an uneasy silence. "So, did you get any good pictures of the eclipse?"

"Didn't want to take my eyes off the road in the fog. I did manage to snap a few with our roof-cam after the sky cleared up east of the Valley," Tommy said with a shrug. "Image quality kinda sucked, though. Got some better ones while we were parked."

Top followed his finger toward a time-lapse montage of brilliant lunar images rolling across his screens. Richer and darker hues replaced pale blue gray until the entire face of the moon was as red as blood. He stood transfixed at the sight, remembering that moment nearly a decade before when so much in their lives had changed.

"So then, Dad—what does this slimeball *here* go and do?" Barry nodded in Top's direction and squinted up at Dory. "He foists a basket case like me off on his fiancée!"

Top felt heat rise up to his ears as his two friends doubled over with laughter. "Now wait a minute, sir." He waved his open palms in front of him and glared down to where Barry sat in his wheelchair hugging his knees. "Your son isn't telling the whole story."

"Sorry I missed the punch line!" their server said and reached in between them. The buxom young woman made too quick her work of exchanging their empty beer bottles for full ones, careful not to let the flowy silk scarves attached to her arm and bicep touch the tabletop. "Be right back with the ladies' drinks. Little more *oomph* for your next round of wings?"

All of them had travelled to Green Bay to watch Barry's kids Pawly and Tommy play in the Ambassador's Invitational high school ice hockey tournament. Barry having been released from Bethesda the day before they left, Top had planned to go easy on the post-game festivities. But the rash of shit Barry dished out now and all afternoon at the Resch Center suggested his shipmate was back to his old self. The kid gloves were off.

"Sure. Bring us the Meltdown Wings this time."

The sheer fabric covering their server's face could hardly conceal her toothy grin. "Your wish is my command, master!" she said and dashed off toward the kitchen.

Top eyed his companions as their laughing jag tapered off. Both Dory's face and Barry's entire head were beet red. "I'll have you know Sheila volunteered."

"Well, Topper, maybe she's just grateful," Dory said once he could breathe again and jabbed his thumb in Barry's direction. "From what I read in your mission brief, you only made it back for the wedding at all because of my boy here."

"Well yeah, Dad, but Sheila's been fawning all over me since we left Norfolk!" Barry crossed his arms and stared up at the ceiling. "It's . . . you know. Awkward."

"I can see your beautiful bride being a little, er . . . peeved at your being doted on by some gorgeous . . ." Dory did a double take toward another of the bar's servers dressed in a naughty nurse uniform. Top chuckled at the fortunate coincidence. The wait staff had gone all out in observance of Halloween night.

Barry pulled at the tip of his auburn mustache. "Well, you guys know how Alex is. She may *say* she's not jealous, but we all know—ow!"

His pale blonde accoster reached over Barry's lap and dropped her purse onto the seat next to Dory. "Don't flatter yourself," Alex said and hopped over the back of their seat. Barry rubbed at the back of his bald pate while she wriggled her lithesome body in beside his wheelchair. "But for her nursing you, you big baby, I'd've left you to cry alongside the road an hour out of Norfolk!" she went on while Sheila shuffled over to Top's side of the table and slid up next to him. "Though keep her from Lover Boy there too long, she just might tie you to the bed. Oh, wait, you'd like that, wouldn't you?"

Sheila pursed her lips as Top took her hand, a faint pink hue coming to her golden-brown cheeks. "Warned you years ago about that sassy neighbor girl, now didn't I?" Dory said with a laugh while their server set out two more drinks at the end of their table.

Alex snorted. "He listens to me about as well, you know. Though we can all conclude where Pawly gets her hard head from."

Barry cocked an eyebrow at her. "You're one to talk. And I wouldn't put it past *your* dad to have stayed up this late just waiting to hear from us, either. Isn't it almost two o'clock in the morning over in Poland right now?"

"Three, actually. But Papa was glad to hear Pawly and Tommy's teams made it to the championship round tomorrow just the same. He had just gotten back from Warsaw and was on his way to bed."

Barry's eyes went wide. "I'd have thought Niko'd have made it back to Szczecin hours ago! Why was he on the road this time of night? Ritzi and your mom OK?"

Alex shrugged. "They're fine, but their flight to O'Hare left five hours late.

Papa hung around until they boarded and only then headed home. I know my brother, though—he'll surely wait until tomorrow morning sometime before driving up here. *Eomeonim* will be bummed missing the twins' games, but she and Ritzi ought to get here in plenty of time for the team party afterward."

Barry looked Top's way as his mouth drew into a small, sad smile. "And none of us would be here at all if not for you, my man. Thank you."

Though Top found no small irony in his friend's words he harbored his own selfish reasons for coming. The leaves had turned later than usual this year, affording Top one last chance this season to treat Sheila to the famous Door County fall colors. Tomorrow after the kids' games, everyone would head to Dory's cabin in the old lighthouse on Pilot Island. With luck they would arrive in time for the two of them to take in the spectacular sunset together along the rocky beach.

In time a heaping plateful of Meltdown Wings arrived for anyone who dared try them. "I hear scouts from all the good schools come to these," Top said while he paused to lick his fingers. "Looks to me like Pawly and Tommy brought their A-game for sure."

Alex nodded and sipped at her drink. "And a good thing, too. An athletic scholarship would go a long way toward funding the twins' college."

Barry wiped sauce from his hands and patted at his wife's thigh. "Don't forget, dear. They both qualify for the NROTC program."

Top watched Alex look down and begin to study the floor. Even after maxing out their pay grade for Special Warfare Operators, Barry had confided paying for his children's education would be a stretch. Especially given he and his wife had very different ideas how best to remedy their little problem.

Although a decent hockey player and diligent in his martial arts training, Tommy's gifts manifested in his love for computers and anything analytical or mathematical. Those traits would certainly make him an attractive candidate for an NROTC scholarship in one or another of the engineering sciences. By contrast, Pawly was no scholar, instead being a natural athlete and a gifted martial artist. Though she did well enough in school, "applied physics" to her meant practicing her slap shot. Tasks not involving body movement were a challenge for her and a source of frustration for everyone else.

The rest of their dinner passed pleasantly enough. Alex had let Pawly and Tommy leave to eat with their friends only after promising they would arrive back no later than nine o'clock. Mom's champions needed their sleep, she had reminded them.

At the end of the evening, Dory insisted he pick up the tab. Their server promptly disappeared with his credit card but took her time returning. The elder man drummed his fingers on their table while Sheila and Top both stood and stretched. Top spied the bathrooms beyond the host station and glanced up to the clock above the bar. Five minutes to nine. "C'mon, shipmate," he said and stepped toward Barry's chair. "Let's get you to the head before we shove off."

"Yeah, I suppose that one-holer aboard the rig will be pretty busy once the girls—"

"Tommy?" came Alex's panicked voice.

Top followed her gaze over to where a winded young man with wavy red hair leaned against the empty high table across from them. Dirt and bruises covered his face.

Dory slid out of the booth before Alex could climb over top of him. She took Tommy's face in her hands and examined his head and neck. "Are you hurt? What happened? Where is your sister?"

"Restaurant was closing, Mom, so they asked us to use the back door. Bobcats jumped us in the alley on our way here."

Top's brow knit. Wasn't "Bobcats" the name of the local boys' team Tommy's squad would face off with tomorrow?

Tommy rubbed at a spot on the back of his head. "Must not've wanted me or Nikky taking the ice, I guess."

Alex's lips drew into a thin line. "Is Dominik all right? Do the Raczkas know what happened?"

"Yeah, he ran to the pizza joint down the street after his folks. But then . . . then Pawly . . . she . . ."

Tommy turned away from her and buried his face in his hands. Alex stepped up beside her son and put an arm around his trembling shoulder. "What, dear? You can tell me," she said in a husky voice. "Everything's going to be okay."

"No, Mom! *Nothing's* gonna be okay. Ever again!"

Tears ran down the sides of his face while she took a step back, open hands drawn to her shoulders. Eyes all around stared at them both filled with fearful shock, morbid curiosity, or garden-variety irritation. The boy pulled Alex's ear close and whispered something. Top's brows shot up as the color drained from her face. Her mouth hung open while she turned and met Barry's wide-eyed gaze. Dread welled up within him during their silent exchange, as if invoking a long-developed plan for contingencies so terrifying that neither dared to speak of them.

"I . . . we . . . we will need your help, Christopher," Alex said, her voice eerily calm.

Top blinked and shook his head. "Er . . . okay. Sure." *Help with what, exactly?*

She stepped over to Sheila and laid a hand on her shoulder. "And I need you to take care of Barry. Please?"

"Do as she says, love," Top said softly and drew his fiancée into his arms.

Sheila pressed her lips to his. "Duty calls, it seems," she whispered and stepped up behind Barry. "Guess your head call will have to wait until we're underway, sailor.

Barry sighed and stared up into Alex's face, his good eye misted over. "Be . . . be careful, dear."

"I will. Love you." She leaned over and kissed him.

"Love you, too," he said after their lips parted.

Alex straightened and nodded toward Top. "Ready, Christopher?"

"As I'll ever be. Let's roll."

CHAPTER FIVE

T OP NEARLY LOST SIGHT OF ALEX after cutting through traffic on the busy street in front of Cheese Cake Heaven. When he at last caught her up, she was down on all fours staring at scratch marks in the dirty concrete behind the restaurant. "What're you—?"

Alex lifted up her head and sniffed at the air. "This way!" she said after she jumped up and sprinted back the way they came. Top resolved to revamp his PT routine while she pulled away from him, her long blonde hair whipping behind her like a flag. Barry had introduced his wife to him during their first week of BUD/S training. She had long been a prize-winning martial artist and credited her arduous conditioning regimen for restoring her thin and wiry build after her pregnancy. And now, once again, he found his gaze drawn toward its obvious and enticing results.

Focus on the mission, dumbass! Not the caboose on your best friend's girl!

By the time he came to the next street, Alex was already halfway across. Top bolted through oncoming traffic and glimpsed her duck into an alley down the block. After rounding the corner he managed to skid to a stop before knocking her over. He stood agape behind her outstretched arm while his mind struggled to process what his eyes were seeing.

Four boys in their late teens clung to each other with wide eyes. They cowered at the end of the blind alley cornered by some . . . *thing* covered in gray fur except for the bushy white hair framing its face and black tufts atop its narrow ears. A short tail with an inky black tip poked out between the low waistline of a pair of torn blue jeans and the tattered hem of a Washington Capitals hockey sweater.

Just like the ones Pawly had been wearing.

He gulped. Damned thing stood about as tall as her, too. Blonde hair pulled into thick pigtails over each shoulder did little to dispel the horrific notion, no matter how much the sight of long black claws where her fingernails should be made him want to.

Alex regarded him with a wan smile and pushed her handbag into his chest. "I'll take it from here. Go back to the RV and give this to Barry. He and Dory will know what to do."

Top clutched her bag and glanced down at the stubby fighting sticks she held one to a hand, Korean *tahn bong* if he remembered right. With a cry Alex tossed one up into the air in front of her and sprang. She caught the stick and landed next to Pawly's doppelganger. It started and drew back, giving her an opening. She vaulted over its shoulder and struck at the creature's head. After landing in a crouch, Alex popped back up into her fighting stance. The thing shook its head and turned to face them, affording Top a frightening view of its wild, feral eyes and muzzle filled with sharp teeth.

Regardless of what Alex had in mind, they needed to get these kids out of here. The threat of jail time could hardly scare these juvenile delinquents any more shitless. "Hey! Walk along the wall over here toward me. Nice and easy, one at a time."

One of the boys nodded. He took slow and careful steps in Top's direction before the creature turned and slashed at him. The boy shrieked and curled up into a ball on the pavement. Alex used the unexpected distraction to strike again, landing her weapons perfectly on a pair of choice pressure points—almost. Though her blows failed to immobilize the thing, they must have hurt like hell. It howled and swiped its claws at Alex again. The kids broke cover and sprinted toward Top before blowing right past. "Wait! Where d'ya think you're—"

The creature bowled him over with force enough to knock the wind out of him. He coughed and gagged and rolled up onto his side while Alex crouched next to him, her eyes never leaving the thing's back. "You all right?"

"I'll . . . ngh!" Top hefted himself to one knee. "I'll live."

Alex snarled and took off in a run. "Get back to the RV now, Christopher—got me?" she shouted back over her shoulder. "This is out of your league!"

He said nothing and set off after her, bristling at her assertion. During training he and Barry both had dealt with polar bears and mountain lions, all bigger and faster than this thing. So what if it happened to walk upright on two legs? It had just caught him off guard, that's all. He wouldn't let that happen again.

Which was why his cache of weapons and survival gear stowed aboard the RV was vital. He fished his cell phone from of his pocket and poked in

Sheila's speed dial number. She would need to pick him up if they were to help Alex at all.

"Where the hell *are* you two? Why didn't you—?"

A blood-curdling yowl from down the darkened alleyway drowned out Sheila's voice. Top turned in time to glimpse the thing silhouetted by the blood red moon in mid-air above the wooden fence behind him. He gasped as a second furred creature hopped the fence giving chase to the first, a *tahn bong* in each hand.

Top reached the curb two minutes later. Hands on his knees, he hunched forward and scanned the darkened street left and right. It was deserted, thankfully, save for the RV roaring toward him. He tugged at the latch handle and scrambled up the steps while the big vehicle skidded to a stop. "Which way?" Sheila hollered from the driver's seat as he slammed the door shut.

He collapsed onto the end of the sofa opposite Tommy. "Gimme . . . a . . . moment," Top said after enough of his wind returned.

"Where's Mom?"

"Ran off, son." He handed Tommy his mother's handbag. "She said to give this to your dad."

Barry reached over and snatched the bag from his son's grasp. With eyes wide he dumped its contents all over the dinette table and rifled through her things. "Alex . . . she has her transponder on her!"

"Then we can track her." Dory reached under the seat for his briefcase and took out a notebook computer. He powered it up and plugged a dongle from his briefcase's inside pocket into one of its USB ports. "Tommy, I'll need you to monitor this for me," he said while the GPS tracking application launched. "Just tell us which direction the screen indicates we need to head in and how far."

The boy took a seat in the booth next to Barry. "S-sure." Dory set the makeshift console down on the table's edge and turned it to face his grandson. "Wow, wicked!" Tommy said and pulled the computer to him.

Top shook his head. "So where is Pawly?"

"Alex must be pursuing her. She should be able to follow until Pawly's Rage expends itself."

His jaw went slack. "You . . . you mean that . . . that *thing* really is—"

"Oh, shit." Barry looked up at Dory over his wife's belongings strewn across the table top. His lower lip quivered. "Alex took her darts."

"Darts? What darts?"

"Throwing darts, Topper," Dory said. "They're coated with a substance which is supposed to act like a tranquilizer, though we don't know exactly how they'll work on Pawly. They may be ineffective."

"But Dad, they could also make her—"

"Alex *knows*, son. I'm certain she'll use them only as a last resort," Dory said and shot Barry a stern look. "So let's get on with finding them so she need not. Are you getting a signal, Tommy?"

"A-firm, G-man! From the east . . . er, I mean, to our right."

Dory clapped his hands and rubbed them together. "Alex activating her transmitter is a good sign. She must have Pawly in sight and wants us to follow her."

Top slammed his palms down atop the table, making Alex's things jump. "Now wait one damn minute! I have weapons and gear aboard we can use to find them if someone would just tell me what in the *fuck* is going—"

"ENOUGH!" Barry raised his hand to Top's face. "'In times of war or uncertainty' . . ."

". . . 'my loyalty to Country and Team is beyond reproach,'" Top finished. "All right, Bearcat, fine. But you'd better debrief me on all this crazy shit. Soon."

"Sure thing, brother. But right now, this is Dad's show."

Top blew out his breath. "Babe," he called to Sheila, "do as the man says."

Dory stepped to the front and sat down in the passenger seat beside her. "I stop in Green Bay for supplies whenever I head to the cabin. Tommy and I should be able to help you follow Alex's trail, Ms. Turner. Now, please drive straight ahead to the next intersection and make a right."

She put the vehicle in gear and tromped the accelerator. "R-right, Mister K!"

The color of the moon paled to burnt orange by the time the RV rumbled up to the deserted demolition site. Alex's electronic trail led them to where Dory said a shopping mall had recently been torn down about a mile from the Resch Center. Anyone not focused on the street ahead or a console did likewise to try and spot either mother or daughter. Top held his hands to the sides of his face and peered out a window.

"I see them! There!"

He turned to where Dory pointed out the window opposite the rig from him. Sheila must have also seen; a moment later, she pulled the big vehicle to the curb and killed the engine. She threw off her seat belt and sprang to Top's side in time to witness Alex stepping out into the light cast from the luminary overhead.

Top and Sheila drew in their breath. Though dressed in the same clothes from dinner, their friend's features now matched those of the beast-girl she had fought before. The very one she now carried in her arms. Unconscious.

Pawly. Her daughter, Pawly.

Lucky fucking break it's Halloween!

Top laughed to spite himself while Alex approached the RV. Her canines had grown into wicked-looking fangs, giving her something of an overbite. Short-lived levity gave way to the horrifying realization he'd watched his best friend's wife and daughter turn into cats. Fucking *cats*. Was he experiencing the time-delayed effects of some enemy hallucinogenic agent deployed during his last mission with Barry?

Sheila wagged her finger toward the window. "Sweet Jesus, Christopher ... they're ... they're ..."

Oh, shit. She sees them too.

Top didn't notice his own trembling hand until he slipped his arm around his fiancée's shoulders. "Y-yes ... yes, I can see that," he said while Alex turned and returned her stare through the chain link fence. The thought of a foreign agent spiking their drinks at dinner flew through his mind. Then why wasn't anyone else freaking out? Why wasn't anyone freaking out seeing *him* freak out?

His racing heart sank seeing the pained expression on Alex's face. He sensed not only did she hurt for herself and all her family, but for him and Sheila as well.

For now they knew.

Everyone scrambled out of the vehicle. Top and Dory each took one of Barry's shoulders and helped him down the steps to the ground. Only after they were lined up along the fence did Dory at last ask the question foremost in everyone's mind. "Is ... is she ... ?"

"She should be fine, Dad. I didn't have to use the darts," Alex said in a gravelly voice Top hardly recognized as hers. "Blunt cranial impact trauma was enough, though I'm afraid I'm getting rusty," she said with a nod to Top. "That strike I delivered earlier should have knocked Pawly out right then and there."

Dory clicked his tongue. "Not our immediate concern, my dear. Now let's get the hell out of here before she comes to."

Top squinted into the darkness behind her. "What about the boys she was chasing?"

Alex opened her mouth to say something before a loud crash echoed across the site. Everyone heard barking and snarling and panicked cries from among the piles of rubble. She turned back to Top and flashed a smile. "I needed to attend Pawly, so I found them some new playmates. And I hear *that* bitch, you know ... fights like a girl."

Top brought a palm to his face. Hearing fabric flap above his head, he looked back up to find Alex no longer there. Something went *thump* on his other side, making him flinch. Alex now stood beside him, having vaulted the fence carrying Pawly's weight without even so much as a running start. And she wasn't even breathing hard.

"We don't know what those boys will say or whether anyone will actually believe them," Dory said with a wave toward Alex and Pawly. "Topper, can we trouble you and Sheila to run us up to Door County yet tonight? We need to get over to Pilot Island a little earlier than we had planned."

"Big Top, Tomcat! Copy?"

Top blinked and turned toward the sound of Tommy's voice. The young man sat with his butt pulled up onto the arm of his wheelchair, waving his hands in the air before Top's face. "Worried me, skipper, you running deep like that," he said and dropped back into his seat. "Any more out of it and you'd've fallen over!"

"Just thinking about, you know . . . things." Like Alex ripping the cords from the RV's window blinds to hogtie Pawly for the drive north from Green Bay to Gills Rock. Like Dory and Barry screaming at Alex's brother in Polish, tag teaming him with their cell phones. Like Sheila arguing they wait until morning to swab down the RV while Dory's decommissioned Coast Guard motor lifeboat throttled up into the choppy Lake Michigan surf. Because he could have no longer told himself this all had been a bad dream once he saw the mess in the daylight.

Tommy tossed his crushed soda can into the trash can across the room near the wheelchair lift. "So it's not just me dragging ass, huh? Maybe you ought to get some rest, too." He yawned and wheeled himself over to one of the rig's comfy chairs while his workstation powered down.

Top strode over to the pocket door at the rear of the vehicle and slid it open. The dimmed monitor screens inside the compact bedroom gave enough light for him to make out Pawly's long ears and muzzle. A sheet covered her body from the neck down except for where her hands and feet were lashed tight to the bedposts. Her family had trussed her up the same way that fateful night, concealed beneath wool blankets and bound fast to the towing rails atop the aft compartment of their runabout.

He closed the door and walked back to the lounge area. Tommy had already propped his feet on the recliner's footrest and sat stuffing a pillow behind his head. "Good call, shipmate," Top said as he plunked down in the chair next to Tommy and began to pull off his boots. "She might be a handful when she wakes up."

CHAPTER SIX

B Y FORCE OF HABIT, DORY'S FEET tread the same circuitous path past the
Tomb of the Unknowns as they did every visit. He drew in a deep breath
upon arriving at the Pavilion and studied the edifice before him. The imposing
concrete structure featured a large slab supported by four massive cylindrical
columns with a waist high flagstone fence all around. Simple, yet solid. Like
he needed to be right now.

Dory approached the Columbarium and turned down the first court to
the left. A moment later, he stopped near the end where it opened to the outside. He turned again and placed a trembling hand on a white marble niche
located third from the top, second from the end.

Dory snuck through the side door of the garage-turned-*dojang* and closed it
quietly behind him. On the rubber tiles with their backs to him knelt half a
dozen teenagers dressed in black *doboks*. They paid close attention to Sunny
and Alex as they demonstrated a simple, yet effective, defense technique.

Alex snarled and grabbed at her mother's collar. With a grin the smaller
tan-skinned woman turned and dropped to the floor. Her foot a mere blur,
she struck the back of her attacker's calf with the ball of her heel. Alex's pale
blonde hair flew as she whirled about and landed flat on her back. She bit her
lip and slapped at the mat while her would-be victim craned her arm behind
her back. Sunny made eye contact with Dory and released her grip. "You practice now. With each other."

Unfazed, his daughter-in-law sprang to her feet. "*Cha Ri-ut! Kyung nae!
She jak!*" she shouted at the kids in Korean. One of the girls elbowed the boy

next to her. Tommy shot Pawly a cross look while she jabbed her thumb in Dory's direction.

"Focus, you two! You can visit with Grandpa D afterward. Got it?"

They both groaned and turned back to their partners. "Yes, Mom."

Sunny walked up to Dory and bowed. *"Dobry wieczór, Pan Teodor."*

"Ahn yeong ha seyo, Seon-yeong-ssi." He returned her respectful gesture before turning to her sparring partner. "And I'm happy to see you too, Alex."

She glared back at him. "Why didn't you call, Dad? *Eomeonim* could have spared me for an hour or two. I could have picked you up at O'Hare!"

"The Blue Line station is only six blocks away, my dear. Besides, I can always use the exercise," he said with a wave of his hand toward the group of teens. "I didn't want to keep you from your growing class either."

The short woman chuckled. "It's quite a thing!" Sunny said and nodded toward her daughter. "I thought she and I and the twins only would train here. For a long time."

"Barry and I caught a lucky break moving back to Jefferson Park in time for St. Connie's spring semester. The other kids are some of Pawly and Tommy's new friends."

"Well, I'm glad for that," Dory said while his eyes darted back and forth across the room. "Say, where is that son of mine anyway?"

Alex glanced around and wrinkled her forehead. "He was here when Ritzi showed up, but they must've gone inside already. They had . . . um, 'family business' to talk about."

Dory stepped through the back door of the old apartment house a moment later and tugged the storm door shut behind him. At the edge of the kitchen floor, he stopped and listened to an argument between two men in a room at the end of the hall. He padded up to the doorway in time to catch the last of their heated exchange.

"Bottom line, Ritzi—what do we do about the twins?"

"Well, the probabilities of desirable outcomes are difficult to predict. We're laboring to minimize deviation from our current set of variables, enabling us to—"

"Little words, if you don't mind!"

A long sigh, heavy with resignation. "Barry, I . . . I don't know."

The sound of a fist pounding a table top caused Dory to wince. "The hell do you mean, you *don't know?*"

"Look, our research funding is in danger of being pulled. We're short on manpower, and expenses are killing us. I'm presenting tonight to a group of investors whose capital influx I hope buys us more time to figure out how—"

"'More time'? Seventeen years of this fucked-up brother-in-law deal hasn't been enough time?"

"Papa and I thought we had this under control since before the twins were even born. We never in a thousand years thought Pawly would—"

"YOU THOUGHT WRONG!"

An uneasy silence passed until one of the men said simply, "Go."

"But Barry, I—"

"Just fucking *go*."

A man in his late thirties ran both hands through his curly brown hair as he stomped through the doorway. He swallowed his lips, causing the short hair of his chin patch to stand straight out. Dory cleared his throat. "Hello, Ritzi."

The man opened his mouth as if to say something, but no words came. None could express the abject helplessness and hopelessness all over his face. Dory winced as the distant memory of one horrible night adrift on the North Sea in a tiny boat came flooding back. Once again he stared into the eyes of a terrified twelve-year-old boy clutching his little sister's unconscious form, ankle-deep in the blood of their kinsmen. Dory reached out to clasp Ritzi's shoulder, but the younger man drew back and hung his head. He shuffled to the front door without a word.

Dory stepped into the room and found Barry seated in an overstuffed chair, face buried in his hands. "I suppose you heard all that."

"Couldn't hardly not, son," he replied while he closed the door behind him. "I'm pretty sure they could hear you clear across the Kennedy."

"He lied to us."

"You mean about the symptoms of the twins' . . . ah, 'condition' . . . manifesting themselves?"

"Ritzi said it'd been taken care of, Dad." Barry looked up to reveal a simple patch over his left eye, having replaced the bandage and shield Dory remembered before leaving for Europe. "Said we didn't need to worry about it. He's been saying that all along, remember?"

"Yes, I do, though I don't think for one minute he was being deceitful or dishonest when he told us all that. Ignorant, maybe; overconfident, perhaps. We're all guilty of that from time to time." Dory took a seat kitty corner from Barry on the end of the sofa. "Best friends from since before you both were in junior high. Yet since Halloween, you haven't spoken to each other except to argue. You don't think he *isn't* burning his candle at both ends for Pawly and Tommy, do you? He loves them almost as much as you and Alex do."

Barry rubbed at his bald head. "I'm . . . I'm having a hard time dealing with this, okay? Doing what I do, if something's wrong, you, well . . . you know, just go *fix* it!"

"Or blow it up."

"Yeah, well . . . I still wish Papa Niko were here. He'd figure out what to do."

"I do too, son. He and Ritzi could work this thing out here together much faster. Part of this trip was to help get him back into the country, but we're still—"

"Yeah, yeah, yeah . . . 'doing the best you can, right?'" Barry sighed and stared down at the floor. "Sorry. I . . . I didn't mean to snap at you. I'm just worried, you know . . . for Alex and the twins."

"Their conditions are all stable for the moment, praise be. Nat and Annie both helped Ritzi see to that, remember?"

Barry slumped back into the chair. "It's not only their physical health that concerns me, Dad. Pawly and Tommy love Alex's father as much as you and miss him terribly. Sure he feels the same way."

"Wounds from the scandal involving Alex's early treatments run deep. Getting him home might take months. Years, even."

"Yeah, if he's allowed back into the country at all."

Dory rubbed at his temples. "You needn't be so hard on Ritzi in the meantime. On my way through Szczecin this last trip, Niko showed me his notes going back to before the twins were born. Suffice to say, he was as shocked as we were when he first found out."

Barry turned away and stared out the picture window. "We're both pretty excited about my new billet."

"So am I, now that all of you are back in the old neighborhood. In light of your, uhm . . . limitation, I guess you needed one."

"Well, Mama Sunny's been training me how to defend my blind side while the kids are at school and Alex is sleeping. And my doctor told me yesterday my eye socket was healed enough to fit a prosthesis. Before I report for duty, he says I'll look like nothing ever happened."

"Who pulled those strings, anyway? Topper?"

"Nah. His dad."

Dory whistled. "Saving the life of Vice Admiral Biggs' only son was a smart career move, I'd say."

"Ah, Top would have done the same for me," Barry said with a wave of his hand. "Not going to play the Power Ball anymore, though. Whatever luck I had's been used up two or three times by now."

"Never hurts having friends in high places when you need a favor, son. Especially when the Director of Naval Intelligence gets into his head he owes *you* one."

Barry's face broke into a puckish grin. "Knew the detailer wouldn't call to cuss me out this time as I filled out my dream sheet. What a feeling!"

"So, when's your first day at 'Great Mistakes'?"

"Captain called me on the phone yesterday to set up an appointment day after tomorrow," Barry said while he stood and stretched. "He wants me to supplement their existing PT program with martial arts empty-hand and weapons training. Recruits'll be better equipped to handle hostile vessel boarding scenarios when they go to sea."

Dory got to his feet and joined Barry by the window. "I suppose you'll have to get used to being called 'Chief' then."

"Been in the Navy nearly half my life now, Dad. I think I will just fine."

"The twins seem to be adjusting well enough."

"Well, they were pretty broke up leaving their friends in Norfolk. Their teams were both strong contenders for the playoffs again."

"Have they been fitting in all right here?"

"Nat and Annie got them back on the ice quick in the Northside youth league. Helps the kids of our old classmates from St. Connie's are introducing them around."

"Must have been some of their new friends I saw in the *dojang* tonight before I came into the house."

"We're both proud of those two, making the best of it," Barry said with a quaver in his voice. "Though we told 'em if you guys are gonna help with . . . well, you know . . . we had to live close by." He glanced down and picked up a large manila file folder on top of one of the end tables. "Aw, hell, Ritzi went and left this here. I think he needed it for his presentation tonight."

Dory held out his hand. "Here, give it to me. I'll call him and find out where he's—whoa!"

Barry slumped forward an instant before he snapped his head back upright. The folder slipped from his grasp, sending its contents skittering across the hardwood floor.

"Are . . . are you okay?"

"I'll be fine," he said and brushed Dory's hand from his shoulder. "Sometimes I get dizzy standing up after sitting for too long."

"Relax. Let me gather this stuff up for you."

Barry knelt down to the floor next to Dory and shuffled a handful of papers into a neat pile. "Ah, geez, Dad, I'm not an invalid. Docs think it's an aftereffect of the meds I was on while my eye socket healed. They said it might take—hey, wait!" He snatched a sheet of paper from his father's hand and screwed up his face.

"What're you doing?"

Barry glared at the bust of a man pictured on the investor profile sheet. "Dad, that's *him*."

"That's him who?"

"The son-of-a-bitch who fragged me and my team, that's who!" he said and handed back the paper. "The guy calling the shots aboard the oil platform when we were—"

"Whoa, hey now, those N2 types would shit kittens if they ever found out you were talking about . . ."

Dory's mouth fell open. The picture showed a man in his mid-to-late fifties with a full head of graying brown hair parted down the middle. A long scraggly beard gave the man a curious yet chilling resemblance to an older Rasputin. He shoved the sheet back into its folder and stomped toward the door.

If the fucking shoe fits, eh, Blaznikov?

"What, Dad? Just who in the hell is that guy?"

Dory held a fist to the bridge of his nose and shook his head. "I'll tell you right after I find Ritzi and beat some sense into his thick—"

The door flew open as he reached for the handle. There stood Tommy leaning against the jamb, horror plain in his wide eyes. "Mom . . . just . . . collapsed. *Halmeonim* . . . called 911 . . . but Pawly is . . ."

The boy's voice grew faint after Dory pushed his way past with Barry right behind him. They bolted from the house, nearly ripping the storm door off its hinges. He crossed himself as they crunched through the snow-covered backyard toward the garage.

An approaching siren wailed in the distance.

Vision blurred already by tears, Dory pulled off his sunglasses and jammed them into the pocket of his trench coat. After wiping at his eyes with his thumb and forefinger, the crisp black characters chiseled into the pristine marble came back into focus.

✝

BERNARDYN O
KATCZYNSKI
SOC USN
1969 2006

"Topper and his team found your little girl, Barry. She's coming home at last, but . . . but I suppose you already knew that."

He growled and slammed his fist against the cold plaque. "All that son-of-a-bitch said would happen to Pawly—I won't allow it! And *we* have the MGS back, son. Niko certainly will help Nat find a way now to—"

The report of rifles cut him off. Dory turned to his right toward the rows of grave markers visible through the open portico. In the distance, a color guard held the Stars and Stripes taut near a group of mourners huddled around a casket. Seven uniformed men stood, weapons pointed skyward, and fired again. And again. A lone bugler coaxed reverent, mournful sounds from his instrument, imparting honor and respect for service to a grateful country in ways words never would.

Dory fell to his knees and wept.

CHAPTER SEVEN

LENNY SIGHED AND STEERED THE white SUV onto the on ramp of the Ronald Reagan Tollway. And the day had gotten off to such a great start, too.

Right after roll call, he collected his winnings from the office pool accompanied by groans from his coworkers. He took no small pleasure prophesying to the despondent Blackhawks fans his Bruins would surely dominate *this* year's playoffs as well. Captain told him shortly afterward orders had come through for his permanent change of station to Boston. The two-week countdown would commence once Cap signed the papers this afternoon. He longed for simple pleasures left behind after enlisting in the Coast Guard nearly eight years ago. Like an entire postseason of face-offs at The Garden, for example, seated at center ice beside his father and brother-in-law.

"Nothing's going to spoil my good mood!" he remembered proclaiming to Mueller on his way out to sight in his new service piece over lunch. Right before Captain collared him. *Me and my big mouth.*

One of the junior officers had been rushed to the emergency room overnight. Orders straight from Washington required Marine Safety Unit Chicago to continue supporting the intradepartmental effort. He was current on his vessel boarding and inspection reports and had handed off his pending investigations just that morning. Cap seized upon the opportunity for Lenny to stand in until the regular guy returned. With his name at the bottom of the roster, the stricken young man had drawn the assignment no one else wanted—working with the obnoxious son-of-a-bitch from DHS in the passenger seat.

"Okay, now this part is important. Pay attention, *gringuito*." The man glanced down at his clipboard through a pair of reading glasses perched on the end of his nose. "What we're concerned about here is proliferation of specialized equipment used for microbiological R&D work."

Lenny shot a sidelong glance toward his new and, he hoped, *very* temporary partner.

"I read the brief, Special Agent Latharo. This MGS thingy disappeared. So what?" he said with a wave of his hand while the SUV blew past the I-PASS tag reader. "The US trades with China by the boatload. Shipments get lost every day of the week. Consignee files a claim, shipper's insurer pays out. Everyone's happy except the accountants at the insurance company, right?"

"Because a missing MGS *is* a BFD, though I would hardly expect you Freshwater Navy clowns to figure that out on your own."

His fingernails dug into the faux leather wrapping around the steering wheel. Two. Fucking. Weeks.

Manuel Latharo took off his glasses and glared at him with penetrating dark eyes. "Let me break it down for you, *gringuito*. 'MGS' is short for 'Morphogenetic Synthesizer'. I know enough about the genetic mutation voodoo behind it to say people who don't *like* us could use it to do bad things *to* us."

"The container carrying the equipment was misrouted from a wharf in Oakland to northern China," Lenny said with a snort. "You think the Chinese would smuggle an army of mutants over here in shipping containers to attack us?"

Latharo's cheeks took on a maroon hue. "Trail goes cold after Ying Kou. Where might this thing end up if it went west to the Xinjiang Uygur? Pakistan? Afghanistan? Who-in-the-fuck-knows-i-stan?" he said in a loud voice. "East to Dandong, maybe? Anyone with a decent arm could skip a flat rock across the Yalu River into North Korea from there!"

"Sounds like an old B-movie script someone dug out of the shit can, if you ask me."

"Humor me, Lieutenant. Consider what North Korea or even Islamic State could do with such a device. The Soviets experimented with various human enhancement technologies right up until the end of the Cold War. Anyone making a play for the MGS may plan to do likewise."

Lenny merged into traffic and pretended not to hear. Scuttlebutt went Latharo served for years with CIA before coming to Homeland Security last year. His tossing around doomsday theories was about as predictable as the proverbial bear shitting in the woods. Ensign Hayes had been thrown into the deep end with this douchebag straight out of the Academy this past spring. No wonder they rushed the young man to the ER last night. Listening to this guy all day every day would make Lenny want to keel over too.

"One of the Agency's outside contractors is a director of and lead researcher for the consignee. This morning, he finally returned my call from several weeks ago. He just got back into town yesterday after doing some hush-hush kind of work none of my friends at CIA will talk about. But he agreed to tell us how this MGS works and what it's used for."

Lenny tuned Latharo out and drove on. He pretended to focus on the traffic signs, looking for the exit which would take them to the city's north side. Rather than sit down together at a college, a hospital, or an office building, Latharo's contact asked they meet him at his home. The guy might be as batshit crazy as the whack job sitting beside him. Why else would Latharo set up an off-the-record meeting under the guise of "orientation?" Plausible deniability, natch.

The scenery took a turn for the familiar when they turned off the Tri-State and onto the inbound Kennedy. Lenny seldom ventured beyond his office west of the city or the ports on the South Side since transferring to Chicago. Not being a Cubs fan, he hardly had occasion to head to the high-rent district. But now, with each successive turn, he found himself retracing his steps from months ago while on a wholly different mission indeed.

He sighed. It was going to be a long afternoon.

Lenny parked their SUV in front of a three-story apartment building. The quaint structure built from tan brick stood in a historically Polish neighborhood on the Far North Side. A man in his mid-thirties wearing jeans and a hoodie trotted out toward the street and swung open the chest-high iron gate. He was average height and wore his long jet black hair behind his head in a neat pony tail. "Special Agent Latharo! So good to see you again."

He walked around the SUV's front to the sidewalk while the man shook his partner's hand. A glint of bright afternoon sun caught his eye, reflected off a large metal box fixed low to the building's exterior. Lenny recognized it as an industrial-sized combination dehumidifier and air purifier like those used aboard merchant ships. Why would a tenement need such a thing? Was the water table here that high? Then again, the neighborhood had been built on swampland almost a century before. He shrugged it off when their host offered his hand and introduced himself simply as "Nat".

"Lieutenant Reintz, meet Doctor Natan Opoworo. While you might not guess from looking at him, he holds advanced degrees in physiological zoology and biochemistry. He's renowned for his pioneering research in cellular transformation."

Lenny squinted at the man's eyes while he showed them inside. "My mother's ancestors hail from all across Eastern Europe. Isn't 'Opoworo' a Slavic name?"

Latharo rolled his eyes. "We're here to talk genetics, *tonto*. Not genealogy."

"My father was born and raised in Poland, but my mother is Korean," Nat said with a shrug. "Guess I popped up out of my mom's end of the gene pool. And I don't mind your new partner asking questions, *Toro*. Isn't that his job?"

"Only until Hayes is back on his feet. Right, short timer?"

Lenny mumbled an answer in the affirmative and rubbed at his temples. The prospect of working this crazy case even that long made his head hurt. Maybe he could manage to get himself put on administrative leave for a while.

The interview had gotten off to a good enough start. Lenny commented on the framed photo of Richard Park hanging prominently on the wall of the doctor's office while he and Latharo took a seat. For the sake of pleasantries, he overlooked the Korean-born NHL player's Pittsburgh Penguins sweater.

Opoworo eagerly shared he and his wife had both been youth hockey coaches for years. And that he had been a starting right wing back in college his last season as an undergrad. When his partner cleared his throat, Lenny knew it was time to get down to business.

Over the next half hour, the dialogue spiraled downward from tolerable to torturous. His partner had impressed him at first with his firm command of the natural sciences. Lataro actually kept up with their host's detailed explanation of the device inside the container that disappeared from Ying Kou. But as time went on, Lenny turned again and again toward the window to seek refuge from the onslaught of indecipherable technobabble. What bits he picked out suggested the MGS was useful to, and usable by, only a handful of scientists in the world specializing in molecular biology—and the thing was wicked expensive.

A loud creak from a roller chair jarred him back to the present. "Come with me, gentlemen." Opoworo stood in front of his desk and waved for them both to follow. "I think a little 'show and tell' might be helpful."

The three men descended a flight of stairs into the basement. Their host opened the door at the bottom and nodded for them to step inside. Lenny had been expecting to walk onto the set of some cheap horror flick—a damp, dank and dimly lit room abounding with sinister-looking equipment and vile-looking specimens. Instead, he saw exotic glassware and a half mile of clear tubing shimmering underneath the bright lights.

Lenny whistled and gazed all around with no clue what much of this stuff actually did, though some of the more pedestrian things he recognized. A pair of desk-top centrifuges here, several beakers of ugly-colored liquid frothing away under a ventilated hood there. That accounted for the ventilation unit he had seen outside earlier. Lataro appeared to take mental notes of the size and scale of the good doctor's "off-site" operation. Maybe Opoworo never showed him around down here before either?

"I shouldn't have to tell you how tight government funding is for esoteric research like what we do," their host said as if somehow reading Lenny's mind.

"DoD and CIA both strictly audit us to ensure work is within the terms of their contracts, so we're not allowed to 'play' at most of our facilities. It's difficult for us to know exactly what direction we want to head when we draft our funding requests for the next budget cycle."

Opoworo stopped with his back to them in front of some kind of indoor rabbit hutch. He lifted the lid and scooped up something with both hands. "Most chickens have two wings, right? That's just how they develop." He turned to show them a full-grown hen with a large bandage wrapped around its back and belly. "Before some hungry coyote broke into our neighbor's coop and attacked his prize layers, so did this gal here. My mother is a veterinarian and managed to save the bird's life."

His partner stooped down to examine the hen's side. "But not its right wing?"

"Exactly. So why not simply coax a chicken's body into growing a new one?"

Latharo's eyes went wide. "Is . . . is that even possible?"

"Should be, or so goes our theory. The body possesses all the genetic information to construct them in the first place, right? My daughter has grown fond of ol' Penny here, our newest test subject." Opoworo opened the hutch and tucked the bird back inside. "She begged me to keep her here instead of with the others at our lab in Des Plaines. We've reverse engineered some of the developmental processes in living tissues there which control . . ."

The doctor kept on while Lenny's stomach let out a loud growl. He had promised Mueller he would grab grub from Pappy's on his way over to catch the Bruins game later on TV. All this talk of chickens and wings was making him hungry.

"We could grow an amputee another leg, or a diabetic a replacement pancreas." Opoworo waved his arms in time with the frenetic pace of his words. "A new spine for a paralytic, even! To do so in a reliable and reproducible manner, though, we needed to vet a process we call 'morphogenetic synthesis.'"

Latharo nodded. "So that's what this MGS device of yours was for."

"Right. It's the culmination of decades' worth of research my father began. Later, my elder brother joined him," he said as he walked with Lenny and his partner following behind. "They conducted proof-of-concept here to identify ideas worth slogging through the administrivia for research grants. This was their sandbox."

"Excuse me, Doctor Opoworo . . . it *was*?"

Latharo shot Lenny a stern look while their host let out a long sigh. "My father was deported over a decade ago now. And about a year after that, my brother was killed by a fire following a laboratory explosion. The MGS is part of their legacy. It . . . it pains me that it's gone missing." He shook his head and pointed at a vat of slimy green goo. "Anyway, over here we're preparing a batch of catalyzation proteins. Next week begins another round of cellular development regression experiments so that . . ."

Without warning, Lenny found his senses under assault as a putrid smell dredged up memories he had hoped would remain buried the rest of his life. Through his mind flashed horrific images of disaster, of dismemberment, and of death. "Hey, uh . . . you don't look so good," Opoworo said after Lenny turned to find his two companions staring at him.

"Where is your—" was all he could manage before the heavings started. He twirled on his heel and sprinted toward the stairs. "Left at the landing, then second door on the right!" their host called after him.

Lenny glared at his reflection in the mirror while water from the faucet filled his cupped hands. His face would be all over the "Wall of Shame" when word of *this* got out. Crap-fucking-tastic.

He raised his hands and took a sip. Swishing the water around his mouth helped purge the nasty taste inside. At least he made it to the toilet before all that remained from his breakfast came back up. He wouldn't have to clean up a mess nor feel guilty about leaving one.

Only good thing being paired off with Latharo was few DHS agents ever spoke to him, and fewer still Lenny's fellow Coasties. When they did, it was all business. Someone at CIA years ago had dubbed his new partner "*El Toro*", known to be as hard-charging as a raging bull and twice as stubborn. The clever play on his last name followed. With a smile Lenny realized odds were good none of his coworkers would so much as hear a whisper about this little incident.

He emerged from the bathroom and tensed up, hearing a girl and a woman yell at each other from somewhere upstairs. Were they scared? Angry? Fooling around? The argument originated from the landing atop the stairwell to the second story. One hand atop his taser's holster, Lenny tiptoed back down the hall and peered around the corner.

His back slammed against the wall when a woman tripping her way down the stairs careened into him. She glared and smoothed her platinum-blonde hair away from her face. "Hey, why don'cha look where yer . . ." Her severe expression vanished, replaced by a glint of recognition in her droopy eyes. "Hey, stranger . . . 's been awhile."

Lenny guessed her to be in her mid-forties. Though with her whole body pressed up against his and only her robe between them, he didn't need to guess to realize she was in *great* shape. His mind raced, seeking any possible way out of this . . . awkward situation.

Her eyes went wide. "Zat you makin' all dat noise jus' now, tossin' yer cookies?" The woman had his wrist in an iron grip before he knew it, dragging him behind her down the hallway. "Lesh getcha sum gingery ale, jus' like I used ta give my kids when dey had sad bellies."

He *so* didn't have time for this. Some ginger ale might help keep his stomach calm when he ventured back into the lab, though. Lenny let her lead him past the bathroom and into a spacious kitchen.

She motioned toward one of the wooden stools next to the tall counter. "Siddown 'ere, good lookin', while I getcha some gingery ale." He took a seat but was up again after she wobbled over to the refrigerator and began to rifle through its contents. The lamp inside highlighted multiple bruises on her forearms and face. How many times had she fallen already? And with the way she was slurring her words and stumbling around, why had he smelled no alcohol on her even while they were . . . close?

"Auntie Alex!"

Lenny started at the sound of the young girl's shrill voice. She came into the kitchen dressed in a parochial school uniform, wearing her long black hair in a pair of thick pigtails draped over each shoulder. She would be, what? Ten? Eleven?

Her monolid eyes went wide before her tan face flushed. The girl wiggled her arms free from the straps of her backpack, and it hit the floor with a dull *thud*. "Why are the police here? What did you do *now*?" She stepped up in front of Lenny and stood on her tiptoes with her hands clasped together. "Please, officer, don't take her away! Not now!"

"Aw, shut yer trap, Stuie." Alex backed up from the refrigerator with a bottle of ginger ale in her hand. "I was jus' gettin' dis hanshome young man somethin' ta cheer up his sad bellies. Now lemme getcha sum ishe."

Lenny made a face while she rummaged around in the cupboard for a glass. "Uhm, sorry, Miss . . . 'Stuie', is it? I may be wearing a blue uniform, but I'm not a police officer." He knelt down to her eye level. "I'm Lieutenant Lennart Reintz with the US Coast Guard. But you can call me 'Lenny.'"

"But Mr. Lenny, we don't own a boat . . ." She gasped. "Did Auntie *steal* a boat?"

He couldn't help but laugh out loud. "No one stole a boat, sweetheart. Pretty cold out for something like that, don't you think? And I'm not here to arrest anyone. My, uhm . . . *partner* and I are just asking Doctor Opoworo some questions."

Stuie tugged at the pleats of her uniform skirt. "Oh, you must mean my dad. I'm glad no one is in trouble. My cousin Pawly comes home tomorrow for the first time since she got out of the Navy. See?"

'Pawly'?

Lenny turned to where the girl pointed at the dining room wall beyond the kitchen. It was decorated from floor to ceiling with streamers, balloons, photographs and "*WITAJ W DOMU PAWLINA!*" spelled out in large, pasted-on paper letters.

He gaped at the enlarged picture of a young woman wearing a Navy Working Uniform in Woodland colors. A choppy bob of rusty blonde hair poked out from underneath her boonie hat like red straw from the head of a scarecrow. Her blue eyes gleamed as she flashed a toothy grin toward the camera, porting her Colt M4 carbine at the low ready. His gaze followed her right arm to the stitching above her chest pocket, visible between the stock of her rifle and forearm.

KATCZYNSKI.

Or, to the Navy, MA2(SCW/EXW) Katczynski, Pawlina J.

"Pawly would be heartbroken if her mom wasn't here to greet her when she comes home. Right, Auntie Alex?"

Lenny glanced over to where the girl's aunt stood in front of the refrigerator, ice piling up at her feet.

"Uhm . . . Mr. Lenny, are you all right?"

Alex stepped over before he could answer and handed him a glass filled more with ice than ginger ale. "Here ya go, hanshome!" Her identity came to mind in a surreal moment. He saw Pawly's face in hers, illuminated by the afternoon sun streaming in through the bay window. Alex was her . . . *mother*? Of course! Now he remembered her voice, telling him Pawly disappeared soon after her discharge. The devastating news, however, had come via a doorbell intercom speaker at a different house. So why hadn't Tommy—?

Lenny cupped his hands over his mouth, unsure whether he might throw up again. "Wuzza matter?" Alex said with an indignant look. "Dis'll make yer sad belly . . . feel . . ." Her eyes rolled up into her head as her voice trailed off. The glass fell from her hand and shattered an instant before she crumpled to the floor.

Stuie's scream goaded Lenny into action, his queasiness forgotten. He knelt down beside where Alex lay and checked her vitals. To his relief, they seemed okay.

"NASTUSIA GRACJA OPOWORO!"

Angry mutterings became louder as someone stomped across the wooden landing outside the back door. A tall, fair-skinned woman with dark-brown hair tied up behind her head burst through the door shouting. "How many times do I have to tell you *not* to scream in the house unless someone is . . . ?"

Lenny raised an open palm to her while she stared at him dumbfounded. "Sorry about this, ma'am." He shifted his arm under Alex's shoulder in a clumsy attempt to keep her from dragging them both to the floor. "Please, give me a moment so I can explain."

The kitchen floor shook when the woman dropped the goalie bags from her shoulder, one after the other. She pulled a stick free from one of them and popped the snaps on the front of her puffer vest. "Does this guy have a badge, Stuie?" the woman said, her eyes fixed on him. "Mrs. Piontkowski down the block was beaten and robbed last week by some punk wearing a police uniform."

The woman brandished her hockey stick like a weapon. Well-toned muscles on her arms and midriff, visible beneath her long-sleeved compression shirt, suggested she had means *and* motive to do him serious harm.

Lenny gulped.

"Wait, Mom! Mr. Lenny from the Coast Guard here was talking to Dad and got all sick and stuff before Auntie Alex fell on him and—"

"Coast . . . Guard?"

"He's okay, Annie. Manuel brought him by to talk with me about . . . oh, my God! Alex!" Nat was at his side in an instant taking the unconscious woman's face into his hands.

"Her pulse and breathing seem normal, but I can't say why she all of a sudden—"

"Just *what* is going on here?"

Lenny turned to Latharo and nodded his head toward Alex. "This one ran into me coming down the stairs and led me to the kitchen. I was speaking with her and Opoworo's daughter before she passed out."

"We should be apologizing to you, Lieutenant Reintz. Alex here is my big sister," the doctor said and gathered the woman up into his arms. "She's been dealing with . . . well, issues."

"So, uhm . . . are you, ah . . . investigating the stuff stolen from my husband's company . . . or something?"

"That's right, Annie," Latharo said. "He's with me. And we were just leaving."

Her makeshift bludgeon clattered to the floor. "I'm . . . I'm sorry, Lieutenant. All the crazy things that go on in this city, I . . . I didn't know . . ."

He waved his hand out in front of him. "No harm, no foul, ma'am."

Lenny's partner stepped over and brought his mouth to his ear. "*¡Que demonios!* If you're quite done making the entire Department look bad, I suggest we go. I've got everything I came for."

"Fine by me." He fumbled with the zipper of his jacket. "Can we help you with her?"

Opoworo shook his head. "Thank you, but no. The witch's brew of medications Alex is on does these kinds of things to her," he said and repositioned his arms beneath his sister. "After I get her back to bed, she'll wake up in a few hours like nothing happened. I would appreciate your seeing yourselves out, though. She'll be shocked when we tell her about your meeting, Lieutenant."

Lenny snorted and turned to leave. *Then that will make two of us.*

CHAPTER EIGHT

SUNNY AWOKE WITH A START when her granddaughter began to scream. The older woman placed a hand over her heart, certain it had skipped a beat. Maybe two. Pawly hugged her knees to her chest as if to quell the tremors that racked her body. Sweat from her forehead plastered the young woman's short rusty blonde hair to either side of her face. Gray fur fell off in clumps from her forearms and lower legs. Sightless eyes fixed upon the wall opposite her while she shivered from some indiscernible chill.

After many long hours in the weeks leading up to Pawly's extraction, Top had ordered them all relax on the trip back from San Francisco. Sunny glanced down at her wrist and frowned. Apparently, she had relaxed too much, the endless moonlit winterscape rushing past her window having lulled her to sleep.

No matter. Perhaps it was better this way. Rolling along a rural segment of Interstate surrounded by darkness would work to their advantage should Pawly begin to rage. Her job, though, was to ensure emergency measures remained unnecessary.

Poor dear. She is having that horrible nightmare again.

Sunny brushed her salt-and-pepper bangs away from her face and reached for a brown glass vial on the end table beside her chair. Drawing it near her face, she scanned the label's small print below the word "Carfentanyl" to confirm dosing instructions. Some quick math confirmed what she had administered around dinnertime last night would keep a normal person unconscious until mid-morning at least. But Sunny knew her granddaughter was not normal. Not at all.

❡

In through your nose, out through your mouth. Locate your center, no room for doubt.

Pawly silently mouthed the mantra over and over to help get her breathing under control. Her mother and grandmother had required her recite it during training every day after school and twice a day on weekends for months now. Techniques she had come to master prevented her ailuran form from overpowering her and also helped her find her focus. And the pain shooting up and down her leg like liquid fire would provide a suitable channel on which to concentrate.

"Ngh!"

That and then some.

She reached across her chest and jabbed her thumb into her armpit to direct her *ch'i* toward her pericardium. Mayhem registered all around her after the ringing in her ears began to fade. Never did she imagine she would fight off one of their own to save her family. She circled the floor in a low defensive stance, wincing every time she put weight on her right leg. Red haze on retreat toward the edges of her vision, she glanced down to inspect the deep gashes in her thigh. No wonder why it hurt like hell. And her favorite jeans were a complete loss, too—ripped denim was *so* on its way out. Between training and summer school, who knew when she could corral her girlfriends into shopping with her for a new pair?

Panic chased her flippant thought away after she realized the flickering light reflected from the walls was no aftereffect of her bloodlust. The lab was on fire, and it was spreading quickly.

Pawly crossed herself and mouthed a prayer. Had her Rage continued, she and her whole family could have burned alive. Getting slashed may have been their lucky break, though pungent smoke filling the room underscored they were still in grave danger. She had to move. Fast.

She chanced her depth perception was working normally once again and pounced. With a grunt she hoisted herself to her feet atop one of the instrument racks above her head. From there, Pawly spied Alex lying prone near the wall of windows and leapt down to her side. "Mom! Are you all right? Can you stand?"

Her mother replied with a groan and pushed herself up to her elbows.

"Where's Dad?" Pawly cried as she shook Alex's shoulders. "And Annie? And Uncle Ritzi?"

"You mean you . . . don't remember?"

"Mom, I . . . I can't. Everything's a blur since I—"

"Oh, dear God! BARRY!"

Pawly followed her mother's horrified gaze across the room to the spot her father laid face down in a puddle of his own blood. An instant later, she crouched next to where he grabbed uselessly at the floor. "No, Dad!" she said as she took his trembling hands in hers. "Don't move! I'll go get help." She pushed on his shoulder and rolled him up on his side. "I don't care if anyone spots me so long as we can get you to—"

There before her lay her father's entrails in a gruesome heap. She turned her head away. And puked.

Her hands drew to her mouth by reflex. Barry's forehead smacked on the ceramic tile beside her before she realized she had let go of him. She scooted around and cradled his head in her arms. "Oh, Dad, I'm sorry!"

When he gazed up at her, Pawly noticed his prosthetic left eye was missing. "Pawlina . . . get you an' your mother . . . outta here."

"But we need to get *you* out of here, Dad! Before that . . . monster comes back!"

"Don't . . . hate . . . him," he said between fitful coughs and waved a hand toward what was once a wall of full-height windows. Long shards of broken glass now hung from the ceiling aside a gaping hole. Her memory was a blank right after the horrible thing had lashed out at her. Maybe it was gone already?

Her long, slender ears drooped while she stared at her reflection, backlit eerily by the flames drawing nearer. Tears traced dark trails in the tawny fur covering her face. Blood stained the bushy white fur along either side of her mouth all the way to her chin. Bile welled up in the back of her throat. She had no right calling anyone a monster.

"Dad, we need . . . I need you. I . . . I can't do this . . ."

Barry reached up and took her face in his quivering hand. "Only easy day . . . was yesterday . . . lil' fighter," he said in a weak voice.

She squinched her eyes shut and shook her head. If she never opened them again, she would never . . . never have to ever think about—

Behind her eyelids, she saw bright flash of red the instant before she heard the blast. She opened her eyes and raised her head toward where the chemical storage cabinet hung on the wall nearby, now engulfed in flames. The metal door flew past and landed next to where Alex lay passed out on the floor. Shock from the fire and latent effects of her meds must have been more than her mother could bear. "Dad, I wanna bring Mom over and—"

Barry's hand slid down the side of her face. Time slowed to an agonizing crawl while Pawly stared down at her father. His head lay in her lap, the corners of his mustache curled upward.

"Dad?"

His right eye was vacant. Cold. Lifeless.

"D-dad?"

A primal scream tore from her throat as Pawly surrendered to the rage and pain consuming her.

❡

Sunny wrapped her arms tight around Pawly's shoulders. Now and again, she would glance down to check whether the IV was still securely fixed to the back of her hand. She coaxed a tinkling sound from the pair of stainless steel balls she twirled in one hand, each about the size of a golf ball. The young woman breathed deep through her nose and expelled her air through puckered lips.

Now that's a good girl. Sunny smiled and drew her mouth close to Pawly's ear. "Shush now, *sohn-nya*. It is okay. I am here."

"*H-halmeonim?*" Pawly clutched her grandmother's arms while her eyes darted about the room. "Wh-what are you doing here?"

"I could ask the same." She pushed Pawly away and set the balls back into their felt-lined wooden box atop the nightstand. "Or why you fled. It is quite a thing. You went to San Francisco. You told no one why. Never write, never call. Now hold still." She popped the tube and carefully withdrew the needle. "We did worry the whole time."

"But *Halmeonim*, I—ow!"

Sunny pulled the tape free from her granddaughter's arm, bringing with it a clump of shed fur. "Put yourself in danger. And all of us to bring you back. You chose to listen to Blaznikov. Not us. We must all give you hell." At the sound of footsteps from the hallway outside the door, Sunny placed a cotton ball over the tiny wound where the needle had been and motioned Pawly to hold it in place. "I will tell the others you are awake. You can clean up in—"

The door flew open and crashed up against the wall. Top stood inside the threshold, slack-jawed at the sight of Pawly before him. Though back in her human guise, lumps of fur trapped beneath her purple sports bra and yoga shorts bulged out all over.

Sunny snarled and dropped down to all fours. The tranquilizer gun flew from Top's hand after her spinning kick connected with the back of his calf. She took him down and rolled him onto his stomach with one fluid motion.

"You lout! Eyes to the floor. My granddaughter is not decent. I told you to knock."

The big man groaned while Sunny drove her knee into one shoulder and craned his arm to the other. "With all that screaming? I thought sure she was raging again and broke free."

Her nostrils flared. "Yes, Dory put you in charge. But I will deal with this."

"Didn't seem to me like you were! She worked her restraints loose once already—"

"You will stop second guessing me! *I* loosened them when we took fuel in Salt Lake City. With them tight, I cannot do a proper exam. Too, they could cut off circulation. I am surprised you asked after Cheyenne."

Top sighed. "Fine, have it your way. Now let me up, willya? This is embarrassing!"

Sunny glanced over at Pawly and nodded toward the robe hanging on the wall opposite. "Not until she covers up."

The young woman cast a furtive glance back and forth between the two of them before she turned and snatched the garment from its hook. "Top? Is that you?" she said while she tied up the robe's front.

He averted his eyes. "Long time no see, sailor," he said while he got to his feet. "Upright and taking nourishment, I see? That's good. Got a lot to talk about before we get back to Chicago," he said while he got to his feet.

"I'm going . . . home?" She wobbled over to the window and peeked through the drawn shades. "Where are we, anyway?"

"Between Omaha and Des Moines on I-80. Pretty sure we passed East Bumblefuck about ten miles back."

"What day is it?"

"Saturday."

She gasped. "I've been out for an entire day?"

"Over twenty-six hours, actually. Be dawn in an hour or so. We should arrive in Chi-town early this afternoon."

"Wow. Must be why I have a headache." Pawly rubbed at her temples. "What the hell kinda stuff did you shoot me with, anyway?"

"Horse tranquilizer," Sunny said. "Though other punk did not—"

Her gaze met Top's after he nosily cleared his throat. "What's important is that you're back with us, sailor. And that no one's any the wiser." He glanced at his watch and turned to leave. "It'll be my turn to drive after we pull in to the next truck stop."

Sunny drew her granddaughter aside and put her arm around her shoulder. "Sink and shower and toilet are in there." She nudged Pawly toward the pocket door in the corner of the room. "Soap and shampoo and brushes, too."

Top paused in the open doorway with his back to them. "Let us know when you're shipshape, sailor. There's someone else here I think you need to talk to," he said and closed the door.

Pawly sighed as she exited the tiny bathroom, savoring the feel of the cool air on her skin now that her shed was complete. Fresh undergarments along with a hoodie and a pair of sweat pants lay on the bed where her grandmother had set them out. Next to them, atop a pair of bright purple sneakers, sat a dark blue ball cap sporting the US Navy Seabees' "fighting bee". She picked up the cap and traced her finger across familiar letters embroidered in brilliant yellow thread spelling out "NMCB 33 PAVING THE WAY ASHORE."

Memories from her original unit came to mind as Pawly donned the dowdy yet comfy ensemble. She did her time in the scullery like everyone else after reporting to Port Hueneme. The stew burners she had hit it off with became her closest friends during their long deployment to Korea. In time for the Lenten season, they comshawed all the ingredients her mother's favorite Fat Tuesday recipe called for. The forbidden bottle of *Spirytus* discovered during a surprise inspection had nearly gotten them all masted.

Later, with their skippers' consent, she and her friends baked up a pile of *pączki* in their field kitchen for their fellow sailors to enjoy. The hungry and homesick men and women hailed Pawly a hero after they devoured the sweet treats like a pack of ravenous hyenas.

She went back into the bathroom and sniffed at the gobs of wet fur covering the walls and floor of the shower. *There I go again, shedding like a roomful of fucking Persians.*

Rummaging through the cupboards yielded a small plastic trash can and a roll of paper towel. She knelt down and scooped up one handful after another of the slimy stuff. Then she wiped down the stall, filling the little can with waste nearly to the top. Once finished, she stood to examine her handiwork, satisfied her traveling companions would appreciate their bathroom being more or less presentable again.

She fished a dark purple canvas clutch from the heap in which her fighting gear and battle dress uniform lay. Sliding open the room door revealed a narrow hallway. Peering through the windows as she tiptoed along, Pawly realized she was inside some kind of large recreational vehicle. Fortunately, the rig stopped shortly after she had undressed. Brushing herself out while bouncing around the cramped shower stall would have been a royal pain in the ass.

Beyond lay a room almost completely taken up by tactical displays and a tricked-out computer workstation any self-respecting hacker would drool over. Sofa chairs, a dining table, and a tiny kitchen surrounded a set of steps which led down to the door to the outside. Whatever Top and *Halmeonim* did aboard this rig, they were prepared to be at it for some time.

She froze when she spied the high-end customized wheelchair parked atop the lift platform beside the wide entry door. It matched the picture she had seen on Annie's Facebook page, but where in the hell was its owner?

Pawly drew up her hood and stepped out of the RV. A dry chill bit at her nose, making her wince while the throaty rumble of diesel engines reverberated all around. Drivers of the rigs parked the length and breadth of the gigantic parking lot likely bedded down hours ago. Her sneakers crunched into the snow with every step as she wandered beneath the brilliant lights. Though a few people made their way about, she recognized none of them.

A red octagonal sign perched atop the truck stop's main entrance featured the words "Maid-Rite" in flashing white neon. The thought of the signature loose meat sandwiches made her stomach growl, reminding Pawly she hadn't eaten in nearly a day and a half. Several of the restaurants had been regular stops on family vacations. She and her friends from "C" School frequented another up the road from Camp Lejeune whenever they availed themselves to weekend passes. They'd put 'em down by the sackful with every visit.

Such happy memories. All the more reason Pawly knew she needed to get the hell out of here, get as far away from her friends and loved ones as she could. What they didn't know *would* hurt them. What the hell were they thinking, anyway? No one could possibly know she was with them already, and she would see to it no one found out.

Do Greyhound buses make meal stops here? A one-way ticket back to San Francisco couldn't cost more than—

A barely audible *pish* near her feet stopped her short. She glanced down in time to spot the glowing end of a cigarette butt go dark and sink out of sight into the snow.

"Don't bother," came a familiar voice. "Kitchen's been closed for hours. If you're hungry, we've still got a hoagie or two and some pasta salad in the fridge."

She drew in her breath and stared at the man. Face. To. Face.

"Tommy! H-how can you—"

Her brother tapped at the metal exoskeleton around his legs and waist with one of his crutches. "Stand up? With this thing. Helps me walk now, too. Wicked, huh?"

Pawly felt her throat clench as she reached out to embrace Tommy. He blocked her, porting one crutch across his chest. "Fall off the face of the earth for months, then act like everything's okay when we finally catch up to you?" The freckles on her brother's face disappeared as he flushed.

"I'm—I'm sorry."

"'Sorry' ain't gonna cut it, Sis."

"So what would you have me do, then?"

"Stop running away, for one." Tommy unbuttoned his pea coat and patted at the holster under his shoulder. "Just so we're clear—had my eye on you the moment you stepped out of the rig. One more step, I'd've tagged you with another tranq dart. Woulda dragged you back to the RV myself to keep you from pulling another disappearing act."

Pawly studied the snow at her feet. "I . . . I had reasons."

"Yeah, we all have 'reasons' to find the motherfuckers who attacked us. Haight-Ashbury will still be there after we take them out, so you can go back to daisy-picking."

"Oh, you think I was out there on some kind of vacation, do you?" She narrowed her eyes and jabbed her finger into her brother's chest. "Well, good thing you're standing so I can say to your face how much I—"

"AT EASE, SAILOR!" Top kicked up little whisps of snow as he shuffled up to them with Sunny right behind. "Listen, you two—I've never liked the idea of siblings deploying to the same theater of operations. But I need *both* of you for what we're trying to do. Yeah, you've got issues to sort out. Do it on your time, not mine. Now, pipe down and saddle up."

Steam wisped from the tops of four foam cups wedged into the cardboard carrier in Sunny's arms. Top thanked her and took a sip after she handed one to him. "Can't wait to get back to civilization so I can get a decent latte," he said and made a face before the two of them disappeared into the vehicle.

Tommy hobbled over next to Pawly and leaned his face close to her ear. "You must have known we would come for you, Sis. Just like Lenny did." With a knowing grin he tossed his crutches up into the RV one after the other. He gripped the railings and hefted himself inside, dragging his exoskeleton along like so much deadweight.

She gaped after him. "But how . . . how did you know—?"

A couple toots from the rig's horn drew her gaze to where Top's reflection glared at her in the passenger side mirror. She knew that look—"get in or find another ride." With a sigh, she scrambled up the steps and slammed the door behind her.

"Kept up with the Hawks, right?"

Pawly turned and spied Tommy behind his console cleaning his glasses. "No, I wasn't exactly keeping a regular schedule," she said between the last several bites of her sandwich. "Hardly time to catch one period, much less a whole game."

With specs again perched atop his nose, Tommy tapped away at his keyboard. "Let me bring up the highlight reel from the Cup playoffs last year. Here, check it out."

Pawly wadded up the wrapper and tossed the ball toward the trash can. It bounced off the rim and landed next to where his exo sat parked up against the wall. She groaned and knelt down to pick the plastic up off the floor. When she stood again, her eyes fixated upon one of the several monitors Tommy used while he worked. Though one indeed featured video clips from the Blackhawks' postseason, the one which held her attention looped through a different series of images. A certificate of graduation from the Coast Guard's Officer Candidate School. Discharge papers from Walter Reed National Military Medical Center. A photo ID of a lieutenant newly assigned to the USCG's Maritime Security Unit Chicago. Her brother made sure to highlight one name on each form prominently: LENNART EMIL REINTZ.

She gasped. "L-L-Lenny?"

"I know, quite a shot by Kane, right?" he said in a loud voice. "Never would guess Rask could deflect that one, but he did. Series went downhill from there."

Pawly stood speechless. Tommy clicked his mouse to launch a movie clip in a new window. It featured the porch in front of the house her folks moved them all into upon returning to their old neighborhood from Norfolk.

Somehow he must have hacked into Chicago PD's surveillance video shot by the camera atop the streetlight by the curb. She gawked at the grainy footage showing a man speaking into the intercom near the front door. The video froze as he turned to leave, his dejected scowl clear in the enlarged image. It was Lenny. At Mom's house. Coming for her, just as he had promised. Not even a week after she skipped town.

Another screen displayed her grandparents' house down the block where her extended family still lived. Two men walked along the sidewalk beside one another engaged in some kind of argument. Tommy stopped the video and zoomed in as the driver got into their unmarked white SUV. Lenny again. The cursor twirled around the recording date on the bottom right of the frame. Yesterday.

The screen went blank for a moment before a still photo appeared. Two Navy servicewomen smiled and posed in their dress whites, minutes after their graduation ceremony at Great Lakes had concluded. Tommy had snapped the picture a moment before her best friend Sally broke her promise and started bawling.

Pawly had quickly followed suit. A short time later, she would be on her way to Texas for "A" School at Lackland. Sally and Tommy remained behind for their own advanced training and began seeing one another. The night before their deployment to the Gulf of Oman, he proposed. Tommy kept up his ruse, prattling on about stats and figures supporting his theory—this season's Cup playoffs would be a Chicago-Boston grudge match.

His voice grew distant before Pawly collapsed atop the credenza desk next to his console. Top himself appointed her squad leader upon their arrival in Chah Bahar. Within days his reputation would be ruined. Lenny would be wounded. Tommy would be paralyzed. And the woman she loved like a sister would be dead.

She broke down in screaming sobs. "No . . . Sally . . . oh, God, no!"

CHAPTER NINE

WHAT THE HELL AM I DOING HERE?

Lenny slumped down onto a bench near the park's small playground where a couple dozen children laughed and squealed and ran amok. He understood enough Spanish to pick out several choice tidbits of *barrio* gossip from parents and caregivers lounging nearby on the other benches.

After the tenth glance down at his smartphone in as many minutes, he swooshed at the screen to pull up last night's message from Special Agent Latharo. Without saying why, the text urged him meet his partner at ten o'clock this morning at this public park on the South Side. He closed the message and saw "10:33" displayed in big white numerals.

He growled and jammed the phone back into his jacket pocket. This was not how he had intended to spend a rare Saturday off. There was the laundry list of chores he promised Aunt Nessie he would finish prior to his move back east. Like repainting his upstairs apartment, for example, with time enough to catch a shower before Mueller came by tonight. They planned to grab a burger together and hoist a few at the Center Tap before the Wolves faced off.

The unseasonably mild morning led him to wonder whether Chicagoland was in store for a green Christmas this year. He stretched his arms across the back of the park bench and closed his eyes to enjoy the comforting warmth of the sun's rays.

His phone chimed to announce an incoming text. He sighed and fished the thing from his pocket, expecting a note from Latharo to cancel their meeting or offer some lame-ass excuse for his running late.

hey lemony rinse! tomcat here. hear you heard polecat's coming home. sry I couldn't spill. busy with cloak n' dagger shit. texting u as she's crashed out.

Lenny gaped at the message. He and Tommy Katczynski had become friends during their sea tour together aboard the San Jac on patrol off the Iraqi coast. "Tomcat" and Sally, Tommy's shipboard steady, had hooked him up with Tommy's twin sister Pawly for a double date shortly after they all reported to Camp Lejeune for shore duty. So why had he been keeping her whereabouts from him all this time?

At length, he swooshed upward to view the sender's phone number. Unfamiliar, but he recognized the "563" area code. He remembered it covered most of eastern Iowa from his past workings with Marine Safety Detachment Quad Cities.

His friends at CGIS-HQ texted this morning while he made his way into town aboard the "L". Wheelchair-bound Tommy had gone to work for CIA after his rehabilitation, but that was all anybody outside of the Agency was allowed to know. Was his old shipmate "out in the cold" and under orders to contact no one? Or was he ignoring him? Maybe he was using a burn phone even now to reach out on the down low. Lenny began to tap out a reply when another text came:

polecat needs new cell. might give her this one. expect her busy w/family stuff for a few days, but she wants to c u soon. enjoy the photo reel itmt! l8tr tmk

Indignation gave way to surprise when his device chimed again. And again and again and again. His finger flew across the screen while more than two dozen new messages arrived, each with a picture attached.

There she was. Piercing ice-blue eyes framed by ruddy freckles and topped by a choppy bob of strawberry-blonde hair. Frosty emo butch chick. Deadpan snarker. Blackhawks fan. Pawly. *His* Pawly.

Instead of singing in the shower every day, Lenny rehearsed telling her off when, and if, she ever came home. She would understand in no uncertain terms how he had agonized over whether they would ever be together again. Now the very same photo he had seen blown up on the wall of Doctor Opoworo's kitchen yesterday gave him pause. There she stood with smile full of zeal, eyes filled with hope. Hope for her future. Their future, he knew.

He had been the one holding the camera.

A flicker of light caught his eye. Lenny glanced up to view a bright white void swallow up the children, the playground and everything else before the shock wave slammed into him. He flew over the back of the bench into the air. His arms and legs flailed about until he impacted the bulkhead behind him. Pain radiated from his trunk to every extremity and back again. The whiteness faded to black while he slumped to the deck below.

¶

Ow.

Hurts.

Lying here hurts. Breathing hurts. Blinking hurts. No sense blinking anyway. Can't see a thing. Can't hear, either. Ears ringing. Like that damned school bell at the end of recess. Riiiiiiiiiiing. Oh, wait, can hear the other men now.

They're screaming. Holy shit. Wailing like banshees. Are they dead? Am *I* dead? Ow. Oh, fuck no. Hurts. Can't be dead. Dead doesn't hurt. Dead doesn't hurt so fucking much. Ow.

They're still screaming. At least they're alive. Maybe they'll be... oh, wait. "Get them off?" Get *what* off? They're eating their eyes? Maybe that's why I can't see. Worms crawling around in their ears? Chewing into their brains? Poor bastards're seriously fucked up. And why are they over...

Ow. Breathing hurts. The Iranians! Must've blown their wad. Saw those cat people and blew their wad. *Taste the rainbow, motherfuckers!* How could OPCOM have... oh, shit. Hurts. The blast came from OPCOM!

"OPCOM..." Ow. Hurts to cough. Stop fucking coughing! Ow. "OP-COM... Dolphin Leader..."

Holy shit. Is that *my* voice? Throat hurts. Along with everything else. Fucking static. Try again.

"OPCOM... Dolphin Leader... copy?"

Ow! My ear! Hey, where'd my earpiece go?

"Don't talk. Save your strength."

Fuck that. Gimme back my damn earpiece. Gotta job to do. "Hafta call in, get help..."

"No one left but me *to* help, Lenny. Now hold still!"

Someone knows my name? Who? Ow. Voice... man or woman? Can't tell. Like someone's been gargling battery acid.

"Gotta call in... OPCOM..."

"THEY'RE DEAD!" Drops. Warm drops. On my face and neck and chest. Is it raining? Never rains here.

"OPCOM was Ground Zero! Rip, J.C., Kender, Sally... Tommy... they're all... all dead."

They're... *what*? Oh no. Oh no no no no. Ow. Hurts. Stop touching me! Wait... fur? Too fucking hot to be wearing fur. Hoshit. Cat... person? Here? Talking to me? Gonna play with me before you kill me like a fucking mouse? Maybe he'll eat me. Ow. Hurts. Go ahead, pal. Almost dead now. Get on with it, then.

Wish the rain would stop. Wait... how does Cat Dude know who's at OPCOM anyway...?

Oh, wait, dude's got nails. Long nails. Duh, he's a fucking cat. Go figure. Ow! Why are you touching me? Hurts! Oh, wait . . . not so much. Mmmm-mmm. Feels . . . better.

"You'll be dead too if I don't get you out of here. You are *so* not dying on me, understand?"

Whoa. WHOA! Upsy-daisy . . . here we go again. This is gonna hurt! Oh, wait. Wind. No screaming. Nice. We're falling. Slowly falling. Can Cat Dude fucking *fly* or—?

Oof! Tight. Holding me *real* tight. Paws off, fella. Don't swing that way. Oh, wait. Are those? So they are. Coppin' a feel from Catwoman. Yay me. Groin . . . wet. And cold. Holy shit. I wet my pants. Well, fuck me. *That's* impressive.

"No. No! Oh, God . . . this can't be happening!"

Yes, cat lady, I pissed myself. Thankyouverymuch. I'm pretty put out about it, too. Still raining. Hope I won't smell. Ow. We landed. No more flying. She's . . . ow . . . walking . . . ow . . . with me . . . ow. And laying me down. Hurts. Not as much, though. Is it still raining?

"Too many close to me die, Lenny. Not gonna let you too."

Close to me . . . woman . . . oh, God!

"P-Pawly. Where . . . where's Pawly?"

Ow. She whistled. Whistled loud. Now my ear hurts. Like every other fucking part of me.

"CORPSMAN! OVER HERE!"

Who the fuck is she yelling at? Footsteps? Musta been these guys. They speak English? Our guys, then. Good. Ow.

"Thought you swept this area, Vaz!"

At least the rain stopped.

"Yes, Commander, I did. This guy wasn't here five minutes ago, I swear!"

Wait. Where'd Catwoman go?

"Oh, so you want me to think he just fell out of the sky, Corpsman?"

Well, now that you mention it . . .

"Whatever. Give him the once over while I raise the helo. Back Office, Big Top! Another casualty along the pier. Need medivac for six, repeat, six men."

Ow. Now *you're* touching me? Hurts. Stop it!

"And tell the Coasties their XO is accounted for. Big Top out."

"Wa . . . ter . . ."

"Velasquez, hand me that bottle. Thanks. Here, Lieutenant, take a sip."

Plastic. It's wet. Feels better. Swallowing hurts. Everything hurts. Ow.

"Who's the cutie?"

Lenny felt the cold wind on his face and looked around. A shabbily-dressed man walked around the bench and plunked down on the end opposite him.

"Never mind. Don't suppose it's any of my business anyway."

He eyed his uninvited guest while the man sat a brown paper bag down between them, the neck of some kind of green glass bottle inside plainly visible. A scarf and floppy, wide-brimmed felt hat obscured the man's features. Patches dotted his tattered overcoat. Pawly's pert face disappeared after Lenny closed the message and stood up to leave.

"You should try some, *gringuito*. The taste will grow on you."

The familiar voice halted his departure mid-stride. Eyes wide, Lenny turned to find Special Agent Latharo regarding him with a bemused grin, his scarf pulled down around his neck. "What? You expecting some other bum to offer you a pull off his hooch?"

With a sidelong glance, Lenny grabbed the bottle his partner held out toward him. He took a swig and made a face. "Ugh!" he said and handed it back. "The hell is that horrible stuff?"

"My own concoction. It's like what the Brits call 'bitter lemon', only I use genuine *limones peruanos* in mine."

He chuckled and sat back down. "Explains why you're such a sourpuss, then?"

"¡Choteado!" Latharo took a sip and turned back to where the children played. "Been drinking this stuff nearly fifteen years now. Not a drop of alcohol in it. Started when I was in rehab."

"You were . . . an alcoholic?"

"I still am, only managed to keep sober that long. My father's recipe here helps me stay on the wagon and off the sauce. Kind of a cure-all, supposed to prevent malaria."

With a snort, Lenny pictured mosquitoes with their little beaks puckered so tight from a snootful of the stuff they could no longer pierce skin.

"Your initiative is commendable but unexpected for a short timer," his partner said. "Something you'd like to tell me?"

"I . . . I don't know what you're talking about." Lenny cursed himself. No doubt Latharo picked up on the quaver in his voice.

"Don't play coy with me, *gringuito*," the man said like an artisan might address a dimwitted apprentice struggling to grasp an elementary concept. "When I left CIA, I was a field liaison officer to NSA. My friends there called late yesterday afternoon saying a certain query from Coast Guard Intelligence might well pique my interest. Guess *that* cost you a favor or two, eh?"

He sat and stared straight ahead in a vain attempt to avoid further arousing his partner's suspicions. His cheeks betrayed him while uncomfortable warmth rose upward to his hairline.

"Your hunch is well supported by simple observation. Opoworo and his expensive gadgets doing freaky stuff beneath his big house in a swanky neighborhood. Living there with his extended family and his looker of a wife. Daughter attends Catholic school. So you ask yourself 'where does Poindexter here get that kind of *dinero*?'" Latharo waved his arms around to emphasize his point. "Trust fund baby? High-stakes bookmaking operation? On the payroll of some foreign government? What?"

Latharo paused and took another pull from his bottle. "Each of those is a reasonable theory, which is why I vetted them all months ago. Man and his financial records both came up clean. Rare combination of gifted scientist and smart businessman is all I can figure," he said with a shrug.

Silence passed while Lenny worked up nerve enough to reply. "I thought . . . I thought he might be in cahoots with the guys who stole that morpho-whatever thingy."

"So Opoworo can have his cake *and* eat it too after the insurance policy taken on the device's shipment pays out?" His partner slapped the seat next to him and wagged a finger in front of Lenny's nose. "Now you're thinking, *gringuito*. Resourcefulness and initiative are rare traits in young people these days." He set the bottle down on the concrete and slid one arm behind the bench. "I didn't expect a guy running down the clock to do that, so I dug a little deeper. Found out your captain rescinded your change of station. Makes sense, considering Ensign Hayes suffered a mild stroke. Come to find out he has family history. He won't be fit for duty for weeks if he's not medically discharged first."

Latharo drew his hand up and rested his chin in his palm. "But frankly, I'm at a loss to explain why you put in a chit to fill his position. You realize you'll be stuck with me and this fucked up case for God only knows how long, right?"

Lenny stared at his feet while his partner reached down and took another drink. "It's the girl, isn't it? She local? Or back in Boston?"

He blew out his breath. Since the text last night, he had dreaded this moment. "It's . . . complicated."

The man jammed his hands into the pockets of his overcoat and turned back toward the playground. "I come here every now and again when I want to think about things," he said at length. "Everyone thinks I'm just another drunken vagrant while I keep to myself right here on this bench. Parents keep their kids away, and the cops can't be bothered."

He sipped at his bottle again. "This is the neighborhood where my ex-wife and I raised our daughter for the first eleven years of her life. I used to bring her to this very park." Latharo pointed at the jungle gym opposite them. "That one there was her favorite."

One gregarious little girl atop the bars squealed and called in Spanish for her friends to follow. "I was at the height of my career with CIA," he said with a sad smile. "High flyer. Mover and shaker. Mean, mean drunk. One day, my wife took our kid and left town. A week later, a process server handed me divorce papers."

Lenny fidgeted in his seat.

"Two years go by before I get wind my ex remarried," he went on. "Then eight years ago, my daughter shows up at my front door. Said she'd taken the other man's name and was on her way to Great Lakes so she could earn enough to go to college and get on with life."

"Your daughter was Navy?"

He nodded. "From that time on until the day she died. At Chah Bahar."

The muscles in Lenny's neck tensed. Of course, he *would* know about that. With buddies at CIA and NSA, Latharo could find out whatever he wanted about whomever he wanted. Including—and especially—him.

"Now that's complicated, *gringuito*." He threw both arms over the back of the bench. "I mean, I've seen some Weird Shit in my day, but nothing like what happened during *that* operation. No wonder why you blew chunks the other day at Opoworo's place. You were there."

"Yes. I was," Lenny said and turned to glare at him. "What of it?"

Latharo met his gaze. "Figured that had to do with why you wanted to work this case so bad. I . . . I got a second chance to be a father until my daughter was cut down in her prime. But having missed so much of her life—I *will* avenge her. Pathetic, but it's all I live for now."

He stood and slid the bottle into a pocket of his shabby longcoat. "Figured a guy with his whole life ahead of him like you would find something worth living for by now. Like that girl in the picture, for instance. But no, here you are playing defense to clear your good name."

Lenny sprang to his feet. "I was never court-martialed, you know!"

"No, but you were under suspicion and still are," his partner said with a sardonic grin. "I've suspected for months Opoworo and his family are somehow connected with what went down at Chah Bahar. And whoever made off with his MGS could well be planning armies of mutant soldiers like the ones they say killed my daughter." He shook his head and stared at the snowy ground. "That's why I volunteered to head this investigation in the first place."

Latharo turned and walked away. "I saw you staring at that picture of Opoworo's niece the other day. And on your phone now," he said over his shoulder. "You have as much skin in this game as I do."

"Your daughter," Lenny called out after him. "What was her name?"

"Petty Officer Second Class Salvación Ruiz," he said without turning around. "But to her friends, she was simply 'Sally.'"

CHAPTER TEN

SWEAT RAN DOWN THE SIDES OF Pawly's face. Bright sunlight awakened her moments before when Tommy drew open the shade of the RV's bedroom. She had tried to sit up but found her arms and legs bound fast to the four corners of the bed. Profanities and threats of physical violence came out as unintelligible mumbling while she pulled at her bindings. Someone had put some kind of gag in her mouth.

Tommy stood beside one bedpost with a shit-eating grin on his face. Pawly decided then and there to someday soon return the favor by super-gluing his smart ass to the seat of his wheelchair.

"Don't give me that look." He walked around to the window, the servos in his exoskeleton's joints whirring quietly with each step. "You did this to yourself. After *Halmeonim* sedated you, Top insisted we truss you up again in case you started raging."

Something along the road appeared to catch his attention. Though she ceased to struggle, her eyes continued to shoot daggers into him.

"Just passing Joliet Airport now," he said to the glass before facing her again. "Oh, don't worry. I'll help you out of your bindings soon. Gag was my idea, by the way. *Halmeonim* agreed it would keep you from biting through your tongue."

Tommy tiptoed toward her bedside, careful to avoid her gear strewn about the floor. "So what I was trying to say before you went into orbit was..."

Pawly raised her head and watched him rummage through the pouches on her utility belt with both hands. Something landed a moment later with a soft *thud*.

"Well, what have we here?" He bent over and stood again with a stainless steel pocket flask in his hand. After unscrewing the cap, he held the small bottle up to his nose. "Hmm ... Żubrówka?" he asked before he took a swig. "Wow, that's the real deal!" Tommy capped the container and tossed it onto the pile with the rest of her things. "Holding out on me, Sis? The genuine stuff is really hard to get here, you know."

He sat down at the foot of the bed. "Didn't expect you'd need anything to keep your urges in check, though, living your shadow life in San Fran. Could have shred some random mook any night of the week, and no one would be the wiser. Maybe now that your self-imposed exile is over, you'll take up smoking like me. Or go back on the meds like Mom did."

Oh, dear God, not that ...

"All news to you, right?" Tommy leaned forward and rested his elbows on his knees. "Oh, *Halmeonim* and Uncle Nat helped Mom and I get on best they could after you ditched us. Grandpa D's hands were tied pretty much after what went down at Chah Bahar." He snorted. "Not like you or I would ever be called back to active duty."

She turned toward the window to avoid his accusing stare. No way would she give him the satisfaction of seeing tears well up in her eyes.

"Sally came from a broken home. Knew how important for a family to stay together after hers flew apart." The servos in the legs of his exo whirred for a moment before he rose. "Forget that quickly she's the only reason either of us survived?" he asked in a husky voice. A lump formed in her throat as he paced back and forth along the foot of the bed. "She died trying to keep all of us together so ... so we could live."

Tommy reached his thumb and forefinger underneath his glasses and wiped at his eyes. "Every day you ran from everyone who's ever cared for you, you discounted the sacrifice Sally made for us. *That* pisses me off." The RV rumbled over a new bumper crop of potholes while he stared down at the floor.

"Now you know Lenny is still looking for you. The one person should have given up on you didn't," he said at length and shook his head. "You two *are* perfect for each other. You're both mental."

He opened the door and poked his head out into the hallway beyond. "She's awake," he called out to someone she could not see. "Doubt she'll be any more trouble. Give me a hand untying her?"

Pawly heard muffled voices before someone clomped their way toward the bedroom. "Hope you're shipshape, sailor," Top said when he entered while her brother worked at the bindings around her ankles. The elder man wedged himself between the nightstand and bed and loosed the ligatures holding her wrists. Arms freed, she sat upright and pulled out her gag. "Home port's on the horizon. Would you like a bottle of seltzer?"

"Yeah," she said while she worked her jaw. "That would be great."

"Go to him, Pawlina," Tommy whispered in Polish once Top left the room. "Don't blow your second chance. That's what Sally would have wanted." He held one finger over his lips. She nodded in reply, well aware of how serious his breach of protocol was. Both she and Lenny were still under suspicion in connection with the Chah Bahar operation's disastrous end. Whomever their former CO now answered to would surely prevent her from having anything to do with him.

Pawly grabbed at Tommy's shoulders when the RV bucked after hitting a particularly deep crater. She drew him into a hug and brought her mouth close to his ear. "Thank you."

"Like the playoffs this year, Sis," he said with a wink. "It'll be a season to remember."

"Here ya go." Top handed the juice spritzer in his hand out to Pawly. She thanked him and took a sip just after Sunny called out to Top. With a nod he shuffled off toward the front.

"Gotta make a head call and get my wheels ready," Tommy said and followed behind.

The vehicle slowed and leaned in to another cloverleaf before the main control tower at O'Hare loomed into view. Pawly took another swallow of her fizzy drink. They would be home soon, where she was certain to face her mother. With her free hand she reached down the neck of her shirt and drew forth a shiny chain. At the end of it hung a tiny blob of silver which had been poured and then impressed with a wax seal as it cooled. She held the pendant between her fingers and examined the two words on a banner beneath a rampant griffin and lion pair—"Semper Paratus".

Always ready'. Just like you'd better be, Lenny.

Top returned Pawly's embrace while Sunny parked the RV in the narrow alley. "Thank you," she said to him in a small voice, "for bringing me home."

He patted her back and said nothing. Inane promises like "everything will be all right" would be neither helpful nor appreciated. He had seen manifestations of the twins' Affliction firsthand—their "Talents." The daunting challenges faced by their family since would have crushed those with less fortitude. They had yet to tear their tight-knit clan of warriors apart, but they had come close. Too damn close. They were now about to set his boss' risky plan into motion, though that was tomorrow's trouble. For the moment, he looked forward to seeing a grievous wrong between mother and daughter made right.

Pawly fumbled at the bill of her cap and drew her hood over her head. Once the RV stopped, Top followed her down the steps to the outside. Bright sunlight made him blink; cold air made his nose crinkle. He spied Nat, Annie, and Stuie off to the side before Dory acknowledged him with a grateful nod.

Pawly stood with eyes fixed upon her mother, appearing oblivious to all of them. Shoulders slumped, she shuffled forward. "Mom, I can exp—"

A loud *smack* echoed through the alleyway like a gunshot. Alex drew her trembling hand back across her chest after slapping her daughter as hard as she could. "No need. You ran to avoid exposing us, because you thought you must."

Pawly said nothing. She cupped her cheek in her hand while her face flushed.

"I honestly thought your father and I raised you better than that. Then you go and take all the lies and half-truths out of the mouth of that . . . that *lunatic* at face value?" Alex said as her voice cracked. "The bloodlust is part and parcel of who we are, Pawlina. Ritzi and I knew running away was like trying to ditch your own shadow."

Pawly turned to where Tommy sat in his wheelchair. Top saw her brother shrug in reply as if to say *told ya*. "Mom, I'm—I'm sorry. Can you ever—oof!" was all she got out before their mother threw her arms around her and squeezed. The two of them hugged and cried and laughed, each admonishing herself while begging the other for forgiveness.

Top dabbed at the corner of his eye.

CHAPTER ELEVEN

Niko felt his aging body's endurance stretched past its limit. With a groan he pressed himself up against the wall of the darkened room. He held his breath and listened to his pursuer's footsteps coming down the corridor. After seeing them pass through the door's narrow window, he began to count. Though he aimed for thirty, he gasped right after twenty-four.

He pulled his glasses off with one hand and rubbed at the bridge of his nose with the other. How quickly they had come. How completely they had caught him unawares! A gnawing ache registered deep in his stomach. Was he old enough to start going senile?

Keeping odd hours gave him the solitude he needed to focus on his work and more easily camouflage its true nature. But being alone in the building late at night carried risks as well—ones he had obviously underestimated.

Niko did, however, have an exit strategy. In the twenty minutes he had evaded his captors, he had managed to stop and leave a note behind. If his capture was indeed imminent, his message once found would put the authorities onto his captors' trail. And if not, he'd simply call his students from a safe and secret place to advise them to ignore his warning. Offering plenty of his high quality homemade hooch for their next soirée would certainly buy their silence.

After being deported from the United States, Niko had returned to his native Poland and immersed himself in his research. He had wept and rejoiced when his old friend Katczynski told him Blaznikov was missing and presumed dead. Once reunited with his loved ones in Chicago, he would resume the life he had begun there decades before. Only alongside his bride with their children, grandchildren, and friends gathered around would he feel truly whole again.

He breathed on his lenses and rubbed at them with his handkerchief. His adversaries' identity puzzled him, though clearly it was someone with keen interest in his recent breakthrough. Perhaps they had managed to trace their prototype's "special delivery". The secret nature of their endeavors helped narrow down the list of usual suspects. His stomach began to turn, realizing whom he was likely dealing with. Making off with years of research data *and* destroying the first workable prototype to rid his family of their Affliction forever—whomever their attackers were could have ruined everything Niko and his sons had ever worked for had he ignored Kat's urging to keep the MGS in storage.

Niko tucked the handkerchief back into his pocket and tugged at his chin. Celebrating Christmas here with his family would be wantonly reckless. Sharp minds had sought him out in a well-organized and well-executed maneuver despite the great pains he had taken to keep a low profile after making tenure here. His fellow researchers were welcome to the headlines and the limelight. He busied himself teaching the Institute's biomolecular engineering undergrads and puttering about in the lab after hours. Anyone seeking him out could only intend to exploit his latest accomplishments. After years of setbacks, false starts, and dead ends, his rapid and remarkable progress lately dulled his usual keen sense of caution and wariness.

At length, his thumping heart quieted enough for him to hear normally again. He put his glasses back on and crossed the room to the door. The latch disengaged after he keyed in the entry code. He pulled on the handle and slipped into the larger room, letting the door close behind him.

The dim glow from the myriad test instruments enabled Niko to find his way toward one particular console mounted atop a lab bench. He grinned after reading the pop-up window that had appeared on the screen after he fled. The ad hoc backup had successfully mirrored today's work to his private and secure server back in the States. With his data spirited safely away, there was no reason for him to tarry further.

In the windowless room to his left rose the building's exterior wall. He could slip out the emergency exit there and trot across the parade grounds to the transit station near the campus' main entrance. According to his watch, it was already the wee hours of Sunday morning. He could disappear into the throngs on the streets after closing time and make the night's last tram with time to spare.

Niko's mental list of necessities to pack evaporated after tinkling bells startled him. He turned to see the door he had just come through ajar. Puzzled, he tiptoed back and bent down to examine the door jamb. A tiny wooden block had been wedged there between it and the corner of the door. He certainly did not remember *that* having been there before.

All the lights came up at once. He blinked, trying to pinpoint his pursuer but saw only spots. He rubbed his eyes and turned toward the light switches next to the door on the other side of the room. No one was there.

The bells again. They passed over his head, followed by a *thump* from behind him. "Please do not leave so soon, Teacher Most Honorable. You're the guest of honor at our party!"

Niko spun around. A young woman dressed in a dark battle dress uniform sat on her haunches atop a lab bench nearby, chewing at a lock of her jet black hair. A long wooden staff hung over one shoulder and an automatic pistol in its holster the other. The smug air about her spoke volumes. How could she have possibly known he would understand her every word? Korean was certainly her native language, though her speech patterns resembled Japanese. Softer consonants and the subtle manner in which she inflected her vowels differently, though, drew Niko to conclude she was from the North. Confirmation of his suspicions the Democratic People's Republic of Korea was indeed behind this attack.

"I can have you arrested for attempted theft of government property!" he said in Polish. "This is a secure area!"

"You do so say," she replied in kind and swept her gloved hand toward the instruments rigged up around the room. "Flashy lab equipment for some sexy, but these not are why came we. We come to you find, *seonsaeng-nim.*" Her lips parted into a knowing grin. "Teacher Most Honorable Nikodemos Opoworo," she continued in Korean. "The world's foremost authority on ailuranthropy!"

Niko felt his heart skip a beat. Not only were the North Koreans after him, this woman knew the true nature of his research. Like only a member of Blaznikov's inner circle would.

She leapt off the lab bench and landed on the floor nearby with her back to him. A pair of pearl-shaped chimes clanged together, dangling from her ears by long silver threads. They reminded him of the triangles his grandchildren played in an elementary school recital years before. Hands clasped behind her back, she turned and flashed him a sweet, sickening smile. "Hana."

Niko blinked. "Er . . . excuse me?"

"'Hana' call me," the young woman said in her broken Polish. "Your name I know do. Now you mine."

Her hands blurred as she snatched the staff from her back and twirled it around her head. "Mawro right do," she said after its tip stopped millimeters above his ear. "Opoworo *seonsaeng-nim* shrinking not violet. Most person flinch when I *bong* swing."

His eyes narrowed. "I've trained in the Arts for years. I knew the moment you grabbed your weapon you were quite capable of placing it precisely where you wanted. Someone clearly went through much trouble to send you here. You wouldn't dare risk injuring me."

Hana screwed up her face. The North's intelligence briefings clearly left much to be desired.

"So now you know something about me," he said in Korean. "I suppose now you plan to take me to this 'Mawro' person?"

"Yes, that's right, Teacher Most Honorable," she replied in kind. "Captain Mawro is very interested in the things you do and how you do them. He became our capable and heroic leader after Captain Blaznikov's death."

Niko clenched his jaw to avoid his mouth falling open. So the rumors *were* true!

She produced a small handheld transceiver from a small pouch fixed to her web belt. "Cub to Tiger, over," she said, receiving only static in reply.

He looked down at the floor lest his eyes betray him. She was wasting her time keying up again and again. He researched the impacts of radio frequency emissions on living tissues in this building, constructed inside a massive Faraday cage to prevent any RF energy from coming in or going out. Her two-way would be useless in here.

Hana cursed under her breath and pocketed the transceiver. She toyed with the little orb hanging from one ear between her fingers for a moment then nodded toward the door. Niko played along, and she fell in behind him. Good. She was forced now to improvise. As was he.

He glanced at their reflection as they passed a wall-mounted display case. Her staff's tip hovered above the small of his back, ready to strike. "That's a rather, er . . . unconventional weapon you have to cover me, Hana my dear."

"Captain Mawro insisted we not risk damage to your equipment or to you, Teacher Most Honorable. He knows I might get . . . carried away using anything other than this."

His sympathies went out to her. The girl was doing a lot more talking than he would have expected a trained, professional commando to do. Maybe she was just born batshit crazy? No matter. Niko concluded meeting Mawro now was not in his best interests. Bargaining from such a compromised position was a loathsome prospect.

He pushed the door open and glanced up at a spot on the ceiling. Out of the corner of his eye, he glimpsed her doing the same. With both hands, he slammed the door to trap her weapon against the jamb and hurled his weight against the staff. After her squeal came a dull *thud* and the tinkling of her tiny pendants rolling across the floor. Niko flung open the door and leaped over where Hana lay dazed in a crumpled heap.

Hana got to her feet with an angry snarl as he sprinted for the emergency exit doors across the lab. "That was *rude*, Teacher Most Honorable. Please, do not make me hurt you!" She grunted and swung her staff towards him, moves punctuated by a hollow *click* and an eerie hissing sound.

Niko yelped after his feet ran out from under him. Cloth tore as he fell and landed on his back. He stared with wide eyes toward where a long ceramic blade pinned a piece of his lab coat to the beam above his head.

He craned his neck in the direction of a hollow wooden *clack*. A wicked-looking spear sprouted forth from her staff's remaining segment, and she lunged. He jerked to one side an instant before she drove it into the floor where his shoulder had been. With a grunt Niko jumped up and tugged the blade free from the beam. The swatch of fabric from his coat fluttered to the floor while she came at him in earnest. Though he parried her first several attacks well enough, he knew his aging body's reduced stamina put him at an increasing disadvantage. Hana worked him away from the emergency doors back over to the lab equipment. This was bad. His best chance to ditch his pursuers would be lost if he missed the damn tram. He had to get the hell out of here. Now.

Niko reached his arm out to deflect a thrust from her spear. After its tip flew past his head, he grabbed the shaft and heaved. Hana cursed and dove into a rolling tumble while he swiped upward with his blade. Though he missed her head by mere millimeters, he did sever one of the long silver threads connected to her earlobes. Her momentum sent one of her little pearl-shaped pendants flying over the bench tops. It tinkled as it landed and bounced under the clear shield around one of the test rigs. Meters red-lined and annunciators squealed in alarm when the rig's radiated energy strayed from nominal.

Hana screamed in agony behind him. Niko turned to see her on her knees, clutching her ears in her hands. Blood ran down the sides of her face in tiny rivulets from where her fingernails pierced her skin. Though her strange reaction piqued his interest, he wasn't about to let a chance like this pass him by. While his would-be captor carried on, he bolted across the laboratory and pushed open the emergency door. The sweet smell of cold night air rewarded him. Just beyond the Oder River flowed past toward Szczecin. On the bank opposite laid the village square where, as a boy, he had played *zośka* with the other neighborhood kids. He would miss his friends here; he hoped they would come to forgive him.

Niko started when he felt someone grab the nape of his neck. He was in the air at once and landed roughly on his back. The door slammed shut while he blinked up into the lights above. He gasped, recognizing Hana glaring down at him. She appeared different. Disturbingly different.

Though her uniform and gear were unchanged, orange and white fur now covered her face to her hairline. Black stripes along her cheekbones slumped downward in line with the furrows in her brow. Claws poking through the fingers of her gloves scraped against her weapon's wooden surface as she drew it back over her head.

Niko scrambled to get his feet under him. *Dear God!* She's *Kindred?*

"With regret, I must now be rude in return, Teacher Most Honorable," Hana said in a raspy voice. He heard her staff slice through the air the instant before he saw stars.

Franciszka yawned and tapped in the entry code for the door. She flipped on the light switch and scanned the room to see just what was amiss. The computers monitoring her experiment had autodialed her cell phone after the instruments detected something outside of nominal. After throwing on some clothes, she trudged the three blocks between here and her flat through the snow. Tomorrow, she would bring in a cot.

A flashing light caught her attention atop a device on the room's far side. Franciszka stepped over and bent down to examine a pH probe submerged in a beaker half-full of murky greenish-yellow liquid. She gritted her teeth, seeing it had been unplugged. No wonder why the instrumentation had gone crazy.

With an irritated sigh, she snapped the connector back into place and poked the reset button to cancel the alarm. The indicator LED changed from flashing red to steady green.

"Really, Marek? Prank my experiment the day before we go on Christmas break? Oh, you are *so* dead when I—"

She spied the hastily scribbled note on the white board next to the door. Its message was clear: she was in danger, leave the building immediately, call for help.

A moment later, Franciszka bolted outside through the building's double doors. She pulled her cell phone from the pocket of her hoodie and dialed 112. "I'm calling from the Technological University of West Pomerania!" she said when the emergency dispatcher answered. "Send police to Building 133—I think my professor has been abducted!"

CHAPTER TWELVE

THE SLITS IN HER EYES narrowed. Hana sighed and gazed at her reflection in the mirror of the ladies' restroom. Extending a claw from one finger, she scratched at the fur covering her face and mulled how her transformation had come at a most inconvenient time. The sweet smell of mountain air was palpable in her daydream earlier while the sun rose over Paetku's peak. With their mission complete, she and Mawro would catch the next express to Berlin. Then, only the long flight to Pyongyang via Beijing would keep her from her time alone to train. And hunt.

All she had to look forward to now once they left the campus was the dank, putrid air below deck aboard an ocean freighter. She hated how she and Mawro were forced to travel by way of the leaky old tubs whenever they were "indecent." Maybe if her cycle completed before the ship reached the Strait of Gibraltar, they could go ashore and catch a plane back home like regular people.

Her black-and-white striped tail twitched as she pulled at the waist of her uniform. That sweetheart Sung Jin promptly delivered her rucksack so she could sneak in here. Though her Pearls afforded her a modicum of control over her transformations, her body reverted to its ailuran form whenever one of the tiny round pendants were damaged.

She leaned up against the wall and tugged at one of her spats. Hana wiggled her exposed toes, grateful to be finally free of her tactical boots. Her claws dug into the tender areas between her paw pads whenever she morphed wearing anything on her feet. The base of her back still ached from having her tail cramped into her other pants for nearly an hour. The trousers she wore now were specially tailored to accommodate her unique "features." She had endured the discomforts awaiting Sung Jin to relieve her. Until then, she had been under orders to stand watch over their unwelcoming host.

Her pack hoisted atop her shoulder, Hana pulled the door open. The instant she crossed the threshold, her whiskers began to twitch. There was a different scent now. The aroma of smug confidence she was accustomed to during one of Mawro's campaigns was gone, replaced by the sour, sickening odor of frustration and anxiety. It grew stronger with every step she took toward Dr. Opoworo's laboratory where the rest of the team was working. Upon entering, she understood why. Their Special Operations Force escorts stood together along one wall while Sung Jin conducted their mission briefing. Their combat gear donned, each man held his weapon at the ready. They were on high alert once again. Something big was going on.

"We've been found out," Mawro said from a hardwood chair next to one of the test benches. His arms and legs were bound fast by thick nylon straps—he couldn't possibly intend to proceed with the experiment, could he?

He nodded to his left toward Doctor Opoworo, still out cold from Hana's strike. "Apparently, he managed to get some sort of distress call off before you sniffed him out and subdued him." Mawro had ordered the professor bound hand and foot to a lab stool as their team set up to prevent him from causing a ruckus. A makeshift gag fashioned from a long strip of duct tape wound around his head and mouth.

"For our Great Leader, we will be victorious!" Sung Jin said at the end of his troops' mission briefing. "Yes, Commander Choi!" they shouted back. He dispatched them in groups of two and three while plugging what appeared to be a radio transceiver into the wall. "Aren't our radios useless in here?" Hana asked while the device powered up.

One corner of his mouth turned upward. "If we were actually transmitting over the air, then yes. But each surveillance patrol is equipped with a carrier current unit like this one to transmit over the building's electrical wiring. They'll be able to communicate with one another and with me by plugging in to any outlet." As if on cue, the first squad reported in. They were in position and "all clear." Perhaps the knuckle-draggers Sung Jin insisted on dragging around with them might turn out useful after all.

Several square metal horns fastened to the ceiling pointed down at Mawro in the heavy wooden chair. She figured them to be high-powered microwave antennas, connected by ductwork to the apparatus which had to be their energy source. Mawro tapped away at the keys on two halves of a split keyboard clamped to the chair's arms and twirled a small trackball.

"You needn't worry," he said, his gaze flashing back and forth between Hana's face and the projection screen behind her.

She knit her brow and sniffed at the air again. The stink of fear dissipated after Sung Jin's soldiers deployed, leaving Mawro's reassuring calm and composed scent strong in the room. "Captain, if we've been discovered, shouldn't we hasten to depart?"

He snorted. "We brought Commander Choi's team with us to buy us time if necessary. Opoworo had been close to a breakthrough, which we will now realize!"

Though Hana savored melee combat in her ailuran form, she desperately wanted Mawro to be right. But this . . . this *thing* he finished rigging up while she was out of the room resembled a high-tech version of an ancient torture device. And strapped to the chair, he would be forced once the experiment began to finish. No matter how excruciating doing so might be.

"There, done! This time, I'm sure I've got it!"

For his sake, Hana hoped so. Burns patched the skin on his arms and hands. His writhing about had worked the tail of his shirt free from his pants. He looked like hell. Mawro was driven by a single-mindedness peculiar to both legendary scientists and infamous madmen. Clear now was why Blaznikov had forbidden him carry out such experiments, no matter how many times she volunteered.

Sweat trailed down the sides of Mawro's face. He breathed deeply as if to steel himself. "Now, let us try again, shall we?"

Red lights came on from atop the instrument panel to indicate the field generators were producing energy. He clenched his eyes shut and tugged against his restraints. A small tuft of gray fur formed on the back of his hand, then another above his wrist, then another on his forearm. She glanced up to his face and gasped. The streaked white ruff had already filled out beneath his chin. His ears grew long and narrow before black hairs sprouted from their tips, forming little tufts. Mawro's breathing deepened with increasing ferocity. The corners of his mouth turned up as his canines lengthened into fangs. Whiskers popped out from along either side of his elongating muzzle. Mawro flexed his fingers. Dark claws protruded from underneath the fur covering them.

His eyes fluttered open. His pupils had become slits like her own, indicating his transformation was complete. The lights above the machine went out as it powered down.

"I was right, Hana!" came Mawro's gravelly voice. His eyes shone with delight as he examined the fur on his hands. "Blaznikov would have never permitted my getting close enough to the doctor to test my theory. We should have done this ages ago!"

Opoworo groaned and blinked before she could reply. He shot her a cross look before turning his attention to Mawro. At once, his eyes went wide. He struggled at his bindings, making the lab stool's metal parts clank together. Hana knit her brow as the doctor and his stool hopped toward the wooden chair. The professor's glasses had been knocked off during their tussle earlier. Was he having trouble seeing? What about this transformation agitated him so?

Mawro's eyes remained glued to his screens despite the antics of their reluctant host. "I am disappointed, Hana. You must not have made our gracious host comfortable enough." The acrid scent of his anger bit at her nose.

Red lights lit up to indicate Mawro had engaged the next stage. He clenched his fists and grunted as his transformation commenced. Teeth and nails returned to their human likeness. Then the ears. The strands of gray and white fur receded back into their follicles while his muzzle disappeared into his cheekbones. He rested his head against the back of the chair after the lights went out. The sides of his face glistened with sweat. "Hana . . . please . . . untie me . . . now," he said toward the ceiling between gasps.

"You're next, my dear," he said after she released his straps. "I expect the process to work just as well for you, though it might be a bit . . . uncomfortable."

She reached into her pocket and produced a pair of silver pendants. "But Captain, Opoworo's equipment damaged my Pearls! Even if that machine restores my human form, how can I be sure I'll maintain it with these broken?" Lying side by side in her palm, Hana poked at them with one finger. "It would be, um . . . complicated if I morphed in a crowded airport. Or even on the plane!"

"You really only need them during periods of intense stimulation, like combat or hunting. Something pedestrian like flying home shouldn't be a problem until I make time to repair their neurostimulators. Think of this as a 'proof of concept' with no messy molting! Then you and I can fly back to Pyongyang as we first planned."

But Hana didn't hear him. Opoworo's strange scent had captured her attention instead. The professor stared at Mawro in silence, eyes filled with some strong emotion she couldn't quite put her finger on.

"Hana! That means 'sit down in the chair' . . . now." Mawro reached over and plucked the tiny orbs from her hand. "You would be well advised to not be so careless in the future. Never underestimate *anyone* named Opoworo." He stooped over with the Pearls between his fingers and held them up to their host's face. "Isn't that right, Doctor?"

Opoworo screamed wide-eyed into the duct tape covering his mouth. His eyes rolled up into his head, and his chin slumped to his chest.

"His eyes! His eyes!" Hana cried after the professor fell silent. The combination of pungent anxiety and foul revulsion emanating from his unconscious form threatened to overcome her senses. "Teacher Most Honorable appears to have seen a ghost!"

Mawro drew himself up to his full height and cast a rueful look down at the man bound to the lab stool. "He has."

Hana's hackles rose when the shock wave tore through the room. Sung Jin barked into the mic of his carrier current unit, ordering his teams to fall back and take up defensive positions around them. They responded and went offline one after another.

With a snarl Mawro yanked the thumb drive free from his console and stuffed it into his pants pocket. "Change of plan. We'll flee now with Opoworo's data. I should be able to recreate some of his work aboard the boat back to Namp'o."

Hana blinked while he seated himself again in the heavy wooden chair. "Captain, what are you—"

"Under the circumstances, I believe our ailuran forms afford us our best chance of escape, my dear," he said and tapped away on his keypad.

Before Hana could respond came gunshots and another explosion. Opoworo's would-be rescuers were close, and regular police didn't rate that kind of ordinance. Their escorts had to be fighting soldier to soldier. Though this was just what they trained for, their opponents outnumbered them and were fighting on familiar territory.

Their commander met her gaze, answering her unasked question with a simple nod. "Whatever you're going to do, Captain, I respectfully suggest you do it fast," he said in a wavering voice. "I can't raise two of my teams and fear them lost."

"Right, then," Mawro said, his fingers a blur above his keyboard. "I will need hardly a minute to make adjustments before we begin."

Sung Jin's console came to life. Hana listened while his troops relayed their position and status. All of them were hopelessly pinned down and taking fire. At least they had positively identified their opponents—*Jednostka Wojskowa* 2305. He cursed and turned to her. "GROM!" they said together. The Poles must have been expecting them if their Special Forces counter-terrorism team had been deployed on such short notice. But how? "Captain! We may not even have that long!"

"Let them come," Mawro said over shooting and yelling from down the corridor. He made a spectacle of pressing the final keystroke of his console's command sequence. "I've got something I've been just dying to show them."

"Cover the doors, Lieutenant, if you please." Hana nodded to Sung Jin and slung her staff over one shoulder. Atop the nearest lab bench, she launched herself toward the wooden box trusses running the length of the lab's ceiling. She landed between a pair of risers and drew her pistol.

"No firearms!"

She glanced down to see Mawro glaring up at her from his chair.

"Damage to the equipment may precipitate dire consequences for both of us."

Hana flashed a sheepish grin and replaced the weapon in its holster.

Gunshots rang out from outside the lab door. It was time. Sung Jin crouched behind one of the benches and trained his hand-held laser dazzler on the lab doors. She laid a hand against the quillon of her ceramic blade. Their plan consisted of him blinding whoever entered before she swooped down from behind and "neutralized" them.

The red lights lit up once more. Mawro grunted in response to the energy field sweeping over him. Hana did a double-take toward his restraints lying in a pile on the floor before realizing he had hooked his feet around the legs of the wooden chair. His trembling knuckles turned white as he clutched at the chair's armrests. Veins bulged from his arms and forehead. He screwed his eyes shut and screamed through gritted teeth, *willing* himself sit still. Despite being cooked from the inside out.

Fur covered Mawro's arms while his muzzle formed again. Hana winced after another explosion blew the doors off their hinges and across the room. Two members of the GROM team bolted through the smoke and dust and took up positions on either side of the door. Two more came running in, their MP5s trained on the three of them. One barked a demand for their immediate surrender—in Korean.

Shit! They really do *know who we are!*

"Now!" Sung Jin popped up and keyed his dazzler. The point man clutched at his eyes and fell while his teammate and the other men opened fire. Her partner's body jerked side to side from bullets tearing through his limbs and torso.

"NO!" Hana sprang and landed behind the first shooter. An upward swipe of her blade severed the hand with which the man held his rifle's fore-stock. He screamed and dropped to his knees after its magazine emptied into the apparatus next to Mawro. She dove for cover behind a lab bench. Their opponents let off several bursts before they ran to aid their wounded comrades.

Her breath caught in her throat when she turned toward Mawro's pained cry. One hand to her mouth, she took in the frightful sight of him. He lay curled up into a ball, hands pulling savagely at the fur on the back of his head. His arms and legs were huge. His canines reached almost to his chin. Every successive breath came from deeper within his chest until he was practically growling. Something had gone wrong. Something had gone *horribly* wrong.

Her nose discerned a scent she had never encountered before. Though it resembled Mawro's strong, masculine air, it was also frighteningly primal.

Hana gritted her teeth and peered beneath the benches. The two remaining GROM men bolted into the room. One ran over to cover Mawro, the other checked Sung Jin's vitals. Her jaw clenched when the man rolled her partner's limp form onto his back. One remaining man helped the trooper whose hand she had sliced open get to his feet. With blood squirting from his teammate's ruined hand, the would-be rescuer cursed and tapped at the side of his helmet. She smiled in spite of herself—their mission planners had apparently also overlooked the uselessness of their radios in here.

She snuck through the maze of lab equipment while a plan to distract them turned in her mind. Their wounded comrade whom Sung Jin had blinded lay moaning with his hands over his eyes. The odds were now in her favor.

Then she heard the screaming. Drawing her pistol, she peeked out between the uprights of an instrument rack. There was Mawro, down on all fours, fangs clamped around a GROM trooper's ankle. With a twist of his head, he sent the man flying headlong across the room. He plowed into the back of the fellow tending his comrade, bowling them all over.

Hana knew an opportunity when she saw one. She brandished her weapon and leapt out from behind cover toward the man nearest her partner. She gasped, seeing Mawro tower above the lab benches. A torrent of blood splashed across her face and chest after a swipe of Mawro's massive paw sent a trooper's entrails hurtling into the wall with a sickening *splat*. Where in the hell had he come from, anyway? She cursed herself for letting her guard down while the man's eviscerated body slumped to the floor.

Mawro swung again. The last man standing shrieked and fell after rapier-like claws gouged his face from hairline to chin. Genuine primal fear arose within Hana while he scanned the room, eyes wide, angry, and deadly wild.

He threw back his head and roared.

Chapter Thirteen

Mawro worked his eyes in the dim light to regain his bearings. He lay prone on the cold ground, debilitated senses struggling to process the stimuli assaulting them. The strange sensation of warm drops like a summer's rain falling on his back, for instance. Ridiculous. He and his team had come to Poland in the middle of winter!

Searing pain tore through his right arm the instant he put weight on it. He collapsed and planted his face in the fluffy white snow beneath. It was then he noticed something above the base of his spine, like someone had set a sack of flour on his back. Was someone sitting on him? As the ringing in his ears subsided, he recognized the sound of a woman crying.

Oh, shit! Where is—

After jabbing his other elbow into the snow, Mawro gritted his teeth and pushed himself up. Hana straddled his back with her pistol upside-down between her hands. When he rolled onto his side to face her, she dropped the weapon and threw her arms around his neck.

"Back you are!" she sobbed in Polish and buried her face in the fur on his chest. "By the Rage you consume."

That explains a lot. "Wait! H-how did you . . . ?"

Hana sniffed and stood. "Against your body I press my barrel of pistol, hot from shooting as we GROM fled."

He felt his face flush beneath his cheek fur. "Who . . . who told you about that?"

"Comrade Blaznikov speak when last you . . . 'indisposed.'"

He sniffed at the night air, his olfactories instantly overcome by the strong odor of ammonia. In an instant, he recalled muzzle flashes. Men screaming. Bones snapping and flesh tearing. Bodies going limp in his arms.

They had somehow managed to fight their way out of the lab but were still short of their goal. He scanned the dead rushes behind Hana, looking for their trooper escort. But where were they? They weren't expendable just yet. He would need their help getting him and Hana back to the ship without being seen.

"Is . . . is it just us?"

"*Ne, apa.*"

"What about Choi?"

She shook her head and stared at the ground.

Mawro bared his teeth and turned back toward the campus across the river. Soldiers and police had spread out across the grounds to look for them. During his delirium, Hana somehow had guided him to this secluded spot downriver from the Institute near a forest preserve. Good girl.

With a grunt he got to his feet. He stared down at Hana and gasped— even at her full height, she barely came up to his chest. Mawro held his huge hands in front of his face and examined them front and back. Mouth wide open, he tapped at the end of one canine tooth then the other with his tongue. He realized they stuck out almost to his chin once he closed his mouth.

"Hana-*ttanim*, listen," he said as he squatted down and patted at his front pants pocket. "Take the thumb drive from here and hold onto it. I don't trust my big hands to not fumble it. For what this operation has cost us, I'm not taking any chances with Dr. Opoworo's data."

She shook her head as if to clear it and did as she was asked. "What happened back there, Papa?"

"That data I gave you might give us some clue," he replied in Korean without bothering to correct her. "I won't know until I comb through it all."

"You needn't for me to understand that was no normal transformation!"

Memories from the terrible day Werecat's Rage overpowered him for the first time flooded his mind. The day he had become a monster. The day he had lost the family he loved. He would have certainly gone feral but for Blaznikov's men. They had encircled him like adjurists at an exorcism, lancing him with white-hot pokers until his Affliction's manifestations subsided. And on *this* day, history could well have repeated itself. *Thank you, Dear Father, for keeping her safe. Amen.*

Mawro rubbed his face with his hands, careful to avoid poking himself in the eye with his long claws. "I knew something like this might happen. The process Professor Opoworo was working on wasn't like our regular patterns." He drew a circle in the air with his finger. "When you and I change back into human form, it completes a cycle." Then he traced a semi-circle in one direction and back to the point he began. "What we saw during the test runs was not a completion of that process. It was a reversal."

Hana's eyes went wide. "So that's why you didn't molt?"

He nodded. "Neither would have you. Morphogenetic indices are present in every cell's DNA, and each one exists in a given state. Certain stimuli coax their metamorphosis into whatever form suits the body's current needs."

She palmed her temples and shook her head. "All very interesting, but what does this have to do with—"

"I told you about stem cells and their inherent morphing capabilities, remember? Certain chemical compounds introduced into the body break down following exposure to specific types of RF emissions. These stimulate the cells into moving back and forth between adjacent states in their developmental continuum. In my case, between my human and ailuran forms."

"Then why did your body respond . . . *this* way?"

"After GROM shot up the instruments, who knows what manner of out-of-band emissions I was exposed to? They must have triggered some sort of global reaction. And, well—"

The night sky lit up behind them. They ducked down just before a searchlight beam passed overhead. Mawro and Hana pushed the rushes around them aside and spied the beam's origin—a patrol boat motoring upriver along the bank. GROM's thoroughness was impressive. They were leaving nothing to chance.

"Do you think they saw us?"

"I certainly hope so." Shouts came from the deck of the craft before it throttled up and headed toward them. "I've got an idea. Come Hana, quickly!"

The patrolman snarled and batted at the chest-high vegetation all around him with his nightstick. "Kuba, you shit-for-brains. I told you there would be no one here!"

"Fuck you, Kaz." A man atop the boat's flybridge pointed down near where his partner stood. "I *know* I saw something tall and hairy in that patch of reeds when I swung the spot over here."

"Ah, pipe down, you two. Those GROM guys must've spooked you morons fierce at the briefing." Their chief shuffled to the stern and lit a cigarette. "We've been chasing ghosts for an hour!"

Mawro held a finger to his lips and glanced over at Hana. They waded together through the cold water opposite the patrol boat from where the crewmen searched the shoreline. This particular craft had a fiberglass hull and a shallow keel enabling it to navigate close to shore. Its crew had done exactly that, just as he had wanted them to.

Keeping his knees bent, the two of them trundled along, although Hana could barely keep her nose above the surface. Their fur would protect them from hypothermia while submerged in the frigid water, but only for a time.

Hana's muzzle twitched. He knew she would not want him to see her teeth chattering lest he worry for her welfare. They had to work fast. Her manic desire to please him would drive her to remain at his side until she keeled over.

He cocked his head in the boat's direction. She replied with a nod, silently indicating she was ready. Good.

"Bolek, someone or some*thing* was hiding in these rushes just a moment—"

The voices muffled after Mawro ducked his head below the surface. Feet planted into the muddy river bottom, Mawro bent down into a squat and laced his fingers. Hana brought her knees to her chin and swept her arms behind her. When her feet settled into his palms, he thrust his hands skyward.

She twirled out of her pitch tuck and dove toward the deck. Lunging with her staff, she delivered a crushing blow to the pilot's head. The man fell out of his chair and rolled off the open back of the flybridge, landing in a heap on the afterdeck. Mawro lost sight of her after she pushed off the railing nearest the patrolman on shore. He beamed like a father at his daughter's dance recital when he heard her weapon contact its target with a loud *crack*. But as the man collapsed to the marshy ground came the horrifying sound of a pistol's safety flipping off.

The crew chief leveled his service piece at the back of Hana's head and reached inside the trigger guard. Mawro drew back and connected a hellacious haymaker with the side of the man's head, driving him into a wooden piling behind the boat. His eyes shot daggers into the chief's back as the man slumped backward and splashed into the cold water.

"Playtime's over, Hana." Clutching his throbbing arm to him, Mawro kicked the unconscious man lying across the transom overboard. He drummed his fingers on one rung of the ladder up to the craft's flybridge. Despite being soaked, Hana would insist she join him if he climbed up there, putting herself at risk for hypothermia while they made their escape. "Radio *Pe Gae Bong* and let them know we're coming," he said and seated himself at the main helm.

She nodded and leapt atop the foredeck. Flipping every light switch he found off, Mawro intended to exploit their innate advantages operating at night. He pulled the clutches back toward him and cracked open the throttles. The boat's engines purred while the darkened craft backed away from shore. With a twirl of the wheel, he pointed the bow downriver and idled the motors. He notched the drive selectors forward and whistled to Hana before grasping his wrist above his head. She jumped over the windscreen and grabbed the gunwale opposite him as Mawro mashed the three red levers to the console. The craft lurched ahead with a throaty roar and sped off into the murky darkness.

Earlier with her now-functional transceiver, Hana radioed their ride back to

Namp'o. The ship had already cast off from Szczecin and motored up the Oder River several miles ahead of them toward the Lagoon. She stood watch astern since to alert Mawro should GROM or anyone else pursue them. So far, they seemed to have the element of surprise working in their favor. All the better. She had a date to keep with a certain People's Army intelligence officer. Once back in Pyongyang, they would take a nice, relaxing walk in the woods together. Then she would go completely feral on him.

Never did Hana think she would long to board another noisy, dirty freighter. But the captain and the chief engineer's cabins aboard *Pe Gae Bong* had genuine bathtubs. She would soon commandeer one of them, fill it to the top with steaming hot water, climb in, and fall asleep.

Warm thoughts came to mind while she hugged herself tight. She had remained at her post steadfast, despite her fingers going numb over twenty minutes ago. No matter. Mawro was counting on her. They were a team. They were . . . family.

"HANA, COME HERE!"

Mawro's voice barely registered over the roar of the three massive outboard motors behind, all running near wide open throttle. She turned toward the cockpit and saw him wave her over. Her transformation, their dunk in the freezing water, and now keeping watch in the chilly air had altogether taken a heavy toll. She shuffled over to where he stood and cursed herself for zoning out.

The strange effects of his last change still puzzled her. He appeared bulkier than usual, even in his ailuran form. Standing for him was probably more comfortable than trying to squeeze into the pilot's chair.

"Here," he said and indicated the steering wheel. Hana sat down while Mawro disappeared into the boat's small forecastle. He returned a moment later with a pair of heavy wool blankets. One he draped over her shoulders and tucked its free ends under the seat cushion. After bundling up with the other one, he reached out to take the helm again.

"I've got this," she said with a shake of her head and peered down at the gauges. "We have plenty of fuel. At the rate we're going, we should catch *Pe Gae Bong* up in about ten minutes. Maybe you should sit down and rest?"

He chuckled and stuffed himself into the chair across the narrow aisle. "I suppose you're right."

Hana bit her lip and focused on the slalom course of blinking red and green channel markers ahead.

"What happened to me is *not* your fault, understand?" Mawro rose and stood next to her. "I'm sure I can figure a way to—"

"What if you *don't*, Papa?" Hana waved a hand toward his monstrous form. "What if you stay like this forev—?"

They both started when a high-intensity spotlight shone down from beneath the nose of the helicopter following them. Reverberations pounded within her chest as it passed overhead. Though it looked like a Polish Land Forces utility craft, swivel-mounted machine guns outboard of each side door equipped it well enough to scuttle their escape plans. Permanently.

Mawro snarled. Both of them had been careless enough to let this damned thing sneak up behind. "Hana! Eyes on the water!"

"HEAVE TO! PREPARE TO BE BOARDED!" a man's voice boomed in Polish over the helicopter's external speaker. With a nod from Mawro, she palmed the throttles forward to their stops. The three motors crescendoed while the chopper came around for another pass.

Tracer fire lit up the night sky around them. "Get down!" Mawro leapt out of his seat and threw his huge arms over her head. Wood and fiberglass splintered as bullets ripped the flybridge above their heads to pieces. The boat's windscreen disintegrated, pelting them with tiny shards of polycarbonate.

He loosened his grip after their attackers flew past. Hana popped her head up and spied a bend in the river ahead. "You pilot the boat," he said and cracked his knuckles. The helicopter circled around to charge them again. "I'll handle this."

She adjusted their course a little to port to follow the jog in the channel. After ducking into the forecastle again, Mawro emerged with a large extinguisher under his arm. He stepped to the stern, eyes fixed on the attacking craft. "On my signal, cut the power!" he said just as its crew opened fire. Hana glanced up at the small mirror above her head to see the tracers closing in on them. With a grunt he snapped the neck of the red canister. White chemical powder spewed forth from the hole. "NOW!"

The bow of the boat pitched downward when she pulled the throttles back. Mawro raised the extinguisher over his head and hurled it toward their attackers as their craft whooshed by. It flew through the open side door past the door gunner and bounced off the compartment's back wall. The craft rolled right and left as the makeshift rocket ricocheted around until the cockpit's windscreen blew out from the inside, venting a pale-colored cloud of caustic material. After veering toward the riverbank at a rakish angle, the main rotor topped several trees and snapped off. The stricken craft whirled around and crashed tail-first into the river.

Hana sat behind the helm, transfixed on the sight before her. Mawro panted while pieces from the chopper disappeared into the cold water. "Let's go," he said and plopped back down into his chair.

They caught the North Korean freighter up near the mouth of the Lagoon downriver from Police. Patches of thick fog had rolled in shortly after dispatching their pursuers. Hana had missed the ship's running lights at first, mistaking them for loading piers jutting out into the water from the chemical plant on shore.

"Look! There's *Pe Gae Bong*!" She throttled down and steered their boat in its direction. Hearing no reply, she glanced over to see Mawro slumped forward in his seat. She gasped and jabbed her hand in front of Mawro's nose. At least he was breathing. Physical exertion and his out-of-control transformation must have left him vulnerable to fatigue. Getting him aboard ship might be a trick, though. Maybe she could secure the tatters of his field uniform to the boatswain's chair with a couple karabiners.

She drew the small transceiver from her pocket and updated the freighter's crew as to what special accommodations Mawro might require. The lights along the weather deck blinked in response once the officer-of-the-watch initiated radio silence.

After stowing her device, she spied a blue glow in the fog to their starboard side, like some kind of will-o'-the-wisp. Another patrol boat rocketed toward them an instant later, the light bar atop its pilot house flashing. Hana cursed out loud. The other crew must be flying by instruments—how else could they have found a darkened craft like theirs in this soup?

Their pursuers opened up as soon as they came within range, sending tracer fire across their bow. This boat had been nimble and fast, to be sure. But seeing the craft following them plow through the choppy water, Hana knew it trumped theirs in horsepower. It was only a matter of time before they caught up. Death was not nearly as horrifying as the thought of her and Mawro being taken prisoner. Their return to Namp'o depended upon getting aboard their ship unseen. She needed a plan. Quick.

Hana bumped her forehead with her fist. She glanced over next to her to find Mawro lolled backward in his seat. How in the hell could he sleep at a time like this?

After rummaging about in the cubby beside her console, she found a bungee cord with which she lashed the boat's steering wheel into place. A gentle tug set their course toward the freighter just beyond its port bow. That gave her time to retrieve a pair of life vests from their locker in the forecastle. Grunting and cursing, she coaxed the larger one over Mawro's big body. The other patrol boat closed in as she snugged up her vest's own straps. No more time.

She spied a small anchor laid up against the transom with a length of mooring line coiled beside. Hana took one of the thick plastic tie wraps attached to her belt and cinched it around her ankle. She grabbed the scruff of Mawro's neck and pulled him out of his chair with a mighty heave.

Inspiration came in a flash while the bow of the ship disappeared into another fog bank. Hana loosed the bungee and followed suit. She began to count after the murky darkness swallowed up their pursuers' boat. At ten, she gritted her teeth and rolled the helm hard over to starboard. If she had turned too early, she and Mawro would die a quick and relatively painless death upon impact with the freighter's hull at breakneck speed. But if too late, they were sure to run aground on the rocky riverbank beyond. Capture would be all but certain.

The fog broke. Hana whooped and pumped her fist seeing "PE GAE BONG" spelled out in English and *Choseon-gul* above her head along the ship's starboard side. Though confident she had given their pursuers the slip for the moment, they couldn't hide for long from their radar. With a glance down at the compass, she adjusted course to just clear the larger vessel's stern. She picked her staff up from the deck and clipped it to the webbing on her back. Hana secured the wheel again and opened the throttles wide. With considerable effort, she dragged Mawro's bulk to their boat's diving platform.

She lifted the anchor and its line over the transom and set them both on the platform's edge. Another thick tie wrap went around Mawro's ankle. One more bound their ankles together before she knotted the rope securely through. Then she knelt down and put her arms under Mawro's shoulders. With a loud grunt, she pushed him clear of the stern and gulped in one final breath. He hit the water face-first. The line snapped taught, nearly ripping Hana's foot off her leg.

Mawro thrashed about while they sank. She took small comfort knowing he must have come to the instant cold water shot up his nostrils. He would have one hell of a headache in the morning. If they lived that long.

The patrol boat passed overhead in pursuit of their now-abandoned craft. She reached down and drew forth her knife from its sheath lashed to her leg. She sliced through the binding between their feet with a flick of her wrist, and they rose. They gasped, gagged, and coughed for some while after breaking the surface while the freighter's crew trained a spotlight on them. The pneumatic deck gun fired a rope over their heads with a hollow *thoomp*. Hana caught the line as it fell to the water and tucked it in her belt. She paddled over to Mawro and hugged him close before flashing a "thumbs up". The windlass hauled them alongside to the waiting boatswain's chair. Reserves gone and running on pure adrenaline, she thrust his bottom up onto the seat and secured his webbing to the lines.

Mawro flashed a weak smile. "Well done, my dear," he said before his eyes rolled up into his head and his chin slumped forward.

She jumped up into his lap and signaled to the deckmen with a twirl of her finger. "Thank you, Papa," she said as they began their ascent.

Hana placed her head on his shoulder and sighed.

Chapter Fourteen

Tommy liked campfires. Happy memories had wafted through his mind all evening, formed during many a family gathering around an open fire on a warm summer's night. Tonight would be an exception to the rule.

Betelgeuse and Rigel twinkled brightly in the tiny scrap of eastern sky visible above the leafless trees and neighborhood buildings. Tommy hadn't been keen on his sister's cookout idea at first, remembering one particular January night at Fort McCoy in Wisconsin for cold weather re-cert training. He and his shivering shipmates huddled together until dawn around a pathetic little fire they managed to light despite numb fingers, soggy matches, and flaring tempers. Now, he found himself grateful to Pawly for talking them into it. Their first Christmas together in three years was bound to be memorable.

Fortunately, she had hatched this crazy plan with several hours of daylight left. He knew something was up when she ducked out of the house and shoveled off the back patio. Nat hefted an armful of split wood from the pile next to the privacy fence while Top built up the kindling. Even Stuie helped out and brushed snow from the logs around the fire pit for everyone to sit on.

Tommy had watched through the dining room's picture window while he and Annie debated the Blackhawk's likely postseason rivals. Seated together at the dinner table, they finished buttering several loaves worth of bread slices for pie iron *pierogi*. Alex sliced up an entire wedge of *twaróg*, Dory peeled a bag of potatoes, and Sunny brought out some of her special spicy sauerkraut. Top had earned himself an earful on his way through the kitchen to use the bathroom, calling the stuff *kimchi*.

They all shuffled out to the backyard once darkness fell. Nat lit the tinder while everyone else carried the food from the house. A sheet of plywood supported by two sawhorses the men hauled out of the garage earlier became a makeshift buffet table. A roaring fire soon blazed before them, giving plenty of light to see by while they stuffed their pie irons.

Everyone took their seats as the logs burned down. Dory asked for bowed heads and recited a short prayer of thanksgiving in Polish. After he said *amen*, each of them thrust an iron or two into the glowing coals. While they waited upon the heat to work its magic, Dory opened a little wooden chest at his feet and pulled out a shot glass. He handed it to Sunny sitting at his left, who handed it to Nat sitting at her left, who handed it to Annie and on around to Top seated at Dory's right. He produced another one from the box and likewise sent it around their circle. Again and again it went until everyone held one except for little Stuie.

Dory drew forth a bottle from the chest filled with grayish-clear liquid. He stepped over toward Tommy's chair and knelt down to present it to Pawly. She scanned the label and gasped. "Is . . . is this . . . ?"

"Yes, it is. From the batch of *stwucha* your Grandpa N made before he left the country. My last one, actually, which I've been saving for a special occasion." He popped the cork and poured about a jigger's worth of the spirits into Pawly's glass before serving the rest of them likewise. When he got to Stuie, he pulled a juice box from his coat pocket and handed it to her. Everyone stood as tradition dictated after Dory returned to his place around the fire. Except for Tommy, of course.

"Even on a cold night like tonight, friends and loved ones warm the soul like the fire warms the body. While we celebrate our wayward daughter coming back to us, may the fruits of Brother Niko's labor lighten our spirits until his return home." Dory held his glass high and beamed at Pawly. "*Sto lat, Pawlina!*"

Everyone shouted a hearty "*Na zdrowie! Do dna!*" The adults tipped their glasses up while Stuie sipped at her juice. Alex let out a loud *whoop* after downing her shot and broke into song. Tommy reached an arm around Pawly's shoulder and hugged her sideways while they joined in.

> *Sto lat, sto lat, niech żyje, żyje nam.*
> *Sto lat, sto lat, niech żyje, żyje nam,*
> *Jeszcze raz, jeszcze raz, niech żyje, żyje nam,*
> *niech żyje nam!*

"Betcha missed this out in Haight-Ashbury, Sis," he said after Dory refilled everyone's glass.

"Of course I did, fool," Pawly replied as she pulled two pie irons from the glowing coals. "Been craving *pierogi*, too. Sure feels like a hundred years since

I last had one." She flipped one iron open and breathed in the pleasant aroma of their clan's unique contribution to Polonian cuisine. "Now that's what I'm talkin' about!"

Pawly worked the two halves of the iron to coax the toasty treat onto a pair of thick paper plates Tommy held in his lap. After she repeated the process with the other iron, he slid them one to a plate. "*Smacznego!*" he said and handed Pawly hers. He bit at his dinner carefully to open a hole in one corner. A cloud of fragrant steam drifted up into the cold night air while she took a seat and nibbled at her own meal. Experience had taught them both a lesson one night on Pilot Island long ago: biting recklessly into melted cheese and hot potatoes was a sure way to blister one's tongue.

While their food cooled, Tommy figured this was as good a time as any to give Pawly her gift. He set his plate down next to her and fished around in the side pocket of his wheelchair. With a frown, he realized her present must still be in the house. He whirled around and rolled toward the patio door.

"Whe're you going?" she asked after him.

"Be right back. Need to get something."

Once inside, he made his way to the living room coffee table. Atop the stuff piled there when they cleared the kitchen table sat a small cardboard box delivered earlier that day. He opened it and took out a hockey puck. One side bore the Katczynski family crest, the other the logo of Pawly's old ice hockey team from Norfolk—the Arctic Vixens, sister club to his own Arctic Foxes. Tommy placed the order online coming back from San Francisco with a local outfit which furnished promotional pucks for Nat and Annie's teams. They were known for swift and sharp-looking work. Now Tommy knew why.

He flipped the puck into the air and caught it in one hand. Spying Annie and Pawly through the picture window as they shared a joke, he hoped his gift would remind his sister she was part of this team, this family. All of them needed her, loved her, and would never give up on her. His fist clenched around the puck Tommy vowed to brain her with it should she ever run out on them again. Maybe that would drive the point into her thick skull.

The outside door slid open as he closed up the box. Dory walked inside with his cell phone to his ear and threw the door closed, cursing in Polish at some poor slob on the other end. From what Tommy could tell, the caller brought *really* bad news.

"I don't care what you must do. Patch me through to Colonel Luczasik *now*! I'm well aware it's the middle of the night there . . ." Dory snarled and pulled at his face. "No, it can't wait until morning! Besides, GROM has certainly rolled him out of bed already. Yes, I'll hold, thank you." He paced the kitchen floor and waited. "Dariusz, it's Teodor. Yes, I know. I just got the call. Were you contacted right after the assault?"

The room fell silent. "Look, this changes everything," he said at length.

"And how the hell does a North Korean commando team get close enough to capture Opoworo anyway?"

The muscles in Tommy's neck clenched. Was Grandpa Niko safe? Was he hurt? What the fuck was going on?

"That's *your* job to figure out, Darek! I told you after that Chah Bahar incident Pyongyang would put Mawro up to it, remember? *You* told me he'd be safe until I could . . ."

Tommy shook his head, unable to believe what he was hearing. The North Korean ailuranthropes had ambushed their unit while supply convoys bound for Afghanistan came ashore at that asscrack on the Iranian coast. Then came the explosion, and Sally did . . . and he . . .

He shook his head and glanced over to where Dory leaned against the kitchen counter, rubbing at his forehead. "Okay, Dariusz, okay. I'll head to O'Hare right away. I, uh . . ." He stole a quick glance up at the clock. "There's a nonstop on LOT to Warsaw out of JFK I should be able to make if I can make a flight out of here in time. I'll call before I board and let you know. Talk to you then."

Tommy rolled up to the sliding door before his grandfather could pull it closed. Dory waved him through and slid the door shut. Tommy's stomach let out a long growl, though he didn't much feel like eating.

Dory had collared Top by the time Tommy rolled up near the fire beside his sister and mother. He bit into his still warm *pieróg* while the two men exchanged harsh whispers next to the privacy fence. "I'm leaving for Poland tonight," Dory said in a loud voice after waving his hands to silence everyone. "North Korean commandos have staged an armed assault upon the Institute. Eyewitnesses at the scene report seeing a creature fitting Mawro's description."

Alex gasped. She launched into a coughing jag after inhaling a mouthful of her dinner. Pawly patted at her back, but their mother waved her off. "Is . . . is Papa . . . all right?" she managed at length.

Dory blew out his breath. "Niko's pretty shook up about his lab being destroyed, but is otherwise fine. He'll have a goose egg for a while from his captors beating him over the head before they tied him up, though."

Tommy glanced at Pawly sidelong while he chewed, a low growl emanating from her throat. "And we know wherever Mawro goes, that striped skank Hana is bound to follow," she said and clutched at the air in front of her. "Makes me want to stand on her tail and pull her claws out one by . . ." Her voice trailed off after Nat nodded to where Stuie sat beside him, poking a marshmallow onto the end of a stick.

"You'll have your crack at her soon enough, sailor," Top said. "Though at the moment, we don't know if the usual suspects were even in country at the time. I'll do some digging now and keep at it while you all take your holiday. Let's brief at first light tomorrow so I can lay out the plan Dory and I—"

The elder woman cleared her throat.

"Oh . . . er, yes. It will be Sunday, won't it?" he said in response to her unspoken grievance. "No harm in starting after everyone's back from early Mass."

"And breakfast," she added. "None of us will feel like cooking. Not at that time of morning. We will be up late tonight. There is much to catch up on. Right, Alex?"

Pawly shook her mother's shoulder and broke the heavy silence. "You all right, Mom?"

"I'm sorry," Alex said and blinked away her thousand-yard stare. "I just don't want to think about Papa being—"

"Then don't, *moja córka*. Let us handle this." Dory bent down to hug her neck, then leaned over and kissed Pawly's forehead. "And so glad to have you back too, little fighter." He went around the circle to say goodbye to the others before stepping up behind Tommy's chair. "May I borrow this one a moment, girls?" he said as he pulled him back from the fire.

"Finish your dinner, son," Dory whispered after they were a discreet distance from the others. "You now have 'need to know.'"

Tommy gulped down his last bite and licked at his fingers. "Great, Christmas *and* our mission both shot to hell. Do you think someone might find the, ah . . . 'cargo?'" he replied in kind.

"If Mawro is running the show, who knows? And we're not there to do anything about it!" Dory bumped his forehead with his fist. "Watch *Toro* and the Coastie close. If the Poles open the container, they'll see the interior and exterior reporting marks don't match."

Tommy's eyes went wide. "And after they run the number *inside*, then—"

"Then we'll be off Dariusz' Christmas card list, won't we?" Dory pushed him over to the stoop next to the wheelchair ramp and sat down. "He'll know this container went missing from Ying Kou and tip off DHS. Latharo and Reintz would be on the first flight bound for Warsaw they could get."

"What about you? And Grandpa Niko?"

"Hard to say, son," he said with a shrug. "But there will be plenty of time to hatch a plan aboard the plane. I told your mother and Top both I'd call when I land. He'll be sure to tell you what I've got in mind. Focus on mending fences with your sister until then."

Annie slid open the sliding door before Tommy could reply and held out a plastic bag to Dory. "Mom put yours in a foam box so it would keep warm."

He accepted the offering with a broad smile and stepped over to the gate in the privacy fence. "Thank you," he said as he worked the latch and stepped through.

"Please, stay safe," Tommy whispered as the gate slammed shut.

Dory had just stuffed his duffel into the overhead bin when his cell phone rang. He pulled the device from his jacket pocket and made a face at the number on the display. Dariusz and he had reviewed his itinerary before his plane pushed back in Chicago. And it wasn't Milda, so who else could be calling from Poland? Dory wriggled out of his winter jacket and fumbled at the small screen with his thumb. "*Słucham?*" he said as he jammed the device into the crook of his neck.

"It's me."

He started and banged his head on the bin above. "Wh-where in the hell are you?" Dory hissed in Polish, rubbing at his head as his coat dropped into the empty seat next to him. *Fuck, that hurt!*

"Oh, never mind," he said and took his seat, not bothering to wait for an answer. "I'm in New York, about to take off for Warsaw. Didn't I say not to call until you reached the safe house?"

"The government men were all busy mopping up, so I excused myself and took a taxi to the warehouse in Ustowo. Then I made arrangements to have our container picked up."

"Without talking to me first? The hell are you thinking, Ni . . ." Dory drew a hand to his mouth and closed his eyes. "Look, we need to stick to the plan. My employer has a lot riding on this. And you know full well that 'cargo' is the best chance Alex and the twins have to—"

"'Don Michael' led the attack."

He gasped. "How can you be sure? Did you see him?"

"Y-yes, I saw him. He . . . talked to me."

Dory swore under his breath. He would have words with Dariusz about this. None of Blaznikov's known associates should have been allowed within a mile of Niko's lab. Especially Mawro.

"And I realized you were right, my friend, insisting we keep the cargo hidden until I made it back to the States. We don't know how large a contingent he brought, but they'll have a harder time trying to hit a moving target, right?"

Dory glanced down at his watch. "Then why did you take so long to call me?"

"And here you thought I wasn't paying attention during your security briefings," Niko said with a laugh. "I hailed another cab back to town and bought an overseas calling card at an all-night market. But I never anticipated I'd wander half the city trying to find a damn payphone!"

He sighed and buckled his seat belt. "What's done is done, I guess. Now get your ass over to the condo and keep quiet. This flight's a little over eight hours, and Luczasik and I will be another ninety minutes or so into Szczecin. Give me an hour or so to debrief the GROM troopers. We'll go hoist a few afterward, my treat."

Niko sighed while one of the flight attendants announced the cabin door had closed. "At least the two of us will be able to share a little Christmas cheer.

Have you told everyone yet?"

It was Dory's turn to chuckle. "Told them what? How excited you'll be to see them?"

"That's not funny! They can't possibly come see me after everything that's happened!"

"Just like the container, old man. 'Don Michael' can't nab you if he can't *find* you. And the Christmas get-together Millie and I have planned is in what you might call an out-of-the-way place."

"Oh, I . . . I don't know what to say. You know how much this means to me!"

Dory snorted. "You say that now. But you'll change your tune when I start cracking the whip. I'm gearing up for you to start working with the 'cargo' the day after Christmas."

"So soon? But we'll need time to—?"

"Time is a luxury we can no longer afford. We're in something of an arms race now, so I tagged Nat and Annie both to help you accelerate our—"

He glanced up after a woman cleared her throat. One of the cabin crew stood in the aisle by the seat ahead of him, drumming her fingers on the headrest. "I'll explain more over dinner, old man. Gotta go or they're liable to kick me off the plane."

Dory flashed the attendant a sheepish grin and powered off his cell phone. She wagged her finger and grabbed the safety instruction card from the pocket beside his knees. Turning back toward the aisle, she flipped it open while her coworker recited the standard verbiage over the PA in English and Polish. The plane lurched a moment later and rolled backwards away from the gate.

Though she had made good on her promise to herself, Hana's long soak did little to calm her tumultuous mind. She had settled into the tub in the chief engineer's cabin and languished in the hot water until her fur started coming off in clumps. To avoid making a mess, Hana covered the bathroom floor with towels and sat scrubbing her skin nearly raw with a stiff brush for nearly twenty minutes. The inadvertent invigoration left her tossing and turning on her rack for hours afterward.

She stared at the overhead of her small cabin while the big ship pitched to and fro beneath her, slowly making its way over the open sea. Footsteps from the passageway outside went ignored until a piece of paper skittered across her cabin floor.

Abandoning all hope of trying to sleep, she threw off her blankets and padded over to pick up what appeared to be a note. After reading the scribbled message, she cracked the door and peeked out. Hana glimpsed the steward rounding the corner before noticing a steamer trunk by the door near her feet.

With a furtive glance up and down the passageway, she pulled the chest into her cabin and slammed the door shut.

This was one of several trunks in which she kept her personal effects, one aboard each vessel in ChongPol's fleet. Hana knelt next to its hasp and twirled the combination padlock dial. After opening the lid, she rummaged around for a clean bra and panties. She covered her naked body with them followed by a camisole, a pair of wool socks, a knit sweater, and heavy felt trousers.

The hand-me-down men's clothes laid out for her in the chief engineer's cabin were bulky in some areas and tight in others. She had stripped them off as quickly as she could once alone in her compartment. Likely, the stewards would have to wash her uniform several times before all the blood came out. At least she had something decent and comfortable to wear in the meantime.

Hana pulled on a pair of teal blue racing flats and headed topside. The brisk salt air bit at her nose while she trotted off into a loose, leisurely stride. She knew every rivet in the deckplates of these leaky old tubs, having taken up running to avoid the crushing boredom of being at sea. On clear days she loved to watch the endless ocean belch forth the sun, only to swallow it up again hours later at the end of its lonely trek across the sky.

During her first lap around the deck, Hana spied what she thought to be Denmark on the horizon. *Pe Gae Bong* must be making good time across the Baltic Sea, though it was a fool's game to guess just how long she and Mawro would need to remain aboard. Though surely helped by her hot bath, she was surprised her human form returned so quickly. Obviously, her fight-or-flight reflex must have run its course. His, however, had apparently not.

He had floated between consciousness and unconsciousness in the small sick bay below the bridge since they were hauled aboard. Before her bath, Hana requested the ship's surgeon rouse her should his condition change. But she had yet to receive further word. And his molt had yet to begin, or so she believed—no one had said any different. She placed her fingers on her temples and shook her head. Papa would come to and be fine soon enough, or as close to it as their Affliction allowed. He *had* to.

Hana found her stride her third lap around deck and settled in. She stopped counting fifteen laps later. Once the sun burned every last bit of gray out of the sky, she shed her outer garment. The painful tingling in her lungs from the cold sea air exhilarated her. Her body was not about to let her mind dwell on the unthinkable.

Several sailors stood around talking and smoking near the stern, on break after standing watch. As she rounded the corner, she heard Mawro's name and saw the steward attending him wave her over. His grim face told her what she needed to know while he flicked away his cigarette and went back inside. She picked up her sweater and followed without a word.

They entered the sick bay together a moment later. Mawro lay moaning on the examination table, flat on his back. His neck twitched, his jowls trembled, his eyes darted back and forth behind his eyelids. Hana pulled her sweater over her head and stuck her arms through the sleeves. "What is he—?"

The ship's surgeon held up one finger to silence her, then pointed at Mawro's muzzle. "He's mumbling on about something now and again for the past fifteen minutes or so, Lieutenant. Can you tell us what he's trying to say?"

She placed one hand on his chest and brought her ear close to his mouth. After parroting his murmured sounds several times, she recognized the syllables from his native Polish. *Poison pill! Poison pill!*

Her clenched fists drew to her sides as she stood. "Is the radioman still on the bridge?" she asked without taking her eyes off Mawro.

The surgeon glanced up at the clock on the cabin wall above them. "Forenoon watch will be relieved soon. You should be able to catch him before he heads to the galley."

Hana's lips drew into a thin line. "Good. I won't be long," she said and stormed toward the passageway. "Right now, I have an urgent message to send."

Chapter Fifteen

"**G**ET UP! GET UP!"

Niko batted away the hand shaking his shoulder. "G'won, Dory," he murmured and pulled a pillow over his head. "We'll order in and have a drink . . . later."

"Come on, old man!" He felt a chill and realized the sheets were off him. "Get your ass out of bed and grab your things." His friend stepped over to the window and peeked between the drawn curtains to the street below. "We must go. Now."

Niko sat up and rubbed his eyes. "Look, I got over to the damn safe house as soon as I could. And I just now got to sleep, for fuck's sake!"

"Weren't you tired before? I told you on the phone from JFK about when I'd get here. Maybe you were all worked up after what happened, but I thought sure by now you'd be—"

The sound of a truck's air horn cut Dory off while Niko stood and scratched at himself through his boxers and A-shirt. Several large trucks rumbled one at a time up to the busy four-way stop three stories below. Horn blaring, the first truck crept into the intersection and stopped amidst the myriad bicycles, pedestrians, and automobiles darting every which way. "That shit has been going on all day," Niko said and pulled at the stubble on his face.

The big truck took the corner wide after traffic finally yielded. "What's in them?" Dory asked.

"Rye, I believe. There was an outbreak of ergot fungus in the local crop. My friend at the distillery up the street said they're importing grain from Russia. A ship must've docked earlier today. The stuff is convoyed over by truck as soon as it's unloaded to prevent contamination."

"So what were you doing all this time, then?"

Niko sat down on the bed and pulled on his pants. "Chipped away at my backlog of journals. I found a morphogen study in FEBS Letters I thought you'd find particularly interesting."

"That's, er . . . fascinating. Hope you brought a few more because we need to take a road trip." Dory walked over to an overstuffed chair and grabbed the strap on his friend's duffel. "This your only bag?"

"That and my shaving kit. Mind telling me why we're in such a damn hurry?"

"Dariusz and his men are coming for us."

"So what?" Niko said over his shoulder as he stepped into the bathroom and picked up his razor. "It's a protective escort, right?"

"Yeah, while we're escorted to jail."

His razor fell into the sink with a clatter. "'Jail'? For what?"

Dory sat on the arm of the easy chair. "I forgot your lab is a black hole for cellular signal, old man. My phone went nuts after I finished with Luczasik's people and stepped outside. Tommy had sent a dozen texts and left two voice mails to say the game's afoot." He sighed and leaned forward, resting his elbows on his thighs. "Local police and ABW executed a search warrant at the warehouse before the riggers you hired to move the container arrived."

"Then they must have opened it!"

"And tipped off DHS, which is how Tommy found out. Now hurry the hell up and get—"

A fist banged three times on the apartment door. "Katczynski!" came a man's angry voice from the other side. "We need to speak with you and Dr. Opoworo!"

Dory slammed the bedroom door and locked it. "Give me a hand." Niko shouldered up to the oaken dresser beside his friend and helped shove it to the threshold. In the corner, behind floor-length vinyl shades, a sliding glass door led to a private balcony. Cold air billowed in while Dory slid the door open and scanned the narrow street three stories below. "Good. Our ride is on the way," he said as he swooshed at his smartphone.

Both men started at the sound of the entry door splintering. "That dresser won't hold them long," Niko said while more voices called for their immediate surrender. He heard a *psst* and turned to see his friend wave to him from the balcony railing.

"See that?"

"It's a grain truck," Niko whispered while Dory pointed down the street. "What of it?"

"On my signal, we jump and land in the back. Should be soft enough."

Niko gaped at him. "Are . . . are you out of your fucking mind? If we're off by even a split second, we'll both be be—!"

A loud *bam* resonated through the room. Men identifying themselves as ABW shouted and banged their fists on the bedroom door behind them. "We're out of time," Dory said and eyed the oncoming truck. "And options."

Niko grasped his duffel with both hands and glanced over his shoulder. The dresser jumped with each blow of the battering ram. "NOW!" Dory cried when the door gave way. He took Niko's shoulder in an iron grip and pushed him over the balcony headfirst.

Tommy's ears perked up at the sound of his name being barked out over the PA the length of Terminal 5. He rolled to a stop in front of the food court and tilted his head to listen. The flustered gate agent rattled off the rest of their party's names before issuing a stern ultimatum:

"This is your third and final boarding call for LOT Polish Airlines Flight Four, nonstop service to Warsaw, Poland. Please proceed at once to Gate M20 for your on-time departure. The cabin door will close in five minutes and will not reopen."

"Which way now, Dad?"

Nat let go of Stuie's hand and pointed toward the ceiling of the terminal. "To the left," he said. Tommy followed his uncle's finger to the signboard and groaned. Gate M20 was clear down at the other end of the concourse.

"I told you we should've gone straight to the airline ticket counter," Annie said as she stepped up behind her husband and daughter. "We'd have saved a trip going back to get Mom a new one."

Alex huffed and stomped off toward their gate. "This would have never happened if one of *us* had made the reservation!"

"It was unfortunate, yes. Patti booked our reservations using my nickname. My given name appears on my passport. She could not have known. If Dory did not tell her."

Tommy agreed with Sunny's defense of his grandfather's overworked and underpaid admin—after all, she had worked with him long enough to know his foibles. Likely, he dropped a list scribbled on a piece of scrap paper on her desk and asked her to "just handle it." Good thing Patti used to work at the Polish Consulate. They would be arguing with TSA still if she hadn't spelled the rest of their names right.

But he wasn't about to let his sister off so easy. "Bastard Chief would've docked you a whole pay grade, you know!" he said as he rolled up beside Pawly. "Maybe next time, remember you were in the brig the day they covered document inspection *before* you start cocking off to TSA?"

"All right, all right, shoulda checked our boarding passes closer after I printed them. Got it!" She glared at Tommy and waved her hands toward the concourse ceiling. "You want me to apologize over the damn PA or something?"

"Dad, are we going to miss our plane now?" Stuie asked in a manner suggesting she didn't want to hear his answer.

"I think we'll still make it," Nat said and took her hand in his. "Besides, the flight will still be delayed if they close the cabin door before we're aboard."

They would, of course. The ramp rats would need to dig their checked bags out of the plane's hold before pushing back. Tommy hustled along the near-empty concourse, grateful most of the outbound flights on this side of the terminal had left earlier that evening.

Nat waved to the agent at the podium beneath the "Gate M20" sign as she reached for her mic. Pawly bumped her way past Tommy's chair while the woman scanned their passes. She strode off in a huff down the jet bridge, followed by the rest of their family.

Think she'd be more grateful for all the trouble I went through. Least she coulda done was keep her big mouth shut.

Tommy leaned his head back and stared up at the ceiling. His texts had gone ignored and his calls unanswered since tipping his grandfathers off to the warehouse raid.

He started after a door slammed shut behind him. A young man wearing a maroon vest and tie appeared and rolled an airplane aisle chair up next to him. "Boys're up one-nothing," he said and pointed at the logo on Tommy's Blackhawks sweater. Having lagged behind, Nat held the smaller chair steady while the attendant helped him transfer from one to the other.

"Hey, U-Nat, your smartphone didn't play 'Chelsea Dagger' when the Hawks scored. What's up?"

"Oh, I must've forgotten to turn it on after we left security." He fished the phone out of his pocket and poked at its power button as he rolled Tommy down the jet bridge. "And what's this 'contingency plan' all about?" he whispered after they rounded the corner.

"G-man said keep dibs on Latharo and Reintz, right?" Tommy replied in kind. "Pain in the ass to choreograph, but they're going to lead us right to him and Grandpa N."

His eyes went wide. "What did you—?"

A chime from Nat's device announced he had a voice mail. He glanced down at his screen and made a face. "Looks like *Toro* left me a message."

Tommy couldn't help but smile. "Really. Is that so?"

Nat shot him a puzzled look as the gate attendant made her way up the jet bridge toward them.

"We can get your companion settled in the cabin if you need to check a message," she said, "but do hurry. We're scrambling for an on-time departure tonight."

"Oh, uh . . . thanks. This will only take a moment."

The gate attendant wheeled him to the cabin door while Tommy brought up an electronic copy of their flight's manifest on his own device. Pawly snorted and turned away toward the window as the woman navigated his chair up the narrow aisle to his seat. He pasted their flight number into a new text message along with a particular pair of seat assignments:

193.	REINTZ	L	25-C	WAW
194.	LATHARO	M	25-D	WAW

The cabin crew droned out their passenger safety briefing in Polish and English while Tommy sent the text. He gazed across the cabin to where Nat stood stuffing his carry-on into the bin above Annie's head. "Manuel left me a message," Tommy heard him say to her, "saying he and his partner are en route to Poland to—"

His pocket chimed again. With a disgusted grunt he pulled out his cell phone and poked at it with his thumb. Nat gaped at the screen and turned to scan the faces of the passengers all around him. He plunked down beside his wife and cast a confused glance across the cabin.

Tommy flashed him a thumbs up.

Lenny awoke and stretched about as well as his economy-class seat allowed, noting how the cheap seats seemed to get smaller every couple of years. If he flew more often, he might rack up miles enough to try out the plush half-sofas he and Latharo saw passing through the Dreamliner's forward cabin as they boarded. Before dozing off, he had read in his copy of *Kaleidoscope* how every seat in Business Class folded flat into a bed. Flying on Uncle Sam's dime, though, Lenny knew he would never enjoy such luxury. He rubbed the back of his aching neck and leaned back in his chair, trying to make himself more comfortable. Fat chance.

Latharo slumped back in his seat at the end of the row across from Lenny, Akubra hat pulled down over his eyes. The man had been out since even before the plane's landing gear came up. Lenny peeked at his watch and cast an envious glance at his partner. How would he keep from going stir crazy over the next six hours?

As good a time as any to stretch his legs. He ambled his way to the lavatory at the rear of the plane while all around his fellow passengers did their best to get comfortable and relax. Bedtime fast approached for most of them. A few had settled down into a good book. Some viewed a movie on the small screen built into each of the seat backs. One resourceful young foursome appeared to play a game of electronic euchre. The rest simply tossed and turned in their seats trying, most without much success, to sleep.

After washing his hands, Lenny made his way over to the opposite aisle and sauntered forward to where a heavy blue and gray curtain marked off his section. He turned and retraced his steps until he spied Latharo across the cabin, still slumbering peacefully. He noticed the girl sitting beside the window of his row stand and lean against the headrest in front of her. The woman in the seat next to his, likely the girl's mother, rose also. She unfolded one of the air sickness bags and held it out to her daughter. The girl shook her head, as if not wanting to cause a scene, and pushed her way past. Then she hunched over and threw up all over Lenny's seat.

He rolled his eyes and turned away. The mortified mother stammered apologies to everyone around them in broken English and another language Lenny did not recognize. Their cabin crew quickly converged on Ground Zero. One led the pair away to the lavatory while another two cleaned up the mess as best they could. He resolved then and there to be disgustingly nice to every single flight attendant he met in the future. Having to deal with shit like this made however much they were paid nowhere near enough.

A middle-aged woman looked up at him as he approached, a broad grin pasted atop the revulsion on her face. "Oh! Is this your seat, sir?"

He couldn't help but smile in return. "Yes, ma'am."

The attendant and her partner exchanged words a moment before turning back to him. "We have stuff to spray on the cushions for the smell, but you won't be able to sit here the rest of the flight." She stood up and brushed out the pleats in her uniform's skirt with both hands. "We're pretty full with all the pre-Christmas travelers, but there is one seat left up front. May we reseat you in our Premium Club?"

"Uh, sure," he said. Latharo fidgeted and resumed his soft snoring. "Though I would appreciate your telling this guy whenever he wakes up where I went."

"Certainly, sir!" She waved her arm toward the forward cabin. "Right this way, please."

Lenny reached up and pulled at the latch of the bin overhead. "Oh, no no no," she said and placed her hand atop his. "I'm sorry. The bins up there are packed full. Your carry-on must stay where it is."

With a sigh he grabbed the paperback he had started to read earlier from the seatback pocket. He flipped through the book's pages as he followed along behind her. Good, the aerial barrage missed them.

The attendant pulled the curtain at the front of the economy cabin aside and waved Lenny in. She ushered him to a seat next to the aisle in the back row. After buckling in, he opened his book and reached up for the light switch overhead. The lamp came on instead above the girl seated beside him.

"Oh, excuse me, miss," he said, realizing his mistake after the girl pulled the hood of her pink-and-teal sweater she wore backwards down to her neck. "I . . . I didn't mean to—"

"Mr. Lenny? What are *you* doing here?"

His paperback flopped to the floor, forgotten, while she rubbed at her eyes. "M-Miss Stuie? I . . . whe're you . . . ?"

The girl's Auntie Alex sat to her right, sound asleep. He spied Dr. Opoworo sitting across the aisle opposite with his arm around his wife's shoulders, both oblivious to everything on account of their headphones. Some kind of comedy played on a small screen attached to the armrest between their seats while they giggled and tried to snuggle.

"Long time no see, eh, puddle pirate?"

Lenny's mouth fell open as he turned toward the familiar voice. Tommy was here too? The seat between his old friend and the window was empty save for a bright purple ski jacket stuffed between the headrest and the cabin wall.

Then she *must be—*

A woman gasped. He glanced up to find Pawly standing in the aisle beside him, one hand drawn to her mouth. Though her red-and-blonde hair had grown out somewhat, there was no mistaking the whirlwind of emotion that swirled behind her blue eyes.

Nor the all-too-familiar heavings of his stomach.

He popped the latch on his seat belt and squeezed past her. Through the curtain he dashed, bound for the first open lavatory in first-class he could find.

Lenny looked up at his reflection as the flow from the lavatory faucet slowed to a trickle and stopped. He had debated for months what he would do when, and if, he ever saw her again. Rip off her clothes? Cuss her out? Circumstances, hurt feelings and repressed anger counted against the former. But they made his case for the latter all that much stronger.

He reached out for the door handle but stopped short. Pawly's voice came through from the other side in a language he didn't understand, discussing something with another woman. He slid the door open find Pawly standing there, a plastic cup in her hand filled with red liquid. "Might want to work on some new pick-up lines there," she said and held it out to him while the flight attendant walked away. "Hurling at the sight of a girl is certainly a novel approach, but might send mixed messages."

With a snort Lenny took the cup and raised it to his lips. The unmistakable bite of alcohol complimented the drink's tart sweetness. "Slice of lime and I'd have me a Cape Codder," he said and narrowed his eyes. "Oh, that's rich, Pawly."

"Coincidence, really. I read somewhere cranberry juice kills the taste of vomit. And vodka'll get rid of the smell."

Heat rose to his hairline as Lenny took another swallow. "Too bad it's not the only thing leaving a bad taste in my mouth!"

Pairs of eyes from around the first class cabin fixed upon the two of them.

Pawly clenched his wrist and dragged him across the aisle into the galley. "Bad enough standing me up after I came for you halfway across the damn country! But would it have killed you to call and at least let me know you're alive?" Lenny said as she slid the pocket door closed.

Her shoulders heaved as she stared down to where her hands clenched the door handle. "It's ... complicated."

He downed the contents of the cup before crushing it between his trembling fingers. "Yeah. Complicated. Like the mixed signals you've been sending since putting in for permanent change of station back at Camp Lejeune. Without even telling me!"

"You pig-headed ass! Get over yourself!" she shot back as she stabbed her finger into his chest. "I wasn't about to let you throw away your best chance to earn your commission because of me. But this ... this is different. I know it will be hard for you, but ... you need to trust me." Pawly sighed and pinched the bridge of her nose. "Oh, who am I kidding? You were always such a lovesick idiot!"

"Maybe I still am," he said softly, leaning in to place his lips over hers.

Pawly's eyes shot open but slowly closed. He did the same and drew her waist to his, savoring the wonderful, exhilarating sensation washing over him. Her fingers and mouth consumed every bit of him they could, seemingly desperate to fill the void in her heart their separation had created. Pawly clamped her hands to either side of his face while their tongues writhed about together. He could tell her body had missed his touch as much as his, hers.

Now who's sending mixed signals, dumbass?

Without warning the galley door slid open. The flight attendant stood in the doorway looking askance at them, hands on her hips. "I might have guessed," she said in English and wagged her finger at Pawly.

"But ... I mean ... we weren't ..."

"*Sure* you weren't. A little boy here in first class needs some warm milk to help get back to sleep," she said and pushed her way past. "But I did say I'd help you enjoy each other's company until we land. Do keep your clothes on, would you?"

Pawly nodded and followed the attendant into the aisle, neglecting to let go of his hand. Tommy now sat beside Stuie, opening up two adjoining seats for them.

Lenny made a face. "I'll bet you had something to do with this."

"Hoped to do the big reveal along the concourse at Chopin, shipmate," Tommy replied while he handed over Lenny's paperback. "Have to cancel the violinist and champagne now."

Pawly glared at her brother while Lenny settled in next to the window. She raised the armrest after belting in and curled up beside him, head laid against his shoulder.

With a yawn Lenny stuck his book into the seat back pocket and flipped off the light above their heads.

This had not been the first time Niko's life had flashed before his eyes, though he hoped the next time—a couple dozen or so years from now—would be the last. He burst out laughing in a catharsis of sorts, though doing so hurt. His body reminded him in about eighteen different places it was way too old for this daredevil kind of shit.

By instinct, Niko had tucked into a forward roll when he hit and ended up on his bottom facing backwards. Dory, however, landed on his stomach, knocking his wind from him. "What's . . . so damn . . . funny?" he wheezed.

Niko took a moment to find his voice after his laughing jag subsided. "You must be holding out on me, you son of a bitch! If you timed the stock market like that, we could buy our own sovereign nation in no time!" He wiped tears from his eyes with his forefinger and thumb. "What will you do for an encore?"

Dory opened his mouth to say something when a car's horn blared from behind them. He scurried to the back of the trailer and peered over the top. "This is but the first act! See? Our ride's here."

Niko crawled on his forearms up next to him. A small silver grey estate wagon followed behind the truck's bumper. He gasped when he recognized the driver. "What the hell is Jakub doing here?"

"Saving our sorry asses, old man. Lucky break he was in town on union business."

The man's lips flapped in silence while he waved and pointed toward the back of the truck. Something sure had the big lug all worked up. Niko got to his knees and leaned against the rear of the dump box. "Say, Dory," he said over his shoulder, "did you have a plan for getting us down from here?"

"Same way *I* got up, Professor!" came a gruff voice from behind Niko an instant before his world went dark.

CHAPTER SIXTEEN

A LEX WAS BESIDE HERSELF. Though never a fan of flying, her years as a Navy wife required her spend a fair share of time stuck inside airborne tin cans. Long durations in the pressurized cabins made her throat hurt. What passed for food she often found inedible.

By comparison, these non-stops on LOT to Warsaw out of O'Hare were a marked improvement. Their meals had been quite tasty. Seats in premium economy were more than simply a step up from the cattle-car accommodations at the back of the plane. Both improvements helped her drop off into a deep sleep somewhere high over Newfoundland. Even Stuie's antics when Lenny first made his appearance failed to rouse her.

Stuie was up, needling Pawly for details as soon as the "fasten seat belts" light went out. Where did she meet this guy? What did they do on their off-time? Did he work out? On and on and on through the cabin door, up the jet bridge, across the terminal. When the girl asked for "beefcake" photos of him, Pawly made clear she had had enough. Alex wondered just how closely Nat and Annie monitored what sorts of books their daughter downloaded to her Kindle.

Pawly had said little since. She walked along with her daypack hanging from one shoulder, glancing now and again out the concourse windows back toward their plane. Lenny planned to retrieve his carry-on after the rest of the passengers deplaned, she had told her. Before he and his partner rendezvoused with their Polish contacts, he would meet her by the baggage claim to exchange cell numbers. And to discuss whether they might delay their respective return flights a day or two.

Alex's son was her bigger concern at the moment, or, rather, whatever her father-in-law was saying to him. Tommy had muttered something about not recognizing the number when he fished the ringing cell phone out of his pocket, but he took the call anyway. When he began jabbering in Korean, she concluded he didn't want passers-by to overhear Agency business. Such a call so soon after their flight landed did not bode well. Not well at all.

"Dory will not come to us?" Sunny asked as he hung up.

"Right, Grandpa N is with him. Not at liberty to say why they can't come themselves. Milda should be waiting for us at the Courtyard." He pointed out the big glass windows toward the airport's hotel. "Grandpa D said to head straight there and bypass the baggage claim."

Annie glared at him with her hands on her hips. "He knows we have more than just our favorite lingerie in those bags, right?" She nodded toward Alex. "Like medications?"

"Someone's supposed to pick them up and meet us at—"

"Now wait one damn minute!" Pawly waved her arms and stepped in front of Tommy's chair. "I was going to meet—"

"Can't be helped, Sis" he said with a shrug. "Lenny's number should still be in my phone, though. I'll send him a text for you . . . later."

"Don't bother, I'll do it right now!" she said and pulled out her own device. She stopped a few keystrokes into her message and made a face.

"Mine works on the network over here," he said with a sly grin. "One I gave you won't. Bought it at a truck stop in Iowa, remember?"

Pawly snarled and jammed the phone back into her pocket.

"Who here could identify Milda, anyway?" Alex asked.

"Grandpa D texted a photo before he called. Shown her lots of pictures of us, too. She'll likely pick us out before I recognize her."

Nat put an arm around Sunny's shoulder. "Rabble like us would be pretty hard to miss. Especially us Koreans, right, *Eomeonim*?"

Alex's cell phone rang before her mother could answer. Though she expected no call from the States, the number was recognizable in its unrecognizability. Previous efforts to trace, dial back, or otherwise identify the origin of such calls all led to dead ends. She reached a used car dealership in North Carolina one time, another a scrap metal dealer in Ohio. Most recently, a monk at a Buddhist temple in California answered.

"Um . . . I'll be along in a moment. I should take this."

Alex was in no mood for these games right now. She dashed into an alcove and swooshed at the cell phone's screen, intent on making that point quite clear. "Lovely view of the Warsaw city skyline, don't you agree?" came the gravelly male voice as she ducked behind a vending machine.

"Breathtaking, thank you very much, but I don't need a fucking tour guide," she said and switched to Korean. This caller would understand her just fine.

"Temper, temper, Aleška," the man replied in kind. "I got to thinking of you when I dropped in on Professor Opoworo a couple days ago."

"You bastard! Papa's on the run, isn't he?" Alex said through clenched teeth. "I'll just bet you had *everything* to do with that."

"You have Agent Katczynski to thank, not me," the man said and sighed. "Why do you people keep complicating things? Who else but me understands what's right for you and the twins?"

"This from the guy who beat Papa and tied him up before shooting up the place?" Alex rubbed at her forehead with her palm. "You want me to believe you're acting in our best interests when you do something stupid like that?"

"We could hardly have walked up and knocked on the damn door, you know. Don't forget, *we* weren't the ones who started shooting! I'm sure your father-in-law left out that trivial detail."

"Doesn't matter who starts it to whoever ends up dead!"

"We accept the risks inherent to what we do," the man said after a long pause. "Maurycy . . . so did he."

Alex's eyes shot open. "Wh-what happened?"

"To explain would take more time than I have, Aleška. But I can assure you you'll never see your brother's face again."

"What have you done to Ritzi?" The tinny beep thundered in her ear when the caller terminated their connection. "No! Don't go! Answer me! Answer me . . . please . . ."

Alex stared down at her smartphone, its screen blurry from the tears filling her eyes. Her background featured a picture taken in happier times of her and her husband posing with their kids and family. She wiped her eyes and focused on the morose-looking man with curly brown hair standing off to the right side of the frame.

My . . . my brother . . . is dead?

She stepped around the corner and spied the rest of her family several gates ahead along the concourse, almost to the main gallery. With a long-drawn sigh, she shoved her phone back into her handbag and hurried after them.

Nat and Annie stood in front of the duty free shop, arguing with Stuie. The girl's plea to purchase some designer fragrance and her mother's steadfast refusal drew Alex's ire. *Who the fuck cares how long Katiana Dudek's mother has let her wear* Jasmin Noir, *anyway? My . . . my brother . . . is dead.*

"Hey, Sis, are you okay?" Nat said after Alex brushed past.

"I will be in a moment," she replied over her shoulder. Feeling everyone's eyes on her back, Alex proceeded across the gallery to the airport chapel. The sound of Annie and Stuie's bickering ceased as she knelt on a hassock and crossed herself. She choked out a sob and leaned forward, forehead bowed to folded hands upon the back of the pew before her.

My . . . my brother . . . is dead!

Hana turned the corner and grabbed for the handle of the first cabin door she came to. One hand on the knob, she stopped and pressed her ear to the door to listen. Her eyes went wide, hearing Mawro's booming voice on the other side. When did he wake up? Why wasn't he still in sick bay?

She opened the door and closed it slowly behind her. From the one-sided conversation, she realized he was on the phone or some kind of live chat. Her brow furrowed, uncertain exactly what he was talking about. Who *was* this "Ritzi" fellow, anyway?

Right after he ended his call, she poked her head through the bedroom door. He was quite a sight. Mawro sat on the bed, still transformed, with his back pressed up against the headboard. The sheets had been pulled out and placed over his waist and legs, exposing his enormous and hairy hindpaws. He had wrangled a pair of closed cup headphones with a boom mic attached over his shaggy head. The tufts atop his long ears poked out comically from underneath.

Various and sundry computer peripherals sat scattered about the room along with communications gear and cryptography equipment. Conspicuous by their absence, however, were any keyboards or keypads.

She knew Mawro must be terribly grieved, depending on Min Soo via satellite half a world away for something as simple as data entry. With one huge furry forepaw, he twiddled at a trackball on a table rolled in next to his bed. He rearranged the tactical displays on his screens, clearly determined to overcome his limitations bit by bit.

"Ah, you're finally awake, my dear." Mawro slid the trackball aside and picked up what looked like a wood rasp from atop the computer table. He extended each claw on his other forepaw in turn and filed at them as he spoke. "I countermanded your order the steward notify you when I came to. You needed your rest after your ordeal."

Hana pursed her lips and glanced up at the monitors. A mosaic of live video feeds from a series of security cameras in some busy airport terminal covered the screen. Large letters emblazoned onto the far wall of the gallery read *Lotnisko Chopina w Warszawi—Witamy!*

"Warsaw?" Hana scrunched up her nose and turned to Mawro. "What's so special about Warsaw?"

"Opoworo gave Luczasik the slip sometime after you fired off our missive to Berlin."

Hana's mouth fell open. "B-but how?" she said after a moment. "And who—?"

"I'm certain he had help, and I'm pretty sure I know who helped him."

Mawro indicated his screens with the rasp before he set it back down on the computer table. "Right now, Min Soo and I are trying to pick up the trail ourselves rather than let those bumblers at ABW botch the job again."

Hana crossed her arms. "Why bother monitoring the airport? Nothing we could do about it from here, even if Teacher Most Honorable did show up."

"Luczasik is sure to follow protocol. If the person aiding Opoworo is who I think he is, he'll certainly know that as well. ABW agents will be canvassing the airports and the train stations already on the lookout for the two of them. They'll cover the ferry terminals as well if they're smart."

Mawro poked at his trackball to bring up a map of all the highway crossings along Poland's borders. "I think the professor's abettor plans to sneak him out of the country over land and hide out until they figure out where to go next."

"So what are you hoping to find, then?"

One corner of his mouth turned up. He zoomed in on the entrance of the airport chapel set back into one of the gallery alcoves. "Our lucky break."

Mawro's gaze followed the image of a lanky blonde woman in her mid-forties from the chapel entrance back to her traveling companions. Hana immediately recognized the facial features of a younger man and an older woman as distinctly Korean. Next to the man stood a woman about his age, their hands clasped together by their sides. Tall and lithesome with long brown hair tied up into a pony tail—obviously a Westerner. On the floor nearby sat a girl of about ten or eleven playing some sort of video game while she chewed on one of her long black pigtails. A red-haired man in a wheelchair rolled up beside the visibly distraught blonde woman and engaged her in conversation.

"Who are those people, Papa?"

"There's one missing whom I think you'll recognize. Ah! There she is now."

A young woman approached the group from off-camera with a bouquet of coral-tinted white carnations in one hand. Hana scrunched up her nose, recognizing the woman's wavy bob of strawberry blonde hair. "I . . . remember her. She's Kindred!"

"Yes. The same one you encountered in San Francisco, in fact, and at Chah Bahar. Yeon-pyeong before that. Pawlina Katczynski, a.k.a. 'Polecat.'"

He waved a hand at the screen. "The rest of those people are her extended family. The young man in the wheelchair is Tomasz, her twin brother. He was at Chah Bahar also and sustained a spinal injury during combat." Mawro crossed his furry arms over his broad chest and sighed. "He hasn't walked since."

Hana groaned and pulled at the sides of her face. "So what does she have to do with the Professor?"

"Doctor Opoworo is her grandfather."

She knit her brow and turned back to the big screen. "I . . . I don't understand."

"It's close to Christmas. Opoworo has been known to host family get-togethers around the holidays," Mawro went on. "Since he can't travel to the US, I figured there was a better than average chance the family would be in Poland or on their way. Min Soo found reservations for Opoworo's wife, children, and grandchildren on a Chicago to Warsaw non-stop last night under the name 'Teodor Katczynski.'"

"'Katczynski'? You mean like—"

"The same. That's Polecat's *other* grandfather. The CIA agent whom I believe is helping hide Opoworo."

Hana clapped her hands together in front of her. "They'll lead us right to him!"

Mawro leaned back and twirled the long white fur under his chin between his fingers. "That's what I'm counting on. By now, our people should be in—oh, excuse me."

She glanced up at the flashing display inset on one of the screens above her head. Min Soo was calling in. Their subjects on the screen made their way through the terminal while Mawro answered.

She listened to Mawro's side of a discussion about a sting operation the Poles had conducted at a warehouse in Szczecin's outskirts linked to Opoworo. What they found confirmed allegations by German authorities of the professor's involvement in East Germany's Cold War era "super soldier" program. The man was now a fugitive.

"So they'll ship the MGS out of Gdansk? All right, raise Ryang at the shipyard when we're done here and tell him I have a rush job for his welders. Now, where is the car with our embassy operatives now? Ah, yes, I see it. Let me try zooming in . . . no, I've got it. Good, good."

The camera followed a small, dark blue sedan cruising along slowly outside the airport's baggage claim. "Someone should be coming to pick them up after they grab their luggage. Be ready to . . . hey, wait a minute . . ."

Hana watched the family bypass the carousels and disappear into an enclosed walkway.

"Min Soo! Did you see that?" Mawro glanced up at another screen showing a plan view of the terminal corridors. "They may be headed for the hotel. Find me those feeds! Quickly!" A moment later, several more images appeared on the screens. They showed their subjects making their way along one corridor toward the hotel's lobby. "Our people are on their way? Good. Let me know when they . . . oh, shit!"

Mawro slammed a massive fist down hard on his bedside table and snapped it in two. Hana winced and glanced up to see steam rolling out from beneath the crumpled hood of their operatives' car, wedged underneath the rear of a shuttle bus.

"Quickly! Look for a clue to indicate where they might be headed!"

"Right!" she said without taking her eyes off from the screens overhead. The group met an older woman in the hotel lobby with graying brown hair dressed in dark slacks and a wool jacket. The elder Korean and the blonde from the chapel ran up and threw their arms around her neck.

"M-Milena? No . . . it can't be . . ." She turned to see Mawro staring wide-eyed at the woman's image. "Min-Soo! Who in the hell *is* that?" He growled, obviously not liking the man's response. "Get creative and find out. Fast!"

Hana chewed at her hair as the travelers exited the lobby toward a white passenger van parked beneath the porte-cochère. A cargo van bearing the LOT Airlines logo pulled up behind, and a couple of porters ambled out. They transferred several bags to the other vehicle while the party climbed in and got seated.

"It's now or never! They're . . ."

A smile spread across Mawro's face as the van drove past the camera. Its side featured the stylized outline of a large, fuzzy brown animal Hana believed was called a bison. Large white letters spelled out "*Białowieski Park Narodowy*" across a green banner circling the logo. He rubbed at the grey fur covering his forehead. "Well, that could have been . . . unfortunate." The vehicle turned right at the end of the driveway and disappeared into traffic, well out of range of the airport cameras. "Oh, so she goes by a different name these days, does she? We'll have to ask her about that when we visit."

Hana stepped up beside Mawro after he pulled of his headset and rubbed at his ears. "So, what's an MGS, anyway?"

"It's short for 'Morphogenetic Synthesizer,' my dear. You know our Affliction will render stopgap measures like your Pearls ineffective eventually. We'll need the MGS if we're ever to apply Opoworo's data and our own research."

"But what does that other woman have to do with—?"

Mawro held up a hand to silence her. "I'll explain more in due time. For now, go back to your cabin and pack your kit. After we put you ashore at Bremerhaven, you'll catch a train to Hamburg and fly to Warsaw from there."

"You're not coming, Papa? I'm sure we could get a van and make you comfortable in back. Maybe a couple of the crew could come with us to help—"

"There's no time for that. I'm certain Opoworo's family is on their way to Białowieża to meet him, but we don't know how long they'll be there. You've done a fine job soloing before. I'm confident you'll do the same now."

"But, Papa . . . what about my Pearls?"

Mawro reached over to the nightstand next to his bed and grabbed a small box, careful not to crush it. "I finished building another pair last time we were aboard", he said with a wink. "The steward had to help me activate them, but they should be working normally."

Hana opened the cardboard container and studied the two small gray-white balls inside. She took one out and unfurled its long metal lanyard as if she were tossing a yo-yo. With a click she secured it to the silver loop piercing one earlobe. "Th-thank you, Papa," she said while she fixed its twin to her other ear.

"I'll have Min Soo track down an address in Białowieża for the woman you saw in the video. The embassy will send someone to pick you up at Chopin. Don't let Opoworo leave the country."

Mawro smiled and ran the tips of his claws through his ruff. "Find the professor's family, and we find him. Find him, and we find the MGS. Let us pray our luck holds out, my dear. We might score two for the price of one."

Niko groaned and opened his eyes. "He's awake," Dory said over his shoulder to someone he couldn't see. He tried to sit up but managed to raise his head only a few inches before his temples began to throb.

"No, no, no." Dory grabbed Niko's shoulders and pushed him back down. "Take it easy, old man. You've had two hard hits to the head in as many days. And an examination at a hospital to check for a concussion might expose us."

Niko sighed and followed Dory's finger with his eyes as it moved back and forth past his face. "Wh-where are we?"

"Well, good . . . you seem to be speaking without difficulty, too. You and I are in the back of Jakub's car headed east on the A2."

"Ten kilometers west of Poznan, in fact," came Jakub's booming voice.

Niko rubbed at the sides of his head. "What happened?"

"After that guy from ABW whacked you but good, their high-flying circus act must've spooked the kid driving the truck. Next thing I know, he's got the rig wrapped around their SUV like a snake strangling a mouse. I managed to grab the side of the trailer, but those other guys must've had one helluva rough landing."

Jakub glanced over his shoulder and changed lanes. "So I stopped and helped Dory load you into my car. We've been driving since."

"Now that you're in the know, shut up and lie still. Sunny and Annie can check you over when we get to where we're going."

"And where might that be?"

"Białowieża."

Niko's brow knit. "Why in the hell are we crossing the damn country to that . . . that backwater?"

"Such manners, old man! Jakub, you and your mother are rather fond of that 'backwater', aren't you?"

The big man chuckled. "That's why Ma invited your whole family to her home near the Forest for a little pre-Christmas get-together."

"I'm sure you'll warm up to the place," Dory said. "There lies our best chance for getting you out of the country, I believe."

Niko grunted and propped himself up with his elbows. "And just how do you propose to do that?"

"Leave that to me," Jakub said before his friend could answer. "I'm the head of the stevedores' union at Gdansk Harbor. I drove truck between Bialystok and Minsk back before I had seniority enough to hold a job during winter layup. Called in a favor with a trucker buddy across the border in Belarus who's agreed to take you to Vilnius."

Dory nodded. "With your Polish identity card, you can move freely once you're in Lithuania. Take a bus or train to Klaipeda and locate a tramp freighter named *Western Archer*. Its captain is an old acquaintance of mine named Ryerson. You'll sail with him back to Gdansk where we'll meet you with the MGS."

"When will the ship be in port? Will he be expecting me?"

"Soon, and yes. I'll give you Ryerson's cell number. Ring him when you get to town. He'll send a man for you."

"Well, I suppose I should . . ." Niko sat up and patted at the pockets of his jacket and pants. "Hell of a time for me to lose my damn phone!"

Dory chuckled and pulled a device out of the car's center console. "No worries. After calling Tomasz, I took the batteries out of both our phones and put them in here. Neither ABW nor anyone else can use them to track us."

"Payphones are getting scarce, remember? Hard for me to say when I might find one after I arrive in Klaipeda."

"I've already taken care of that. While you were out, I purchased a burn phone for each of us. A kiosk had them for sale inside the traveler's plaza last time we stopped to fuel up."

Niko folded his arms and rested his chin in his palm. "I would hardly turn down a chance to go to sea, but couldn't you have just bought me a plane ticket?"

"I told you I was going to start cracking the whip. The ship will provide a place for you, Nat, and Annie to work with no outside interference for at least ten days." Dory slumped back into his seat with a long sigh. "It's the best I can do under the circumstances, old man. The airports and train stations will be covered by Dariusz' men by now, so I needed other way to get you back to the States. Pure dumb luck Ryerson happened to be, uh . . . 'sightseeing' off the coast near Kaliningrad. I'm improvising here on account of Mawro."

Niko pinched the bridge of his nose. "You're not making any sense, Dory! Isn't Luczasik after him too?"

"Yes. But with him and Hana in their ailuran forms, they could well have fled to the port and boarded a foreign-flagged vessel getting underway. The North Koreans could charter a ship from Szczecin as easily as we can one to

Gdansk, right?"

He sighed and held his forehead in his palm. Was a concussion or all the twists in Dory's plan making his head ache so? "I thought you and Luczasik were pals. Why the hell would he and ABW turn on us?"

"Dariusz is my friend, but I can hardly expect him to ignore which side of the bread his butter's on. What puzzles me is why someone up the food chain would order him to—"

"A poison pill!"

"Excuse me?" Dory made a face. "You *are* aware agents haven't carried saxitoxin since President Ford was—?"

"No, not for us, moron! I mean Mawro used *me* like a poison pill."

His friend groaned and pulled at his face with one hand. "Of course! If he can't have you working for him, he'll make sure you can't work for anyone else."

"My research would be over if I went to prison. I doubt a warden would so much as let me whip up a decent batch of rotgut."

Dory palmed at his temples. "It all makes sense now! He must've leaked whatever details Blaznikov shared about your service to the Soviets. After his operation to nab you failed, maybe he thought rubbing salt into old wounds would spur Moscow or Berlin into leaning on Warsaw."

"Oh, uhm . . . yeah! Right! Certainly!" Niko cast a furtive glance toward the floor. "I . . . I guess reports Blaznikov is dead must be true, right?"

"The old bastard would never implicate himself nor permit anyone else to," Dory said and patted at Niko's shoulder. "Mawro went all in on the Poles locking you up. While three government's worth of bureaucracy sorted out what to do with you, he could sneak you out of the country from under their noses at his leisure." He leaned back in his seat and tugged at his chin. "But I still don't understand how Mawro read all our moves. Your cover at the Institute was rock solid, and we've kept quiet about specifics to everyone outside our team. How the hell did he get wise to what we were up to?"

Niko lay back down and studied the stitches in the car ceiling's upholstery. "I . . . I don't know, Dory."

A lie. He *knew* the truth. Every terrifying bit of it.

CHAPTER SEVENTEEN

IT WAS WELL AFTER DARK BY THE time Jakub and his passengers reached Białowieża. He had driven in silence for over an hour after happily obliging Dory's need to rest his eyelids. The man had spelled Jakub at the wheel for the better part of the afternoon, though jet lag and stress appeared to finally overwhelm him once the sun went down.

As they neared the sleepy village, he reached over to shake his passenger by the shoulder. Dory looked around and smacked his lips together. "Get ready to turn right at the traffic light coming up."

"But Ma's house is to the left around the bend up ahead."

"Standard operating procedure, son. I just want to make sure no one is following us."

Ten minutes later, Jakub found himself back on the main road. "This is just a little resort town in its off season, Teodor. I'm pretty sure we're the only car out right now."

Niko squirmed about, still lying across the back of the car. "Can we park so I can get up and walk around? My back is killing me."

"Quit bitching, both of you. Jakub, go straight through the light and then turn left like you normally would."

He did as directed and scanned the deserted street. The moon shining brightly in the clear sky above them illuminated everything almost like daylight.

Dory jabbed his finger toward the windshield. "You recognize those parked cars, right?"

"Of course. They're all ones Ma's neighbor's drive."

"Turn here. We'll go in the back way."

The car putted up the narrow alleyway past the third house on the left. "Pull clear of the trash can, kill your headlights, and let me out," Dory said and grabbed his bag. He walked over to the tall, wooden privacy fence and swung open the gate. Jakub backed the car into the small yard behind the house and parked. Dory swung Niko's door open and offered his hand. "Can I help you there, old man?" he asked, his breath forming a cloud in the cold air.

Niko made a face and threw his duffel at him. "You're one to talk. We weren't stopping every forty-five minutes on account of *my* bladder!" After stumbling out of the back seat, he groaned and stretched and rolled his shoulders.

Dory opened his mouth to reply but turned toward the sound of a storm door slamming behind him. Milda stood with arms crossed on the stoop of her little bungalow and scowled at them. "Get in here, fools," she said, tapping her foot. "The food is getting cold!"

He reached over and put his arm around Niko's shoulder. "C'mon, you heard the lady." Milda's feigned disgust evaporated as they approached. She smiled sweetly and gave Niko a hug. "Welcome to my home, *Pan* Opoworo," she said before sharing a quick kiss with Dory. "I hope the next time you visit, we won't be so . . . rushed."

"Thank you, *Pani* Gwozdek. I'm sorry I didn't bring any flowers." He turned and clasped Jakub on the shoulder. "Your boy here was in a bit of a hurry."

"Not to worry, Pawlina brought me a beautiful bouquet from the airport florist," she said with a nod of her head. "Teodor, take him to the basement, would you? Everyone is waiting. We'll be along in a moment."

Dory ushered Niko into the house. "Sure, love."

The staircase creaked loudly as the two men descended. Milda reached around the door jamb and grabbed a small, oblong package wrapped in brown paper. "Teodor called Tomasz this afternoon on our way here to brief us on the goings-on. He said to look for a parcel near my front door when we arrived," she said and handed it to Jakub as she closed the storm door. "And that you would know what to do with it."

He fished around in his pocket for his keys. "Sure do, Ma," he said over his shoulder while he walked back to his car. The car's lights flashed before its tailgate began to rise. Jakub laid the package beside a shop-worn red toolbox in the back and pulled out a utility knife and screwdriver. After slitting one end open, he gave it a shake. Out slid two blue metal plates with white letters and numbers stamped into them.

Milda wandered up next to him. "Vehicle tags?" she asked, her breath forming a cloud in the night air.

A joyful ruckus emanated from the house before he could answer, punctuated by whooping, laughing, and crying. "Dory asked if he could borrow my car to pick up his associate, and I agreed," Jakub said at length and dropped to one knee.

"You don't mind?"

"I don't drive much in Gdansk, anyway. I've been walking to work lately and catch the tram when the weather's bad." He swapped his car's license plate with one of the ones from the parcel. "Most anywhere else I want to go, I'll ride my bicycle. And you know I couldn't refuse Teodor. He's practically family!"

Milda crossed her arms and tapped at her bicep. "He paid you, didn't he?"

"Oh, yes Ma, and handsomely at that. This old girl had a lot of miles when I got her." Jakub stood up and patted at the roof of the car. "Even if she were wrecked or impounded or something, I'd still be money ahead."

She squatted down and pointed at the blue plate. "Where did he get these things, anyway? I thought our tags have black letters with a white background."

Jakub squatted in front of his car and finished the work. "They do. Guess Teodor called in a favor with the American Embassy in Warsaw. He said these are off a similar-looking vehicle from their motor pool that was wrecked last week." He looked up at her as he put his tools away. "Ma, it's freezing out here. Could you go in and set aside a couple of your famous *gołąbki* and some mashed potatoes for me, please?"

"I hate to disappoint, but our meal comes courtesy of Elena Bodny from up the street. Hurts me having so many guests and no time to properly cook for them."

"I doubt they mind. And I missed Mrs. Bodny's cooking almost as much as yours." Jakub took his mother by the shoulders and shook them gently to goad her into looking at him. "How are you holding out?"

"I'd be worried if I expected to wait much longer to return to the Forest. The length of time I feel comfortable being away becomes shorter with each passing year."

"I . . . I see." Jakub let his hands drop to his sides and glanced up at the full moon above their heads. "One of the younglings should be out tonight with their family. Are you okay covering for Niko and me by yourself?"

"I won't have to. Aleška and I have much to catch up on, so she'll be coming. We've also invited Pawlina to join us." Milda flashed him a smirk while she worked the latch on the screen door. "You needn't worry."

Jakub *hmph*ed and followed his mother inside. "From what Teodor told me about those two, maybe I should."

The van crested the hill and stopped at a chain link fence topped with barbed wire. White letters glowed forth from a red background on the metal sign, warning in Polish:

ORŁÓWKA PROTECTIVE UNIT
ACCESS RESTRICTED BEYOND THIS POINT
AUTHORIZED PERSONNEL ONLY

Darkness consumed the signboard after Milda shut off the headlights and killed the ignition. Their host scrambled out of the van with Pawly and her mother right behind. Together, the three of them stepped up next to a gate lashed closed with a stout chain and padlock. Pawly whistled and turned about, her eyes wide. "What *is* this place?"

"This is the center of Białowieża National Park," Milda said. "For countless generations before the *blitzkrieg*, though, our kind simply called it 'home.'" A low growl emanated from her throat before she crouched and sprang into the dark canopy above. Pawly and Alex both lost sight of her until she landed on the other side of the fence, giving them a start.

Their host bared her fangs in a wide smile as fluffy snow billowed around her. "Would you like me to show you around?"

"Oh, would I!" Alex stared back at Pawly an instant later alongside their host, tugging the fur beneath her chin free of her scarf. "Something wrong, dear?"

"Are—are you sure this is okay? I've never been so . . . so . . ."

"Carefree? I can imagine why you might be hesitant, Pawlina. Unlike your mother and me, you never knew anything about your heritage until you were almost an adult." Milda pulled a nylon mesh laundry bag out of her hip pocket. "This is a place where you can, oh, how might you say in English? 'Let down your hair'?"

"I don't suppose we can have *too* much fun, dear," Alex said. "Remember, we're here to do a job. Milda's son and your Grandpa Niko are depending on us."

"They'll be awhile yet, Aleška." Milda stuffed her jacket into the bag and stripped off her pants. "Hurry now, young one! Being stuck in nearly a week's worth of meetings at Ministry headquarters was utter torture. I need to stretch my legs."

Pawly closed her eyes and found her center. An instant later, she felt fur sprout from every follicle in her skin. She grunted when her nails became claws and quickly withdrew into her fingers and toes. Her tongue rasped against the roof of her mouth before she licked at her canine teeth grown out into fangs.

Her nose and jaw morphed into a muzzle, and her eyes fluttered open. Though her whiskers protruding forth made her itch, she fought the urge to scratch at her face. She pranced about, seeking relief from the uncomfortable sensation from her hindclaws and tail cooped up in her shoes and pants to no avail.

With a twitch of her tufted ears, Pawly vaulted herself over the fence and landed next to her mother. She wrinkled her snout toward the dark, form-fitting jumpsuit covering Alex neck to ankles. It reminded her strangely of the wetsuits she had trained in during her Navy career, lacking a cutout for her tail, of course. "Mom . . . are we wearing, uhm, you know . . . enough?"

"Trust me, these will be more than adequate." Milda waved a hand the length of the similar suit she wore. "Our fur is enough to keep us warm. I had considered we go *nagość na zewnątrz* but the underbrush here is pretty thick. These suits do a fine job keeping cocklebur from sticking to, shall we say, inconvenient and uncomfortable places."

Pawly cocked an eyebrow. "I thought you insisted we wear these to avoid giving anyone a show."

The corners of Milda's mouth drew back into a grin. "Insolent whelp," she said as she bopped Pawly's muzzle. "Your mother can affirm our unique physiology helps us remain trim and toned as we age. I'm not above flaunting it from time to time."

"Didn't you say this part of the forest was deserted?"

"It is, Aleška. As far as my employer is concerned, I'm conducting a welfare check on the scientists working inside the Protected Area. They took an early holiday and won't return until after New Year's. A pity I never got that memo," she said with a shrug and shuffled through the freshly fallen snow. When they reached the gate, she pulled the padlock by its chain around to their side. "Now step over to that big tree there by the trailhead," she said, pointing toward a large oak up the two-track next to a small wooden sign. Then she opened the mouth of the laundry bag wide and held it out to them. "Put your outer clothes in here, but don't take your boots off until we're at the treeline."

"Why not? Aren't your feet uncomfortable too?"

"They are, Pawlina, but stop to think a moment. Anyone coming this way ought to find footprints left by normal people, right? Ones who don't have claws on their feet and certainly don't vault fences, you see. Though I suggest we keep our boots in the bag so snow won't blow into them."

Pawly glanced down at the snowy ground and shook her head. She had much yet to understand about herself and her Affliction. And she would need to learn fast to continue her covert work. In her human guise, she was an adult, yet not even twelve years had passed since when she first transformed. She felt as lost and frustrated now as when she had struggled with geometry in the sixth grade.

Am I too late?

Hana stood up on a tree limb and sunk her finger claws into its trunk to brace herself. She had been patrolling the border between Poland and Belarus the length of the Protected Area all night. Early on, she had indulged herself and stalked a small herd of bison. But the unpredictable winds changed direction faster than she could, scattering the herd the instant they got a whiff of her scent. Later, she encountered a lynx on the prowl for its next meal. The thing concluded their staring contest with an angry snarl and slunk off into the night. Apex predator or not, she was an unwelcomed rival here.

In more ways than one, so it seems.

She sniffed and scanned the dense forest around her, trying to discern movement or suspicious scents. Hana pulled at a tendril of her hair and stuck it between her teeth. Papa said she would arrive in theatre well before Opoworo when he ordered her to Białowieża. The professor could well take time to celebrate Mass with his family, he had reminded her. Regardless, he was certain to reconnect with them over a long meal before he left.

Then again, the Poles may have captured him already. Mawro would have recalled her in that case, right? Hana chewed at her hair, picturing that punk Jin-ho back in the van asleep or engrossed in a video game with his headphones on. Would be just like him to miss such a call.

She sighed and resumed her patrol, eyes roving the forest floor as she leapt from one limb to another. Before long she spied lights from the village at the park's northern border. Hana sat down on a large branch and pulled a small plastic bag of dried fish from a pouch on her belt. She surveyed the architecture of the surrounding treetops and popped the bite size pieces into her mouth one at a time.

A strange scent wafting through the air gave her a start. Hana held the chunk in her fingers up to her nose and sniffed, pinching it in half when a twig snapped beneath her. Her ears perked up as the bits of fish fell to the snowy ground and disappeared. Something was coming.

The wind zigzagged again while she stuffed the bag back into her pouch. Again she caught the scent for a mere instant, stronger this time. Wild animal? Maybe a rank amateur? Whatever. She would finish her dinner later.

She hopped gingerly from the bough of the knotty old oak, careful not to rustle the dead brown leaves clinging to its branches. She dropped toward the bottom limb of a leafless alder tree nearby. Then she would spring back up into the canopy and resume her trek southward.

A flash of grey bolted forth from the underbrush below. Hana's wind left her when the thing collided with her in mid-air. She did a tuck and roll when she landed into a handstand. With a grunt she flipped herself back onto her feet. Hana grabbed at her forearm and launched a trio of black throwing darts with one fluid motion. She leapt up to the alder branch while her would-be attacker collapsed to the ground with a pained yowl.

Her eyes went wide at the sight below her. A human-looking creature covered in gray fur thrashed about on its back, pawing at its face. One of the darts had penetrated deep into its shoulder, another into its cheekbone just under the right eye. Bright red blood ran down between its fingers, staining the snowy white fur beneath its jowls.

Hana drew one hand over her mouth. A *youngling*? Papa had said nothing about any Kindred anywhere near—

A primal roar from the bushes sent a tingle down her spine. She remembered something Mawro did say: a youngling, like a bear cub, was never, *ever* found in the wild without its mother nearby.

She gulped and scanned the canopy, desperate for an avenue with which to make her escape. Two more Kindred sprang forth from the trees lining the other side of the border. Spotting an opening to her left, she bounded off into the darkness with the sound of her own heartbeat thundering in her ears.

Jakub waved the battery-powered lantern ahead of him to light their way. To pass the time, he told Niko how the narrow tunnel they plodded along had been dug by Polish partisans during the Great War. With it, they ambushed the occupying Germans cutting down the Forest's enormous trees for lumber. Later, Poles and Soviets alike used this and other tunnels to evade pursuing Nazis.

Niko returned the favor of Jakub's good company by peppering him with questions about his work. What strange and exotic cargoes had he handled? What kind of ships carried them? The man loved to sail and had been fascinated by maritime lore and legend since he was a boy. Other men's seafaring stories provided fodder for the tall tales he delighted telling his grandchildren.

"Teodor was in the Coast Guard, as was his father before him after immigrating to the US from Poland. His brother Robercik still skippers a tugboat for a Great Lakes marine towing company. Aleška's husband was senior enlisted in the Navy. Both Pawlina and Tomasz served as sailors too."

They arrived at what appeared to be a dead end in the tunnel. The place was empty except for a spindly wooden ladder leaning up against the far wall. Jakub set the lantern on the floor and pointed its beam toward the hatchway above. "So what exactly was Teodor doing in Poland at the time?" He set his foot on the ladder's bottom rung and gave it a good shake. "The Cold War would have still been going on. I'm sure the Kremlin didn't like his being here one bit."

Niko chuckled. "They certainly did not," he said while Jakub began to climb. "But that's all Teodor will let me say about that, you know."

He said nothing, not wishing to pry further. Too many people knew too much about too many things already. That was why they were here now.

At the top of the ladder, Jakub squatted down on the second topmost rung and thrust his shoulder against the hatch cover. With a grunt he straightened up and muscled it to one side.

He scrambled out and turned back to Niko. "Quickly!" he whispered.

While his companion began his ascent, Jakub tiptoed over to the opening in the massive, hollowed-out stump. A full moon hung high in the sky, casting pale silver light upon the snow-covered clearing. "Moon Before Yule" as his mother had called it. The inconvenient timing of its appearance trumped its brilliant beauty, however. As well as they could see, they could also *be* seen.

Several small stone buildings stood at the clearing's edge, remnants of a sawmill dating back over a hundred years when logging still took place here. A green flag flapped in the chilly breeze from atop the roof of the largest one. It would only be up now after his mother and the others scouted the area to indicate it was safe. Good. One less thing to worry about. Jakub had seen firsthand the havoc a youngling could wreak raging out of control on his first Hunt.

After Niko's head popped forth from the hatch behind him, Jakub put a finger to his lips and waved him over. Both men crouched down next to the opening in the stump and squinted toward the old mill. He did a double take toward a fleeting shadow, but whatever caused it disappeared before he got a good look.

"Did you spot something?" Niko whispered.

He shook his head and pointed across the clearing. "It's nothing. Move quickly and quietly to that last building on the right. I'll follow along behind you." Niko cast a wary glance this way and that with every step until they reached the buildings' shadows. "Viktor is a logger contracted by the Belarusian government to remove deadfall from the Forest," Jakub said, hoping small talk might help his companion feel more at ease. "This time of year, he'll be out walking routes for his skidder before the ground freezes. He'll be expecting us."

Niko scratched at his head. "Just *where* is he?"

Jakub pointed to where the trail disappeared into the trees. "His trailer is parked about a fifteen-minute hike this way."

"What do we do when we get to the border?"

"We, you know . . . walk across," he said, making tiptoes with his fingers through the air.

"Into Belarus? What about the guards?"

Jakub rolled his eyes. "Budget cuts, man! Haven't you seen the news lately? I'm not complaining, though. This way, I don't have to haul you over on my—"

A growling from behind the building stopped him cold. A fur-covered form emerged from around the corner, moonlight glinting off two shards of metal lodged into the creature's face and shoulder. The gray and white coat below its neck was stained brown with what appeared to be dried blood. Its two angry eyes fixed them both with a menacing stare. The thing took a step toward them, then another, sending tremors across every square inch of Jakub's skin.

"Run."

"Run?"

"Yes, Niko! Back to the tunnel! RUN!"

CHAPTER EIGHTEEN

DORY STUMBLED DOWN THE back stairs and burst into the kitchen, banging the black plastic case in his hand against the wall. "Oh, good, you're up," Annie said from where she stood at the counter, her back to him. "Tommy was beat and wanted to shower before bed, so Mom took him back to the hotel. When she comes back, we'll cut into this rolled-up poppy seed sweet thingy Milda set out . . ."

"It's called *makowiec*, dear," Nat said as he came in from the living room and nodded toward the window sill. "That red currant wine over there will go great with—oh, Dory! Is . . . is something wrong?"

Annie and Nat stared at him in silence, worry etched into the lines on their foreheads. "Yes. Yes, there is," Dory said and slumped into one of the wooden chairs beside the table. "Millie just called saying Niko and Jakub were attacked in the Forest."

"WHAT?" they said together. "Are they hurt?" "What about Pawly and Alex?" "Who attacked them?" "We gotta go help!" "Wait, who'll stay here with Stu—?"

He held up his hands to silence them. "First things' first, kids. She said they're both OK, but the Forest Clan is holding them captive."

Annie knit her brow. "The local Kindred tribe? Why?"

"A whelp out on his first Hunt was also attacked, and his parents think they had something to do with it. The boy is hurt pretty bad from what Milda said."

"Well then, Nat can stay here with Stuie while you and I go to—"

"I could see gears turning in your head from here, Annie. The answer is 'no'. Absolutely not."

"But Dory, I—"

"I said *no!*" he said in a raised voice as if to make clear he considered the issue settled. "Sunny's knowledge of Kindred physiology is second only to Niko himself. The clansmen should acknowledge a veterinarian like her can help the boy. They're otherwise intently distrustful of outsiders."

She crossed her arms and glared at him. "But Mom's not one of them! Won't they consider her an outsider too?"

"Not after she tells them how Alex and Ritzi were—"

They all turned toward the sound of the back door opening. "So much loud talking. What is happening?" Sunny said as she stepped into the kitchen. "Where is Stuie?"

Nat waved his hand toward the living room stairwell. "Went upstairs to bed already, *Eomeonim*."

Dory sighed. "Niko and Jakub have been taken captive by the Forest Clan."

Sunny's eyes went wide. "Their leader agreed to meet with us!"

"Yes, but that was before they stood accused of harming a whelp out on his first Hunt. Millie and I have an idea how we might reason with them, but we'll need your help." He popped the latches on the black plastic case and laid it open on the table, revealing a pair of pistols. "Annie, Nat—stay here and get Stuie dressed. After I take Sunny to the clearing, I'll come back here and go pick up Tommy," Dory said to Annie while inserting ammunition clips into both of them. "*Someone* knows we're here, but I don't know who. I don't want anyone after Niko trying to use the three of you as bait."

The elder man handed Nat and Annie a pistol each. "Once we leave, go upstairs and put both of your cell phones on the nightstand. Make sure you run that app I had you download, Nat. Turn off the lights, draw the blinds, and barricade the doors. Get down into the basement near the tunnel portal and *stay there* until we return, got it?"

"Got it," Annie and Nat said together.

Dory whisked past Sunny and waved for her to follow. "Come on. I'll explain everything on the way."

Niko turned his head toward the sound of the opening door. His buttocks tingled when he scooted around, asleep after sitting on the cold stone floor for what seemed like hours. It was a trick to get his feet under him with his wrists lashed to a wooden pole behind his back. He groaned, tired and sore, but managed to hoist himself slowly to a standing position.

Whoever had blindfolded him knew what he was doing, so he craned his neck to listen as well as he could. Footsteps approached, several pairs of them. A cane or walking stick tapped the floor in time with one party member's hesitating, almost lame gait.

The Godfather and his entourage have arrived.

The stick bearer stepped in close as the group formed itself around Niko. "So you believe this man is the rogue Soviet scientist from the news last night?" came an elderly man's voice.

"Yes, Monsignor," replied one of his male companions.

"I am *not* Russian! I'm a Pole!"

"We never said you were, Professor." A round and slender piece of wood pushed his cheek this way and that. "Regardless, you are not one of us and have no business being in our Forest. That *does* make you a trespasser."

"Valuable, also." Another voice, this one from a younger woman. "Lucky for you, Warsaw is offering a big reward for your capture. Otherwise, for desecrating Artsyom's sacred rite of passage, we would have torn you to shreds already!"

Niko contemplated whether his captors intended to yet carry out their implied threat until a man groaned from across the room. "Shame on you, Jakub!" the old man said as the party members turned as one. "You would provoke history repeat itself by bringing this . . . this *butcher* here?"

"This doesn't concern him, Monsignor. The whelp was already raging when he attacked us!"

His face screwed up beneath his blindfold. Niko believed the speaker to be Jakub, but his voice was deeper and raspier than he remembered.

"This fellow is one of the people Ma wanted to introduce to you. He's an ally."

"We have been ministers of the Forest courts around us for countless generations, Jakub. Our kind has no need for the likes of *him*," the old man replied with a snort. "Did you forget your lessons, boy? Alchemists bled out our ancestors alive! They believed boiling our Afflicted blood would change dross into gold. Then Nazi scientists goaded my elders into transforming while they dissected them to learn why. Whenever the winter wind howls through the trees, I still hear my mother's screams."

"I protest, Monsignor Dryzek! This is outrageous!"

Niko gasped, hearing the now-familiar voice.

"You would do well to remember your place, Milda!"

"This *is* my place! Your clansmen attacked my son accompanying a man under my protection, one whom you had agreed to meet with!"

"The green flag was up, Ma," Jakub said. "I thought Artsyom and the others were nowhere near the old sawmill."

"No matter! I would not have consented had I known whom he really was," the fellow called Dryzek said. Niko's skin prickled at the hot breath upon his face and throat. "Did you run out of Kindred graves to rob so you could conduct your gruesome experiments?" he said and tapped his stick on the floor. "Is that why you and your cohorts attacked Artsyom on his first hunt?"

"Monsignor, you don't really believe that he—"

"This isn't the first time this fellow has raised his hand against us, Milda. I recognized his photo during the television news tonight. Years ago, *he* desecrated the final resting places of our ancestors and took their remains back to Berlin."

The uncomfortable sensation returned when the man began breathing on Niko again. "What did you do then, huh? Put them in some travelling freak show? Dissolve them in acid? Cut them up like horse meat to feed to your dogs?" he said and spat toward Niko's feet. "Only my vows deterred me from killing you and those Stasi swine myself."

Someone stomped over and pulled the blindfold off his head. Niko blinked to ward off the assault on his eyes by the room's bright lights. He recognized Milda poking at his head and neck as the spots went away. "Are you okay?"

Niko peeked over Milda's shoulder at the three clansmen behind her. The woman and the man standing next to one another had faces covered with familiar gray fur and white ruffs around their necks. Long canine teeth protruded beyond their lips while their mouths hung open. They waved their hands in front of them, affording him a good view of their pawpads.

Though seeing him for the first time in ailuran form, Niko recognized Jakub immediately. The younger man stood bound by his wrists to a pole in the opposite corner of the room. The whiskers at the end of his gray muzzle twitched when he winked back at him.

This Dryzek fellow, however, whom Milda had addressed as "Monsignor", appeared in human guise. Though older than Niko, he was an imposing figure regardless—tall and husky, like Jakub. The cuffs and collar of his black cassock did not quite conceal the many scars peppered about his wrists and throat.

"What are you doing, Milda? No outsider can be trusted seeing us in our Afflicted forms!" The tails of the purple sash around Dryzek's waist fluttered with each tap of his walking stick. "Especially one of *his* kind."

"Ignore them, Niko. Tell me if you sense pain anywhere."

"No more than one does getting old, my dear. I'll be fine."

"We can remedy that." The man standing behind the Monsignor pulled a knife from his belt and stepped toward them. "Dead men tell no tales, but blind men point no fingers."

Milda turned and held out her hands wide. "Harm so much as a hair on his head, Waldemar, and I'll kill you myself! Don't think I wouldn't."

Dryzek thrust his arm between the two of them. "Waldemar, Ewelina, let me handle this." The couple shot daggers into Milda with their eyes while the priest crossed his arms and glared at Niko. "You're acquainted with Blaznikov, right?"

It was a statement, not a question. Niko exchanged a look with Milda but said nothing.

"His family ran a lumber mill near what is now *Belovezhskaya Pushcha*. For the illicit act of felling timber after the Forest was declared a hunting preserve, the Soviets banished the boy's parents to the gulag. On the way, their convoy was swept over a cliff by an avalanche. There were no survivors."

The man's stick tapped at the floor while he paced back and forth. "The boy went to an orphanage in Leningrad. After a schoolyard scrap ended in carnage, he was turned over to the Pavlov Institute. One of the researchers there bonded with young Blaznikov, treating him like a son. When the Kremlin commissioned the man to exploit our Affliction as the Nazis had tried, he turned up dead, too."

Dryzek stopped and stood nose to nose with him, nostrils flaring. "Ferrymen fished him out of the *Malaya Neva* one piece at a time."

Niko gulped.

"Blaznikov's new handler came straight from Moscow, answering only to the Politburo. In time, the young man served in the Soviet Navy and joined the KGB. There he was tasked to find a scientist to continue the work his foster father began—one smart enough to achieve the Kremlin's goals, yet dumb enough to not question their intent."

Dryzek fixed Niko with a withering stare. "He found you."

He lowered his gaze to the floor.

"You scientists never listen! Generations of self-proclaimed sages before you violated our bodies with shiny instruments or poisoned our minds with concoctions and drugs. And for what? Like the alchemists of old, your efforts are destined to fail."

He winced every time Dryzek poked his chest to punctuate each word. "You see, Professor, the Affliction's origins are rooted in the *curse*, not in science. Christ our Savior commands us 'love thy enemy' and 'offer the other cheek,' but I will not permit your hubris to further threaten our clan. Whether the prison in which you rot lies in Germany, Poland, or Russia makes no difference to me."

"We are also forbidden from harming or abandoning one of our own, right?"

Dryzek made a show out of sniffing the air around Niko. "You must have taken quite a blow to the head to spout such nonsense, Jakub. Any of us with a nose can tell this fellow is certainly not one of us!"

"The blood of Nikodemos Opoworo does not make him Kindred, Monsignor." Milda gazed up into Niko's eyes and laid her hand aside his face. "Jakub's does. And mine, too."

¶

Lena hugged her crying baby close to her chest to shush him. Her kin folk stood all around, staring in silence at the stern of their sinking ship. The *Baltic Wayfarer* was the only home she and many among them had ever known.

She wiped at her eyes while the other lifeboat putted about nearby, its crew fishing everyone out of the water knocked overboard by the torpedo hit. Andrzej Stupek stood atop a bench aside the gunwale, barking orders to the boat's pilot. Her great uncle's brother-in-law first learned seamanship as a young man serving on a British ship flying the Polish flag during the War. At his insistence, every man, woman, and child aboard participated in weekly lifeboat drills since he assumed command of the merchant vessel years before. His stubborn diligence had made him a hero this horrible day.

Beside Lena stood her father's cousin, Alfon. He piloted the boat under direction from his father Piotr, the *Wayfarer*'s chief engineer. "We have twenty-seven!" Andrzej shouted when the two boats drew near.

"And here are the other thirty-two, thanks be," Piotr replied after he finished his head count. "All of our crew and family are present and accounted for."

"How is Aleška?"

The engineer glanced to where the girl lay next to Lena on a plank atop two of the lifeboat's benches. "She's still unconscious." Maurycy sat sobbing beside his little sister, her head cradled in his lap while he stroked the short tawny fur on her face. Next to him, Jerzy, the ship's doctor, wrapped the boy's head with bandages where the Soviet sub commander had pistol-whipped him.

Her heart ached for the children. Hardly two years had passed since the stormy night their mother and father were lost during a ship-to-ship transfer of contraband cargo. Now this.

Lena cinched her sash up around her shoulders and unbuttoned her blouse. The baby's crying ceased after she drew him to her chest, and he began to suckle. Still a teenager and the only woman aboard with an infant, she often cared for the siblings while their grandfather Andrzej stood watch. She slid her free arm around Maurycy's shoulders. "Don't worry. This happens to each of us when we come into our own."

He sniffed and raised his head. "It was her time, right?"

"I . . . I suppose so," Lena said before she bit her lip. For Maurycy's sake, she hoped she was doing a better job of lying than she thought she was. Of *course* it hadn't been her time. Girls transformed for the first time in their early-to-mid-teens, and here was Aleška, barely ten years old. Emotional trauma even at such a young age was known to kick the Affliction in the goads, causing it to manifest quickly. And violently.

Boys came into their own later. Maurycy was two years older than his sister, leading Lena to believe theirs might well manifest about the same time.

Andrzej himself would have certainly insisted he tend them during their first Hunt.

Piotr leapt atop a bench and looked around. "Where are those landsmen?" he shouted over to Andrzej's boat.

"Who cares?" asked Grzegorz, the ship's steward. "If we had given them up to the Soviets, we would still have a ship beneath us!"

Their first mate Wacław stood next to Lena. "Little Aleška would have shredded that sub commander creep, anyway!"

"Only because he was about to shoot her brother," said a woman she could not see, though it sounded like Zuza.

"Shoulda left 'em on the dock. We were buying nothing but trouble from KGB, transporting fugitives."

"That's *all* we could buy with as little money we have. And both our fuel and rations were nearly gone."

"Yeah! How could we turn down that kind of cash?

"Genuine American currency, no less!"

Arguments broke out all around from her kin taking sides. Lena and the children had come to like these three passengers. Like others defecting to the West, none of them gave their full names after coming aboard at Szczecin. Niko was a native to the port city. With him was his young Korean wife who went by Sunny. Lena had become quite smitten with their escort, a dashing young American named Dory. He smelled so good!

Deck plate gossip went the United States government offered Andrzej an enormous sum of money to ensure safe passage to Rotterdam for Dory and his two charges. Times were tight—their captain had been quick to toss the dice on his clan's behalf. The sight of the *Wanderer*'s stern slipping beneath the waves made Lena realize how much his gamble had cost them all.

She felt a tug at the hem of her skirt. "We can't just leave them!" Maurycy said above the din when she glanced down. "We just can't!"

"ENOUGH!"

Andrzej's voice pealed like a bell. Everyone fell silent while he glared down at them from atop the helm of his boat. "Talk about this when we are ashore or back aboard ship. None further now, is that clear?"

Lena and her kin nodded as one.

"Good. Now then, first thing we'll need to do is figure out where—"

A wave crashed over the side of both boats, almost swamping them. The Soviet sub pitched and rolled after its rapid ascent a mere dozen meters away while a man emerged from the top of its sail. With a grunt he hoisted a heavy machine gun up through the hatch and sat it in a mount along the railing. "One of you freaks killed one of mine," Lena picked out from the man's deep baritone among countless Russian expletives. Fear gripped Lena's heart when she heard a loud *clack*.

"Get down!" Andrzej screamed and thrust the women next to him to the deck. "Everyone get down!"

Bullets tore through the air all around after the gunner opened fire. "Cover them!" Jerzy stood and pushed Maurycy toward Lena, dumping the contents of his kit bag all over. She clutched her baby to her bosom with one arm and pulled the siblings down with the other. Several of her shipmates struggled to open the small weapons locker behind the boat's helm, all quickly gunned down. "Keep quiet until I say otherwise!" she hissed into Maurycy's ear above the screams and gun fire. The dead and dying piled atop them one after another after another.

Lena's mind began to shut down before a primal, guttural roar came from the sub's direction. The shooting stopped as soon as the screaming started, followed quickly by sounds of tearing flesh and snapping bone.

The stench from a sickening combination of urine, feces, and blood roused her. Relief washed over Lena, feeling her newborn's toothless mouth still clamped firmly to her breast. She groped about in the pile of bodies around her until she grasped Maurycy's trembling hand. The boy started and whimpered at her touch. "Are . . . are you hurt?" she whispered.

"N-no."

She blew out her breath. "Good. Where is your sister?"

"Other side. I've got her hand."

"Can you breathe okay?"

"Yeah."

"Do you think she can?"

Maurycy patted around next to him. "I . . . I think so. Her chest is rising and falling."

Lena prayed Aleška was still unconscious. Perhaps God in his mercy would spare one of Andrzej's grandchildren from witnessing him and their clansmen being torn to pieces.

Their boat bobbed about on the gently rolling ocean. A faint dripping noise crowded out the eerie silence, the sound of their kinsmen's life blood draining from them. Lena thrust her face toward the bilge and threw up.

She didn't have time for this. Focus! Her baby and the siblings depended on her to get them to safety. But where would she take them? Deck gunner or no, that damned sub might well be skulking about even now, ready to finish the job. She cocked her head, hoping for signs of life aboard the other boat. The tinny slap of waves against the boat's steel hull was all she heard.

Light glinted beside her when Lena turned onto her side. Lena reached for the shiny thing and found the small mirror from Jerzy's kit bag. Reflected moonlight shimmered from the clear night sky above them while the boat rocked gently to and fro. That gave her an idea. Lena wriggled out from underneath the mass of bodies, careful to keep her body below the gunwale. She reached up and swept the mirror around one way then the other. After counting fifty, she scanned again to convince herself the sub was really gone. "Come on. Give me her hand." Maurycy did as he was told. A moment later, Lena and the boy each hooked an arm around one of Aleška's shoulders and stood her up.

The tattered, lifeless forms of their shipmates lay strewn about the boat all around them. "Good," she said and smiled at the boy, trying to hide her fear and revulsion. "Can you take her so I can get to the helm?" Hearing no reply, Lena elbowed his shoulder with the arm holding her baby. He faced her, mouthing words he could not bring himself to say out loud. "Yes, Maurycy," she said for him, her own voice cracking. "They're dead. All of them."

Little Jakub broke his hold and began to cry while Lena patted at Maurycy's cheek. *And so will we if we don't get the hell out of here!*

A beam of light cut through the darkness behind her. She growled and spun around, wanting to at least see her killer's face with her own eyes before he opened fire. "Kill me if you must, but let these children and my baby—"

"It is Milena. Right?" came a woman's voice, or so Lena thought. No matter how badly she wanted to believe her senses, was she or was she not still in her right mind?

"S-Sunny? Is . . .is that you?"

The light went dark an instant before the deck lurched beneath her feet. A pole from the other craft had snagged the transom of their boat and was pulling it alongside. Dory's comforting scent wafted over Lena while Sunny stepped aboard their boat, trailed by two shadowy figures she knew must be Niko and the dashing young American. "How-how did you—"

The men flanked Maurycy to help carry his sister. "Just after your captain called for quarters, the second mate hid us under the side benches of the other boat," Niko said.

"We'd have been here by now, but we, um . . . " Dory rubbed at the side of his face. "We had a hard time . . . getting ourselves out."

The Korean woman wrapped her arms around Lena's baby, careful to place her hand flat up against his back. "Please, Milena. Let me take him. I helped care for Niko's nephew. He was a newborn at that time."

Sunny stepped over the blood-drenched deck toward the other boat with Jakub snug at her breast. A shell-shocked Maurycy trailed behind, followed by Niko carrying Aleška in his arms. Lena looked out over the open ocean, unable to spot any trace of their ship. The waves must have carried the flotsam out of sight while they all lay unconscious.

Dory put his arm around Lena's shoulders to coax her along. "We'll get you and the children out of here safely. I promise." She buried her face in his chest and broke down, the shock of the moment finally overwhelming her.

¶

"Niko and Dory were both experienced seafarers. They navigated our boat to the coast of Denmark by starlight. There, scary-looking soldiers I later learned were the Hunstman Corps intercepted us. They gave us quite a fright before realizing we were not the escaping submarine crew they were expecting. Word came later of a Soviet shore patrol sub run aground east of Lübeck, appearing to have been abandoned."

Niko studied Milda's face while she breathed deep and closed her eyes. "After being checked out by Danish doctors, Jakub and I were hustled off to await deportation back to Poland." She opened her eyes and fixed her gaze upon Dryzek. "We were both born aboard the *Wayfarer*. I had intended to raise my son on the ship among our kinsmen and crewmates like my parents. And theirs."

What tumultuous thoughts swirled through her mind? Niko could only guess. The lovelorn teen had been crushed when Dory admitted he had a wife and son awaiting him back in America. She would need to grow up fast to provide for herself and her baby—by whatever means possible. And she would do so alone.

Waldemar crossed his arms and glared at Milda. "You're not actually buying this tripe, are you, Monsignor? Coming from a misfit like her?"

Ewelina snorted. "'Milda', 'Lena', whatever," she said with a dismissive wave. "A liar by another name remains a liar still!"

"I told you to let me handle this," Dryzek said before his eyes turned to the floor. "Besides, I believe she speaks the truth."

The couple gasped.

"Blaznikov came insisting we accept young Milena and her newborn son into our clan, believing them the sole surviving members of theirs," he went on, never once looking up. "I was never able to get him to explain just why."

Milda buried her face in her hands. "My child and I were being forced back to a country I barely knew, run by the very men who slaughtered my clan!" she blurted out after a long moment. "Who was I to trust with our secret? Blaznikov approached me after we landed in Poland and offered to bring me here to raise my son. In exchange, I would change my name—and keep my mouth shut."

Ewelina narrowed her eyes. "Something stinks here still. Why are we finding out about this only now?"

"I-I couldn't risk losing favor with Blaznikov while he was still alive." Milda cupped both of Jakub's cheeks with her hands. "You two would feel the same about Artsyom, wouldn't you? Though he's been a grown man for years, Jakub is still my baby boy." Tears welled in the big man's eyes as he placed his furry hands atop hers and smiled.

Waldemar jabbed his thumb at Niko. "Then why is *he* here?"

"My wife and I took the orphaned siblings with us to America, that's why. We were permitted to foster them because we spoke their language and a fair bit of English as well. In time, we adopted them both. We made understanding their Affliction our life's work, even after their little brother Natan came along. Aleška grew into a fine young woman and married Dory's son. She bore him twins."

Dryzek sucked in his breath and sat down on a wooden crate against the wall. "Then the Stupek bloodline *survives*?"

Waldemar grunted. "Ridiculous!" Ewelina said.

Milda pursed her lips and stepped around the corner of the passageway. She reappeared a moment later with Sunny, Alex, and Pawly following behind. In one instant, Niko's heart leapt; in the next, he cursed himself for involving his family in this.

The wildcard here was Dryzek. The Monsignor stood and stared at their new arrivals, his expression hard to read. At length, he turned and glared at Milda. "You . . . you brought *another* human here?" he said, indicating Sunny with his stick. "This is unforgiveable!"

Waldemar cast a suspicious glance toward the fur-covered forms of Niko's daughter and granddaughter. "Just who are these . . . others?"

Alex's eyes shimmered while she glanced back and forth between her adoptive mother and father. "I . . . I was born Aleška Stupek," she said in a small voice. "My brother Ritzi and I took our new father's name—'Opoworo'. And this . . . " She wrapped her arm around Pawly's shoulder and pulled her close. "This is Pawlina Katczynski. My daughter."

"Seon-Yeong here is an experienced veterinarian and very knowledgeable of our unique physiology," Milda said with a nod toward Sunny. "I brought her here to help heal Artsyom."

Ewelina's face screwed up as though someone had played some sort of tasteless joke on her. "And why should I permit an outsider like her anywhere near my son?"

"'Harm not the Children of Affliction', Ewelina." Dryzek waved his hand toward Niko and his wife. "If any outsiders have demonstrated themselves trustworthy and loyal toward Kindred, these two have. Release the captives."

Waldemar sighed and cast a resigned look between Niko and Jakub, still bound fast to the wooden poles. "Yes, Monsignor." He drew forth his knife and slashed the ligatures about their wrists.

Milda gave her son a quick peck on the cheek while the other women took turns hugging Niko. "Now please," Dryzek said and motioned toward the corridor with his stick, "come help one of our own."

Sunny wrinkled her nose from the awful smell upon entering the dark, dank room. Artsyom lay on a cot set up in one corner. A man pushed vomit and diarrheal feces toward a drain in the floor with a large squeegee fixed to a broom handle. When he finished, he peered at the readout of a pulse oximetry monitor fixed to the boy's hand. "I don't need an audience," he addressed Dryzek with a scowl. "His condition hasn't improved anyway."

Milda gaped at the balding man. "Karol, you're a meatcutter. What are you doing here?"

"He was a medic in his Land Forces unit years ago when he deployed to Afghanistan," Waldemar said for him. "Old Ilya was taken ill last month and hasn't left his bed since."

Karol straightened and pulled off his rubber gloves. "I managed to remove the bolts. His sensory and vital organs appear to be intact."

Artsyom gasped for air while Sunny stepped up to his bedside. "I can help. His vitals stable?"

Dryzek nodded in response to Karol's questioning look.

"No. His breathing has become more labored over time. And about a half hour ago, his pulse rate started dropping fast." He rubbed his hand over his face and turned to Artsyom's parents. "I'm afraid you should . . . prepare yourselves."

Ewelina, overcome with emotion, turned and sobbed into her husband's shoulder. Everyone else save Karol crossed themselves and bowed their heads. Dryzek stepped up beside Sunny and flipped open the small vial he drew from his sash. Chanting a prayer of extreme unction, he dipped his thumb into the oil within and rubbed at the boy's furry forehead.

A lump formed in Sunny's throat when she opened her eyes and stared down at Artsyom. Atop an upended washtub next to his cot sat a plastic basin. She raised it to her face to get a better look at a pair of metal spikes inside, each about six inches long and covered in blood.

"Are these the 'bolts'? The ones you spoke of? "

"Yes. Like they were shot from a crossbow or something."

"No they weren't," Alex said as she peered over her mother's shoulder. "These are throwing darts."

Sunny cocked an eyebrow. "Do they belong to you?"

Alex made a face. "No, I left mine at home. And they're pointed at only one end." She reached into the pan with her bare fingers. "These here could well be—"

Pawly yanked the basin away from her reach. "No, Mom! I've seen these things before. They're likely covered with contact poison!"

The monitor on Artsyom's hand chirped in alarm. Karol glanced down at the display and drew his lips into a thin line. "His heart rate is . . . dangerously low."

Sunny slapped her forehead. "Atropine," she said, holding her hand out to him.

He blinked. "Excuse me?"

"Atropine, I said!" She pointed to his kit bag lying on the floor. "An auto-injector. Do you keep one?"

"You mean like for after a nerve gas attack?"

"Yes. Yes! "

"Well I, er . . . " He dug around inside his kit and produced a combo pen. "Yeah, but I don't know . . . " he said as he squinted at the label.

"Stuff lasts long time. Administer it. Now!"

Waldemar stood nearby, clutching his wife's head to his chest. With a nod from him, Karol snapped the top off the injector and jabbed its needles into Artsyom's thigh. The medicine's intended effect manifested within seconds. Once the boy's pulse rate climbed above the monitor's low threshold, its alarm fell silent.

"No more imminent danger. Monitor him closely. Keep more atropine close." Sunny glanced up at Pawly. "I remember your encounter in Korea. Hunters for centuries brought down large game with small arrows. Dipped in aconitum extract. Darts, too. Need not penetrate far to deliver the poison. Party would track the animal until it fell down dead." She placed her hand gently on Artsyom's forehead. "A normal human would have died by now. Certainly."

Pawly clenched her fists at her sides and nodded toward the dishpan. "I'm sure those things belong to Hana. Mawro must have sent her here looking for you, Grandpa."

"And came upon Artsyom instead," Jakub said and met eyes with Niko. "She'll be out there still waiting to ambush us on our way to the border."

Waldemar led Ewelina over to the side of Artsyom's cot. "I drive truck-load express freight all over Belarus and Lithuania," he said and offered Niko his hand. "Name a place and I'll take you there. Meager way to thank you all for saving our son."

"That would be quite helpful," he said, taking Waldemar's furry hand in his. "Much appreciated."

Pawly snorted. "Hana's not known to give up easily on anything."

Dryzek sneered while gray fur sprouted forth from underneath the collar and cuffs of his cassock. "Leave her to me."

CHAPTER NINETEEN

Hana crouched on the snow-covered tree limb and gulped down great lungfuls of air while her striped tail drooped toward the ground. Once her breathing was under control, she raised her head into the chilly breeze and sniffed. Only after her heightened senses led her to believe no Kindred had followed her did she permit herself to relax.

With a hand out to steady herself, she straightened up against the trunk of the massive oak. Hana poked at the chronometer on her wrist to produce a display of her present lat/long coordinates. Poking it again showed her position relative to where Jin-ho awaited her. Their van sat parked beyond the fence surrounding the Protected Area on Białowieża's outskirts.

Hana spied the thick limb of a poplar tree nearby. She sank the claws on her feet into the branch beneath her and pushed off. Little bits of bark fluttered earthward behind her. High above the Forest's floor, she leapt from treetop to treetop toward the clearing along its southern border. The moonlight shimmering off the virgin snow glowed brighter as she neared her goal. She gritted her teeth and drove herself forward through the pain. There would be ample opportunity to rest once she reached the van.

With rest, however, would come reflection. The encounter with the priest and his followers left Hana rattled to her core. While Mawro and Blaznikov kept no secrets regarding the existence of others like them scattered about the globe, she never guessed they were legion. The cassocked man must have been his clan's elder, appearing to her in his ailuran form with his clansmen behind on either side. Were there dozens? A hundred? How could there be so many? How many more were . . . out *there*, somewhere? Did they hide in plain sight or cloister themselves in catacombs? The unanswered questions assailing her mind threatened to overwhelm her.

On top of all that, Opoworo was long gone. The elder made his point when he demanded she leave—members of their clan had already escorted the professor across the border, so no reason required she remain. Pursuing him into Belarus was no option as her country had no diplomatic mission there. Not like her credentials would do her much good in Poland anyway if she were seen sporting orange fur and a striped tail.

Though it mattered little, Hana couldn't help but wonder whether the clan elder thought she had actually attacked first. He granted clemency this one time only because the whelp was expected to survive. His voice played in her mind on an endless loop, bellowing out a stern warning as she fled. For violations of the ancient Kindred edict "Harm not the children of Affliction!" there stood but one punishment. Death. And with such overwhelming numbers, the priest and his clansmen could well have carried out sentence then and there with only claws and fangs.

At length Hana reached the treeline. A dozen meters to her right sat the van, encircled within a cloud of exhaust. She swung to the ground and rapped on the back door three times, then twice again. Hopefully, that punk Jin-ho had compromised neither their position nor their stealth with his carelessness. At least he had possessed sense enough to turn the van's lights off.

Seconds passed. Nothing. Her whiskers twitched as she crinkled her nose. Hana repeated her signal a bit more firmly, but again the electric lock refused to disengage. She banged on the door for a third time. No reply. With a loud snarl, she bounded atop the vehicle and shimmied up to the edge of the partially open sunroof on her belly.

Jin-ho lay asleep in the driver's seat with the heater cranked up. As a taxi driver in Pyongyang, he had learned to crack a window whenever standing. A fellow cabbie had asphyxiated in his sleep awaiting a fare one cold night.

He groaned and rolled his head to one side before his soft snoring resumed. Hana snaked her hand through the opening and hooked one claw through an oversized link in the gold chain around his neck. She made a fist around a handful of the links and heaved. Jin-ho planted his face on the glass of the sunroof with a hollow *thump*.

"Rise and shine, sleepyhead!" she said, a sweet smile plastered across her face before she let go. The startled young man yelped and crumpled to the floor while she savored the satisfying sound of his pained moans. "Your orders required you stay alert. That implies staying awake as well."

Hana fished a small plastic ampoule out of her bandolier and flicked it into Jin-ho's chest with her thumb and forefinger. "Try some ginseng extract. My treat. Now, open the back door before I get rude with you."

Jin-ho glared up at her, rubbing at his red face with one hand. He stuffed the ampoule into his pants pocket and heaved himself back into his seat. A tinny *click* sounded from inside each door. "Thank you!" she said in a sing-song voice and leapt down.

Hana scrambled through the back door and pulled it shut, immersing herself in the dim glow from the communications console. She made her way to the operator's chair near the front of the compartment and knocked on the bulkhead behind Jin-ho's seat. As she buckled her lap belt, the van lurched forward and headed back towards town.

Feeds from the cameras mounted in the van's front, rear, and two sides gave her a clear picture of their surroundings. She removed the hook from the headset's earpiece and worked its tube into one of her elongated ears. "Park across from ... the Gwozdek residence and ... report any ... movement," she said and wiggled her nose to free her whiskers from the boom mic. "Oh, and drink that stuff I gave you. It will help keep you alert and awake."

They were wasting their time, and she knew it. She dared not break bad news to Mawro, though, before tying up loose ends. Opoworo may be lost to them, but Mawro would demand to know just how many of the professor's extended family had accompanied him.

A few minutes later, Jin-ho parked the van down the block from the house they staked out earlier that day. Hana zoomed her cameras in on the house's front and side windows. The darkened lights and drawn shades came as no surprise; they had seen no signs of life before. None were apparent now, though that hardly meant none existed. She tapped at her keyboard to run the gamut of electromagnetic spectrum regions detectable by their equipment. "Hah!" she cried, spying two Wi-Fi sources near each other in a room on the upper story. Two people, or at least their mobile devices, were inside.

A couple of keystrokes brought up a screen with a pair of crosshairs. With them, she focused the van's laser microphones on one of the room's windows. Hana turned up the gain on her audio feed until she heard the sound of someone snoring. She buzzed up Jin-ho and tugged her mic close to her muzzle. "Subjects present at the premises but appear stationary," she said before she pulled off her spats and scratched the soles of her feet. "Alert me should others arrive. I'm going to rest my eyelids now."

She leaned back in her chair and rested both heels atop the edge of the console. Her eyes fluttered open and closed while she stared up at the compartment's ceiling. After what felt like an hour, she sat up and glanced over at the clock display. She sighed. Not even fifteen minutes had gone by. Who was she kidding? Sleep would hardly be possible even without the adrenalin, and she found the ambient quietness unsettling. Nothing prevented the priest's monologue from hijacking her thoughts.

Tell the whelp that sent you—Blaznikov's foolish dream we leave our Forest died with him! Here, our race was born. Here soon, our race will die.

Mawro would not be pleased. Confessing her failure was scary enough. The thought of relaying the doomsayer's message terrified her. To him and Blaznikov both, the Plan embodied life itself. And now, their own kind bore grim testimony against them—all their labors, all their sacrifices, had been for naught.

"Lieutenant!"

Hana rubbed at her eyes and glanced down at Jin-ho's name flashing across the bottom of her screen. "Y-yes? What is it?"

"Something's not right here. Look for yourself."

She zoomed her camera display in on the living room window as their subjects made their way through the back door. "Where the hell did *they* come from?"

"I don't know! The ones inside never moved, and the others just appeared out of nowhere. Sounds like the CIA man and that guy in the wheelchair left before we got back."

Hana poked at her console to listen in on the laser mic feed. She winced when the back door slammed and trimmed back the channel gain. "Did you copy their intended destination?"

"None of them said where they were headed yet."

Some kind of a heat signature came up on her infrared camera display, but the house obscured her view of its source. "Appears they've started their vehicle, so be ready to follow them. Discreetly."

Jin-ho grumbled his assent while Hana cranked up the gain on the microphone feeds. The sound of a vehicle traversing the potholes in the alley behind the Gwozdek house confirmed her hunch. A moment later, a minivan emerged from around the corner and lit up the darkened street with its headlights. "Here they come!" she said after the minivan's driver gunned the engine. "Are the markers ready?"

"Of course." Jin-ho ducked out of view and popped back up, holding what resembled the control head of a toy R/C car.

"What are you doing?" she said as the Gwozdek's minivan rumbled past. "Deploy the damn markers!"

"I am! I am! Check out your left side viewer."

Hana brought up the van's tactical schematic on her display and spotted a small compartment door underneath flop down to the pavement. Glimpsing the van's side mirror in the external camera feed, she watched a scale dune buggy zoom down its ramp and tear off down the street after the minivan. "Let me put you in the driver's seat!" Jin-ho said before another window popped up on her screen. Hana leaned in close and scrunched up her nose. The thing had a *dash cam*?

The racer caught the other van up quickly and matched its speed. "Steady now," he said as the van's undercarriage came into view. The rear stabilizer fin rose and cleared the fuel tank an instant before the little car spun out. "Gotcha!" he cried after the fin snapped off.

Hana slumped back into her seat with her mouth open. Through the buggy's camera lens, she watched the minivan disappear around the corner. She snarled and slammed her hands down on her console. "So help me, Jin-ho—you lose them and I'll see to it Mawro sends your whole family to the gulag! Our entire operation could be compromised if—"

"Breathe, Lieutenant. I know exactly where they are." Her screen blanked out for an instant before a street map of Białowieża appeared. "We're the blue dot, and they're the red one." A tinny *clink* indicated the R/C car had returned to its compartment home. "Check this out."

Jin-ho made a U-turn and sped off while Hana called up the feed from the forward camera. She glanced up at the video image as the two dots on her other screen converged. The traffic light turned green, and the Gwozdek's minivan pulled away. "The stabilizer contains a tracking device which I deployed before their van snapped the fin off. Even an experienced agent like Katczynski won't think to check for a bug on *top* of the fuel tank. Nifty, huh?"

Hana grinned with begrudging admiration. "Not bad. Not bad at all."

"So let me sleep next time, will ya?"

She felt her face flush beneath her fur. "Oh, yes. Thank you, Jin-ho, I—"

"I'll go so you can call your boss."

With that, her audio feed went silent. Hana sighed and launched her phone dialer application. From the INMARSAT directory she clicked on the one entry highlighted in its registry: *Pe Gae Bong.*

She glanced down at her chronometer before the ship's first mate answered. "Can I speak to my Papa?" she said in a small voice and cut the gain to her earpiece. After a short pause came a long burst of static. "Go ahead, Lieutenant," she heard him shout. "Secure connection established."

"Aye, Commander Suk. Patch me through to Captain Mawro, please."

"Straightaway."

Hana chewed at her hair and waited. "You're late."

"I'm sorry. We were delayed locating the Opoworo party but are now tailing them."

"Is the professor still with them?"

"Uhm . . . no, Captain. I have it on, er . . . good authority Teacher Most Honorable escaped into Belarus already." Hana turned her gain down, expecting him to fly into a rage.

"I expected as much," he said with a *hmph*. "Opoworo had a head start and Luczasik nipping at his heels. But I'm not worried."

Hana's jaw fell open. "Why not?" she asked at length.

"Remember? All we need to do is find the container."

"I-I don't understand." Hana rested her chin on her palm and scratched at the side of her face with one claw. "How do we find a single one in such a busy place? There are thousands like it stacked to the sky!"

"We won't have to. You keep tailing the family, and they'll take us right to it. Aside from the professor, are the rest of them together?"

"Agent Katczynski and that hacker fellow left before Jin-ho and I returned from the Forest."

"No matter," Mawro said after a long pause, enough for Hana to wonder whether their connection had dropped. "They're probably just running interference to throw the Poles off Opoworo's trail. I'm confident he will make his way to a port in one of the Baltic States and catch a freighter back to Gdansk."

"How can you be so sure?"

"I know how Opoworo *thinks*, my dear, and I'm sure I've got Katczynski figured out too. Once their ship drops lines, CIA will order the container put aboard. Then the good doctor and the others can continue their work without distractions or interruptions. With his family there, they can celebrate a long holiday together while heading west across the Atlantic."

"Sounds . . . heartwarming."

"Yes, but we're not going to let that happen. Now listen carefully. Here's what I need you to do."

Hana bit her lip and focused on Mawro's instructions, putting the priest's stark prophecy far from her mind.

Tommy turned off the water at the sound of a knock on the door of their hotel suite. He threw back the shower curtain and grabbed a towel while Dory answered. His grandfather accepted the package from the front desk clerk and fumbled about in his pocket. A moment later, Tommy heard the woman squeal with delight and the door close behind her.

Once toweled off, Tommy pulled on a clean tank top and a fresh pair of boxers before hefting himself back into his wheelchair. The corners of his mouth turned up as he wheeled himself out of the bathroom. "Tipped her pretty well?"

Dory stood at the foot of his bed buttoning his shirt in the mirror. "I figure she deserved a little extra for going above and beyond on our behalf," he said before pulling on his belt. "I'd asked her to bring this to us as soon as it arrived."

He rolled over to the window and peeked through the drapes. "Gets dark early this time of year around here."

The elder man sat down on the bed and laced up his shoes. "Yep. Like back home."

"Don't suppose the sunlight kept you from sleeping."

"You would think, but I was tossing and turning for quite a while after you dropped out. Guess I napped for too long after Top offered to drive."

"Said he slept from wheels up out of Dulles until final approach into de Gaulle, then again to Chopin. Wired enough to bitch me out nearly the whole way here. Surprised he didn't wake you."

Dory knelt down and put a hand on Tommy's shoulder. "Well, I didn't want to say around him how proud of you I am. That was a ballsy move on your part. Your father would certainly agree."

Tommy beamed. "Thanks, G-man. Said keep a close eye on Latharo and Reintz, right?"

"Don't let it go to your head, son. Hacking the airline's reservation system to force them onto the same flight as the rest of you could well have exposed us."

He shrugged. "If Milda hadn't come, sure Pawly would have been happy to tail the Coastie for us."

Dory snorted. "You think she could have kept her head in the game?"

"For about as long as she could keep her hands off him," Tommy said and made a face. "Suppose if she couldn't, at least he'd be out of our hair a while."

"Setting my, uhm . . . *personal* objections aside for a moment, it's still a bad plan. Latharo would lack jurisdictional authority to board ship and expedite the handoff of our 'hot potato' from ABW to CIA. The heat will be off Niko and me once they do."

"That's why I started to freak when I couldn't raise either of you. If we had missed that plane, I wasn't sure how we'd keep dibs on them. I was certain they would lead us to—"

"Your sentiment is touching, son, but we old farts can fend for ourselves. We've had to learn the hard way. And trust me, school is still in session." Dory took a small knife from his pocket and slit open the tape and brown paper covering the long and narrow package. Two metal license plates slid out as he shook it over the bed, each white with black letters.

Tommy cocked an eyebrow and pulled on his socks. "What are those?"

"Jakub's original tags. I'm headed to the storage unit I rented up the street from the train station parking lot. I'll pull the car inside and swap these out so the others can go back to the Embassy. Our ABW 'friends' won't know what to make of his abandoned car turning up on the other side of the country from Szczecin."

"How are you going to get back here?"

"Catch a taxi, I guess," Dory said with a shrug. "There should be plenty around. Oh, and rouse Top after I leave so he can get us checked out."

"Well, I'm up, so I can just go and—"

"No, no, son. He booked the rooms. The front desk will need his credit card before Ryerson's man comes to take us to the ship."

Tommy tapped at his cheekbone with one finger. "I suppose he's not on

ABW's shit list like we are, huh?"

"Exactly. An electronic transaction from Gdansk with his signature shouldn't arouse any suspicions. We'll be halfway across the Atlantic by the time anyone thinks to check hotel surveillance cameras."

Dory wrapped the plates back up in the brown paper and slid them between the straps of his duffel. "You stay here and keep working," he said and grabbed his coat. "I want you hacked into those port video feeds by the time I return."

CHAPTER TWENTY

THE STIFF OCEAN BREEZE RUSHED in when Lenny pushed open the compartment door, nearly blowing off his cap. He pulled its bill down low over his eyes to shield them from the harsh glare of the tall luminares lining the pier alongsides.

For a moment, he leaned up against the handrail and took in the organized chaos playing out below him. Longshoremen rushed back and forth over the deck of the *Western Archer* hauling lines, fastening cables and securing cribbing. Between them darted Agency operatives, interpreters, customs inspectors—even a few of the *Straż Graniczna* troopers he briefed with the day before. ABW agents had met him and Latharo at Chopin and had been driving them hard ever since.

He shivered. The wind had started to pick up before they went below to conduct a routine inspection of the ship's hold and engine room. He zipped up his jacket all the way to the top and checked his watch. 18:47.

Over their lunch, the SG men tried to explain regional variances of Christmas traditions here. Once the little children spotted the first star in the evening sky, the grownups would set them down for their annual *Wigilia* feast. These men's families were now gathering around dinner tables all across Poland, with more empty chairs than the one dictated by custom to welcome yon wayward traveller. No wonder why everyone was racing around to get the hell out of here.

How many kids were due candy and presents tonight from *Gwiazdor*? How many the ominous birch switch? "Ves-oh-wesh Shaunt," he recalled Pawly saying as they exchanged gifts last Christmas Eve across a mess tent picnic table. Perhaps one day, another right jolly old elf would visit the two of them together. As a family.

A hand clasped Lenny on the shoulder, giving him a start. "*Basta ya, tonto.* You've been getting mopey on me ever since what's-her-name stood you up at the airport."

He balled his fists and faced his partner. "You think she would put her brother up to text about some fake family emergency just to ditch me? Man, you are some piece of work."

Latharo snorted. "And *you* are in denial."

"Radio silence ends as soon as this ship clears the breakwater. I'll send Tomcat a reply to have her call me. You'll see. Things will be—"

"Well, Lieutenant, your white glove is surely soiled by now. I trust my vessel otherwise passes inspection?"

Lenny whirled around and met the icy stare of the ship's master. "Oh, um ... yes, Captain Ryerson." He dashed off a signature in his pinch book and tore off the duplicate copy. "I believe everything is ship shape."

"Good," the bearded man said while he skimmed the form. He tucked it into the pocket of his long coat and glanced over to Latharo. "Are the cribs and lashings below deck sufficient to prevent damage to your container's precious contents?"

"Yes, but I still think we should—"

Ryerson turned and walked away. "Forgive me, gentlemen, that I needs must curtail pleasantries," he said without turning around. "My crew and I are on a tight schedule. Please make your way off my ship with due haste."

The two of them headed to the rear of the quarter deck and proceeded down the gangway. "¡Puta *madre!* What did you do to piss him off?"

"Me? You're the one acting like a charm school dropout! I did tell you masters don't take kindly being told how to conduct ship's business, didn't I?"

Lenny and his partner stopped before a dark-skinned man standing in their path, hands buried in the pockets of his leather bomber jacket with a brown *ushanka* on his head. "Your reputation precedes you, Special Agent Latharo."

His partner's eyes narrowed. "Field Agent Biggs, I presume?"

"We meet at last." The man grinned at them and offered his hand. "Please, call me Top."

Latharo ignored him.

The CIA man made a face and shoved his hands back into his pockets. "We, ah ... appreciate all you and Lieutenant Reintz have done to ensure the proper safety and security protocols were followed. Let us take it from here."

"I don't think you realize just what you've gotten yourself into, Agent Biggs," Latharo said with a wave of his hand toward the ship. "To the Agency, I'm *persona non grata*, I understand. But I can't close our investigation without knowing what you intend to do with the—"

"That's classified, and you know it," Biggs said and crossed his arms. "Assessing potential WMD and CBR capabilities of equipment like this falls under our agency's jurisdiction, not yours."

Latharo snarled and pulled at his face. "If you read your damn brief, you'd know this thing was surreptitiously exported without prior DHS authorization. This is a counter-proliferation investigation!"

"No, this *was* a counter-proliferation investigation. So said Langley and Nebraska Avenue two hours ago now the equipment is back in American hands," Biggs said and snapped his fingers. "Ours."

Several heavily armed agents stepped out from between the rows of containers on either side of them. Latharo sidestepped the CIA personnel and stomped off toward shore. "We'll leave these jackals to mark their territory, Lieutenant. It'll get messy once they start pissing all over each other."

Bored, bored, bored.

Bored.

Stuie knew it would be so until she and her family all arrived back in the States. She counted some of her favorite memories from among the Christmastime visits they had made to Poland to visit Grandpa Niko. He and Grandpa Dory would tell tall tales from their sailing days trying to outdo one another. When Mom said they were headed to Gdansk, Stuie envisioned all the cool stuff she would see with her grandpas walking the piers. Tiny tugboats pushing huge ships around. Hulking machines hustling brightly colored boxes around everywhere. Enormous cranes picking up tractors and trucks and trains from ships' holds like they were toys.

Her hopes evaporated not long after Captain Ryerson ushered them aboard the *Western Archer*. He said they would need to remain in their cabins until American inspectors finished their work. To help pass the time, he offered an armful of books from his personal library. But they were all about spies and war and stuff, hardly anything she found interesting.

The adults left quickly once the inspection was complete. Dad said all of them had much to do before some super secret cargo showed up. Grandpa D came by later to say she would need to stay put until the ship reached open ocean. Only then would the men assigned to guard their rooms allow Stuie to go off exploring.

Then came word Tommy would have the ship's wireless and satellite internet connections down until further notice. No Skype, no Facebook, and no Twitter, so catching up with her friends back home was definitely out. Many of the apps for her tablet were useless, too, since her device didn't work with the cell towers here.

Didn't help she burned through most of her battery playing Dots and

Swing Copters on the drive up from Białowieża. And, come to find out, her stupid charger's plug wouldn't fit the outlet in the cabin wall. Mom went below after inspection with her backpack, taking along her power converter inside. So she played World of Goo until her device shut down in the middle of Chapter Three, right as the Corporation launched Product Z. Natch.

Stuie stepped over to the desk in the stateroom she and her parents would share during their voyage across the Atlantic and sat down. Her gaze wandered back and forth around the room while she shuffled a deck of cards featuring Archer Maritime Trading's company logo. Their cabin was quite nice, despite its porthole windows facing away from all the exciting stuff happening alongside the busy pier. Captain Ryerson said this cabin and its mate on the other side of the passageway hosted company officials and guests sailing aboard the small fleet's flagship.

Normally, she would have been fine with such an arrangement. Compared to many of her friends at St. Constance, she enjoyed the frequent solitude that came with being an only child. She liked playing euchre, though, at the impromptu family gatherings after dinner in their big house back in Chicago. Now, the adults all planned to crash in shifts in the *Archer*'s other stateroom once their stupid secret cargo was aboard. When would she get three other people together long enough for even a few hands?

Stuie hoped Mom's converter kit contained a plug to fit the funny-shaped outlets along the wall of their cabin. Over the long voyage, she might make it to Chapter Four yet. She sighed and placed a card face up in front of her. Then another. And another. What a way to spend Christmas vacation. How many across for a hand of solitaire?

Bored, bored, bored.

Bored.

She started as the ship's cat leapt up and sent the cards skittering. The orange tabby mewed and considered her with eager, bright eyes. With a sigh she set both elbows on the desk and cradled her chin in one hand. "Looks like everyone else is too busy for either of us, huh, Oscar?" she said and stroked the cat's face. He purred and slowly twirled about, coaxing her fingers to rub at his neck and back and tail.

A glimmer of light outside the porthole window caught her attention. Across the night sky streamed a glowing trail. She blinked and spied another. After the third one, she was on her feet. No way was she going to miss the meteor shower, too. Tommy said before they came aboard the Ursids activity would peak tonight. She came to enjoy the free light shows after he invited her sit through a couple with him, not that she was an astronomy geek or anything. The view through the tiny window, however, was nowhere adequate to take in the night sky's full splendor.

Stuie tapped a finger on her lips and paced about, racking her brain for a way to escape their cabin. At the sound of scratching, she turned to find the cat pawing at the brass dog to the right of the hatch. A smile came to her face while she stepped over and rubbed his ears. "Good idea, Oscar!" She shoved the desk chair over to the wall next to the hatch and stood on it while she worked the dog loose. A couple of quick glances back and forth between her middle and the open porthole convinced her she would surely fit. She jumped down and stuffed her wool cap into one sleeve of her overcoat. With her coat hung across the chair back, she climbed up and shoved her body through the opening headfirst.

A railing hung down from the awning above the exposed deck. Stuie reached for it and pulled herself the rest of the way through. Taking care not to look down at the frigid water, she leapt and stuck a perfect landing with hardly a sound. Auntie Alex would be proud!

She glanced back and forth and listened. No one was coming, and no one appeared to have seen her. Stuie thrust out her tongue and reached back through the hatch to grab her overcoat. She donned it and her hat quickly to ward off the night's chill. *Clover Ewing, eat your heart out!*

Oscar leapt through the window and landed beside her. "C'mon, boy. Let's check out those meteors!"

Stuie shuffled her way along to the edge of the superstructure but came up short of the best seat in the house. She knelt down in front of the cat and made kissing noises. He sprang up and dug in his claws where she patted at her shoulder. After jumping up, she wedged her feet under the awning's bottom rail and leaned out over the pier four stories below. The spectacle above her head took her breath away.

Dozens of meteors traced wide arcs across the sky, leaving brilliant trails behind them. Stuie hooked a stanchion in the crook of her arm as the stiff breeze played at her pigtails. "Brrr," she said and tugged her wool hat down low over her ears with her free hand. "Are you warm enough, boy?" He simply mewed and nuzzled her face.

From her right came a blinding flash an instant before the shock wave slammed into her like a freight train. Pain coursing through her head, she felt rather than heard Oscar screech in terror and leap away. By instinct, she reached out to grab him. And slipped.

She screamed as the concrete deck rushed up to meet her.

One foot propped up on the railing, Lenny scanned the harbor toward where the *Western Archer* sat at its berth two piers away. Port commerce carried on at a frenetic pace all around him and his partner. Seemingly everyone vied for an early quit, anxious to begin their holiday. Trucks blared their horns, longshoremen cursed at one another, cranes gracefully swung around their loads above like synchronized aerobats. Despite the MGS' importance, he hardly expected one of the busiest ports in Europe to come to a standstill during its passage.

The reflection out over the water of flashing red and blue lights behind him caught his eye. Lenny turned around and saw a police motorcade rolling up to the guard shack. Cruisers drew close to one side or the other while the gate rose, permitting a non-descript tractor trailer to motor slowly through.

Latharo pushed his way through the doors of the vending area behind the security station, a steaming cup in each hand. "Sloppy. Just sloppy," he said as he handed one to Lenny. "After incurring trouble and expense for an escort, why not run them the length of the dock?"

"Oh, thank you." He took a sip and motioned with his coffee toward the convoy. "Actually, that's not uncommon. Jurisdictional issues at European ports are just as contentious as ours. See?"

A group of men and women, armed and armored, converged around the rig. It set off at a brisk walking pace into the labyrinth of stacked containers. "ABW troops. Dariusz Luczasik's people," Latharo said as the barrier came down behind the cruisers bringing up the rear of the procession. "Hopefully, that FNG Biggs won't give them any trouble getting the container aboard."

Lenny pulled his smartphone from his jacket pocket and swooshed at the screen. "Well, there's one way we can make sure." His mapping application opened, affording him a bird's eye view of the port. A little green dot appeared in the center.

"What are you doing?"

He pointed at the display and winked. "That's our container. I anticipated the CIA guys would shag us off sooner or later. Figured this would spare me having to listen to you piss and moan afterward."

"Huh." Latharo's gaze followed the dot as the transport made its way along the pier. "You planted a bug?"

"No, that might be traceable. Remember yesterday when I accompanied the SG guys on their border search? They were asking about smart seals on shipping containers from the States, so I jacked in to the GPS transponder on our container to show them how 'continuous squawk' mode works. Oops, silly me." His face broke into a puckish grin. "Guess I neglected to turn it *off* before I left. Runs the battery down in a hurry, otherwise."

"Well, I'll feel a lot better when the damn thing is aboard and the ship clears the—"

The ear-splitting sound of a nearby explosion reverberated from stacks of containers all around them. Both men dropped their coffee cups and thrust their hands over their ears. Each gawked at the other, seeing the same unasked question plastered across his partner's face. *What the fuck was that?*

Latharo drew his sidearm. Lenny jammed his smartphone back into his pocket and did likewise. As the port's emergency sirens blared all around, the two men dashed off toward a column of smoke rising into the night sky.

CHAPTER TWENTY-ONE

Pawly vaulted the containers stacked five or six high the length of the pier. Top had assigned her to patrol the harbor for any sign of Mawro's people, especially Hana. The night had been quiet until Tommy dispatched her to cover the container following the blast, which had also knocked out his security camera feed. Until told otherwise, she would need to be her team's eyes and ears.

For that, she found herself grateful. At least she could focus on something other than her unsettled emotions. Longing. Desire. Anger. Her pining for Lenny was a distraction, which Tommy had not-so-subtly reminded her during their briefing. Their mission came first. It had to. Lives depended on it. Her mother's, her brother's. Her own.

Pawly held up her finger to her earpiece. "Tomcat, Polecat."

"Polecat, Tomcat. Go ahead," came Tommy's voice in reply.

"On scene. Am engaging."

"Stay frosty. Four combatants in your vicinity. Rest appear scattered. Might be checking out that explosion."

"Roger, I'll have an eye. Polecat out."

A horrific scene played out as she touched down near the idling tractor trailer. The driver and his lumper screamed and tore at their eyes and faces. Two armed men left to guard the vehicle shouted at each other until one drew his weapon and fired on his teammate. The other man responded in kind while she dove behind a stack of containers. She shook her head to clear it, willing away painful memories. No surprise the current situation bore stark resemblance to Chah Bahar. Mawro and Hana must be at work, following

Blaznikov's playbook verbatim.

Pawly chanced to peer around the corner after the shooting stopped. She spied both men lying in puddles of their own blood and bit her lip. That these men's children were spared the horror of watching their fathers die brought her no comfort.

She ducked down as the throaty roar of a diesel engine approached. A massive rubber-tired container handler lumbered past, its operator wearing some kind of gasmask. It straddled the rig, carrying a box of the same color but twice as long. The conex on the back of the trailer seemed to disappear like a Russian doll into the larger one as it descended. With a creak and a groan, its side panels folded up into its roof to allow the first to nest perfectly inside.

The operator hoisted his load clear of the tractor's cab and crept ahead. Once the back lined up above the now-empty trailer chassis, an identical replacement container lowered into place. A false end and two sides deployed from the container's roof, concealing the empty space. Its job apparently complete, the machine throttled up and sped off down the pier.

Pawly wiggled at the camera aperture built into the frame of her goggles. "Tomcat, did you see *that*?"

"A-firm, Polecat. New one on me, too!"

"Polecat, Big Top. Copy?" came Top's voice over their tac net.

"Big Top, Polecat, go ahead."

"Follow that container until we can—"

Pawly craned her neck to the left and dialed down the gain on her transceiver. Two men approached, their weapons drawn. With her body pressed flat up against a box, she pulled a small extension mirror from a pouch on her web belt. A flick of her wrist locked its handle into position at the end of its reach. She poked it out around the corner ahead of her and squinted down its length.

Lenny dashed out from behind one row of containers and sprinted toward another, followed by a middle-aged man with bronze skin and dark hair. She recognized Lenny's new partner now from their quick introduction planeside back in Warsaw. The two of them leapfrogged their way along to the tractor trailer, holstering their sidearms before a pair of men lying motionless on the concrete. He knelt and jabbed his fingers aside one man's neck while the Latharo guy did likewise. The morose glances they exchanged confirmed the worst.

She gasped and lowered the handle when Lenny rose and turned her way. Pawly counted ten and took another peek to find him staring at the display of his smartphone. He waved his partner over and pointed at something on the screen before the men trotted off toward where the handler had sped away moments before.

"Tomcat, Big Top . . . *mea culpa* offline. New combatants traversing target area, posture neutral. Positive ID as 'Lather and Rinse'. Shall I pursue?"

Silence. "Er . . . brain trust here affirms, Polecat. Carry on," Tommy said at length.

"Stay out of sight," Top added. "They may not remain posture neutral for long if they get a good look at you."

Pawly glared down at the gray fur covering the back of her hand and made a fist. "Roger that, Big Top, I'll be Oscar Mike. Polecat out."

Stuie lifted her head and spat out some sandy gunk that smelled bad and tasted worse. With a groan she rolled herself onto her back and trained her eyes on a light fixed to a pole high above. Some kind of red haze obscured almost its entire bright glow. She blinked and raised her hands to examine them. They were red too, along with everything else.

Her mind raced, trying to understand what happened to her. A memory from back home in Chicago came to mind—Mom yelling herself hoarse to not play up on the roof of their family's apartment building. A fall from such a height would kill her for sure. She and Oscar had been up nearly twice as high. Was . . . was she—?

The answer came in a hurry after she sat up. Stuie sucked in her breath and palmed at her throbbing temples. "It hurts? Good. You're still alive, then," Auntie Alex had remarked countless times during her training.

Might have had something to do with her seeing red, too. Through a convenient hole torn in the heavy fabric above her head, she poked her head up and looked around. She stared intently at the gray canvas tarp covering the open top shipping container that had broken her fall. Her field of vision slowly returned to normal, starting with a growing spot at its center.

Stuie scrambled over to the edge and leapt down to the pier below. She tucked and rolled into a defensive stance with her hands at the ready. If only her aunt and *Halmeonim* could see her now! Then again, maybe not. With a glance up at the moon above, she realized her curfew was long past.

The stern of the *Western Archer* lay about fifty feet away, partially hidden by several stacks of containers. Stuie gasped when she spied the logo of one featuring a stylized tiger.

"Oscar!"

She glanced all about, frantic to find the orange tabby. There was no sign of him on the ground anywhere, and she didn't remember seeing him in the container either. She would be in enough trouble if she were caught sneaking out without having to explain why he was missing too. Should anyone find out about her fall, though . . .

Into the maze of brightly colored boxes all around Stuie set off, resolved not to return to the ship until she found the cat.

¶

Hana's tail swooshed side to side as she glared down at the handler poking its way along the quay far below. A tailwind was about the only thing she could hope for to make the damn thing move any faster.

The camouflaged container had left the big machine precariously unbalanced. Papa insisted its operator maintain a cautionary speed on the straight-aways and slow to a brisk walk around corners. Any damage to the MGS device inside might render worthless all their careful planning and precise execution. Though it pained her to sit and wait, Hana understood their complicated logistics were but a minor annoyance.

Bittersweet emotions swirled through her mind while she tugged at a tuft of orange fur on her cheek. Soon with Papa's help, she would bid farewell to this cursed form. Great Leader be praised.

She turned back toward the stopped tractor trailer. Most of the trooper escort had taken the bait after she detonated the decoy charge on the port's fiber hub bungalow. Though Hana would have preferred to neutralize the remainder herself, Mawro had insisted she deploy gas canisters filled with Windfall to save time. Her country had secretly exported the mass produced hallucinogen to the First World for years as a recreational drug. But in concentrated form, Windfall produced powerful and horrific visions to everyone exposed to it. She had seen firsthand family members under its influence tear off each other's skin with their bare hands. Like the mountain sheepherders near *Samjiyŏn-kun* as they led her mother to the Chinese border carrying Hana in her arms.

Kindred were immune to Windfall's effects, much to the surprise of the *Bowibu* who had ambushed them. They would all come to understand manifestations of their Affliction, though, were far, far worse. Hana studied her palm and curled her fingers, watching her claws extend and retract from their tips. Past episodes of her Rage erased any memory of the day her mother died, but she would never permit herself believe she wasn't somehow responsible. Were these very claws the last thing her mother ever saw?

She buried her face in her hands and shook her head. With considerable effort she forced herself review the operational plan again—while port security forces languished in disarray, *Pe Gae Bong*'s crew would put the container aboard and cast off. Back in international waters Hana planned to lap the deck until she collapsed from exhaustion, hoping to forget. Once her human form returned, she would catch a flight back to Pyongyang from wherever a North Korean freighter could berth without arousing suspicion. Mawro would want to be alone with his work, as would she. Only among the desolate mountains of western Ryanggang again on the anniversary of her mother's death would she dare will herself to remember.

The ship's deck crew prepped their crane lines and spreader bar as they made ready for the handler's arrival. She sat down on top of the stack of containers and let her legs dangle over the side, four stories above the quay below. Chin in one hand, she settled in to wait. Nothing more for her to do now until Mawro came over the air to recall her.

Then she caught sight of the two armed men about fifty meters behind the big machine. They advanced from one container row to the next, keeping a discreet distance between them. One wore some kind of dark blue uniform and the other plainclothes. No surprise the mooks posing as stevedores failed to detect their presence. Hana was on her feet in an instant, smiling as she tugged at her bandolier.

This operation might well prove interesting yet!

Manuel had worked with numerous partners through the years, most of them wannabes, nincompoops, and whiners. A few he had grown to respect, and one became a close friend. Experience had taught him to hold people at arm's length until they proved themselves capable and trustworthy. This Reintz fellow was doing exactly that, but he would rather boil in oil before letting on he felt that way. Doing so would only give the young punk a swelled head.

When his new partner wasn't moping about like a lovesick twit, he more than demonstrated his worth as an investigator and operative. The MGS would have been swiped out from under their noses had Reintz lacked intuition or initiative enough to keep tabs on it. Now he led their chase, tailing the container handler like a pro.

Manuel broke from his hiding place and leapfrogged to the next stack of containers. With a smile, he made a mental note to keep his eye on this one. He would be interesting to watch, indeed.

When the machine creaked to a stop near the edge of the pier, he realized the thieves must be on their way to a ship. They wouldn't have lugged the conex this far if they intended to hide it in plain sight and haul it away later. A truck pulled up while the operator lowered his load to the pavement. Several men in blue coveralls jumped out and applied large, rectangular decals over the container's reporting marks with different letters and numbers on them. Their thoroughness was impressive—the damn things were even weathered so they wouldn't stand out. The man in the machine's cab removed what appeared to be a gasmask and climbed down. Once on the ground, he ambled over to bum a cigarette from the truck's driver.

Manuel placed his hand on Reintz's shoulder and nodded toward the machine. "We need to make our move. Their friends must be waiting for them aboard ship down that way," he whispered. A moment later, the ground crew finished their work and turned back toward their vehicle. The man standing next to the driver's window took one last puff from his cigarette and crushed it under his boot heel.

His partner holstered his sidearm and leaned forward like a sprinter waiting for the starting gun. "I've got an idea," he said before he dashed off.

"¡Espera! What're you—" Manuel rolled his eyes and ran after him. They huddled together behind a concrete barrier opposite the machine while its operator climbed back up to the cab.

"Follow me!" Reintz said before he hopped atop the chest-high wall and sprang. After grabbing the container's top rail, he pulled himself up and over. "Cover me while I subdue the guy driving," he said as he reached down toward Manuel with his hand. "I'll use his radio to call for—"

"LOOK OUT, MR. LENNY!"

He turned toward the girl's scream in time to catch a glint of light out of the corner of his eye. A spear blade struck the top of the container and bounced off while Reintz half-leapt, half-fell to the pavement. A woman's voice shouted at them in an unfamiliar language while his partner rolled to safety behind the wall. The ground crew's truck roared up toward the wall and screeched to a halt. Four men piled out drawing handguns from their beltlines and ankles. He and his partner were about to be outnumbered and outgunned.

"Change in plan!" Reintz yelled after he popped up and yanked something from his tactical vest. "I'll handle these guys. You take out the knife thrower!"

Manuel scanned the darkness, trying to pinpoint the woman's location. He glanced back over his shoulder after his partner collapsed with a yelp. Reintz lay face down mere yards away, the knee of a hostile operative in his back. His gaze followed the sound of a tinny rattle until he saw a flashbang rolling across the pier in a lazy semicircle.

He scooped up the grenade, pulled the pin, and threw it in one smooth motion. Mouth wide open, he dropped to his stomach and shut his eyes tight while squashing his palms flat up against his ears. Before the device's earsplitting report, the brilliant light behind his eyelids made him see red—the same color of jumpsuit these fools would be wearing by daybreak on their way to Czarne.

The image of his rib cage being flattened by a truck tire flashed through his mind an instant before pain consumed him. After what seemed like hours, Manuel found himself rolling across the concrete to a stop on his back underneath a luminary. With a grunt he blinked up into the bright light and turned toward the sound of approaching footsteps.

Waves of fear and revulsion washed over him at the sight of a woman dressed in a dark-colored, form-fitting uniform. Orange and white fur covered her face and hands and bare feet. She stopped and glared down at him, her narrow eyes drawn into slits while her long striped tail swooshed back and forth. "Stop us you not will," she said in broken English.

This was one of the creatures responsible for Sally's death. Artist renditions of survivor's accounts from Chah Bahar had been horrifically accurate. The woman's lips drew back the length of her muzzle, revealing long white fangs as she reached behind and grasped the staff slung over her shoulder. With a loud *click*, she twirled it around to her front and brandished a wicked-looking blade. "But here now we kill—AAAH!"

His attacker dropped her spear and flailed her arms behind her, as if trying to scratch at something on her back. Light glinted off the pair of shiny metal strands pulling the woman's ears back along the sides of her head, their ends looped between a young girl's fingers.

"LEAVE MR. MANNY ALONE!"

The courageous *chica* planted her knees between the operative's shoulder blades and held on tight. Long, black pigtails whipped back and forth across the girl's face while the woman caterwauled and pranced about like a rodeo bull. He recognized her instantly.

Manuel sprang to his feet and snatched his hands-free device from his jacket pocket. Finger already on the button, he jammed it into his ear.

"Call Opoworo!"

"Tomcat, Polecat. Roger that, am responding," came Pawly's voice over the speaker within the command center. Tommy's ears twitched while his fingers flew across his keyboard, pausing only to push his glasses back atop the bridge of his nose.

Keeping on top of her rapid movements during a sortie was tricky business. Tommy had come to trust his Talent the summer after their Affliction first manifested. He guided Pawly through wind and waves and darkness and storms so their great uncle Robercik could save his struggling Bob Kat Marine. Much like what he had learned crouched down before a hockey net—watch the action, run the probabilities, execute the best defense.

"Have an eye, Polecat." Tommy pulled his boom mic closer to his muzzle, careful to avoid his whiskers. "Haven't pinpointed the origin of the detonation yet."

"Will do, Tomcat. Polecat out."

"Stay frosty," Top said from behind him. "We don't know if our antags are having a bad day or executing a clever play to set us up."

Several huge video monitors loomed above and around the console in front of Tommy's wheelchair. He glanced back and forth between the monitors to his left and right. One displayed a real-time feed from Pawly's goggles, the other the port's network status map and his command prompt.

"Well, *we're* having a bad day until those video feeds come back," Dory said. "We'd be flying completely blind if Pawly weren't out there!"

The black tufts at the ends of Tommy's ears twitched while he concentrated. "I know, I know, almost got it . . . there."

Black-and-white images from around the port replaced the static on his remaining screens. Top glanced up at them and scrunched his nose. "Er . . . nothing's moving."

"Sure it is. See?" Tommy pointed at a screen as it finished repainting to depict an ambulance turning off the pier toward the security station.

"I thought the fiber was down hard after the blast destroyed the hub."

"It is. Most ports first installed cameras years ago with coax for video feeds and twisted pair for command and control. Gdansk went with multi-mode instead of single mode fiber when they upgraded. It's cheaper."

Top rubbed at his face. "So they left C&C on copper?"

"Right. Newer cameras can transmit video over both for testing and troubleshooting. Twisted pair lacks the bandwidth to stream even three frames per second for more than a couple devices, though."

Dory chuckled. "Though plenty for your Eyes of the Lynx to follow, right?"

"A-firm, G-man. Turned down the frame rate as low as I could and configured the server to continuously poll the cameras round robin. Refreshing nineteen images once every ten to twelve seconds is enough for me."

His grandfather stepped over and clasped him on the shoulder. "That's our boy."

The control center door flew open and banged against the wall as Nat and Niko rushed in. "What is happening?" Sunny asked. Tommy glanced behind him toward his grandmother, rubbing at her eyes in the chair she had fallen asleep in.

The two men panted, their faces deathly pale. "I just got a call from Agent Latharo," Nat said at last.

Dory's eyes went wide. "You didn't answer it, did you? *Toro* thinks we're in Białowieża on holiday. Picking up a call can betray our location!"

"He thought it was about the MGS and let it go to voice mail," Niko said for him. "But then we listened to Latharo's message saying Stuie has—"

"She's gone!"

Annie bolted through the open door, grabbing at her hair with both hands. "We looked everywhere in our compartments. Stuie is gone!"

Top furrowed his brow. "My people would never allow her leave unless you or I—"

"They said they didn't see anything," Alex said, entering the room right behind Annie. "The porthole window was open, but I can't explain how she got over to—"

An electronic warbling from the speakers aside of Tommy's main console cut her off. Heat rose from underneath the fur on his face toward his hairline—he had forgotten to turn off his own cell phone before the operation commenced as protocol dictated. Automatic connection via Bluetooth came in handy, but only during non-classified operations.

Top's eyes narrowed, as if to say *nice going, dumbass!*

"Who the fuck is calling, Tomasz?" Dory barked in Polish. Tommy let out a nervous laugh. "Sorry, I—hey, hold on," he said in English as a familiar number flashed across his screen. "Now Agent Latharo is calling *me*."

"Take it! Take it!" Nat said. "Stuie's with *him*."

Dory froze. "She's *WHERE*?"

Annie pushed her way past everyone to Tommy's side. "Pick it up! Please!"

His grandfather aged ten years before his eyes. "Put it on speaker, son."

"R-right."

"I know you're all around here somewhere, *hijo*. Where are you, Door Kat?" boomed Manuel's voice through the console speakers.

Dory snarled and activated his headset. "Right here, *Toro*. Now, where's Stuie?"

"End of the pier by the container handler. I'll need help. Fast." Then the line went dead.

"Tommy!"

"On it, G-man!" He located the corresponding feed and put it up on the control center's big screen.

"There she is!" Top said. Stuie's long black pigtails trailed behind, frozen in time. She bore strong resemblance to a character from some magical girl *anime*. "Can you zoom in any more?"

"Negative," Tommy said and twirled at his track ball. "That's all the magnification I can get. I'll switch to another camera."

"No! Wait!" Everyone's gaze followed Alex's finger toward the tiger-striped face of Stuie's accoster.

"Oh shit," Dory said in a deadpan voice. Annie and Nat stared mute at the image until a stifled cry escaped her throat. The tigress shook Stuie loose by the next camera update. The image captured her in mid-air, arms flailing about in front of her. Only Tommy saw what happened next.

He cut the feed.

"No! NO!" Annie screamed at the darkened display above. "Don't hurt her! Don't take her!" She turned and grabbed at her husband's shoulders. "Dear God, do something . . . she's our *daughter*!"

Nat reached up and pulled his jacket free from his wife's clenched fists. Then he took her hands in his and yanked them downward to their waists. That seemed to jar Annie from her hysteria. She blinked at him and hung her head. "Sorry, everyone," she said in a small voice.

Niko stepped up from behind and put a hand on his son's shoulder. "Go back to your cabin and *stay there*. Dory will send for you once we know Stuie is safe."

Nat's lower lip quivered. "All . . . all right." With an arm across Annie's back, he led her through the bulkhead door and disappeared into the passageway.

CHAPTER TWENTY-TWO

STUIE SHOOK HER HEAD AND got to her feet. The red haze had crept again into view from the edge of her vision. She managed to duck behind a pallet stacked high with sacks of rice when something swished over her head. The woman in the dark uniform pranced past, slashing at the air with her spear. Stuie gulped at the sight of the claws fixed to the ends of her fingers and toes. The points of her fangs jutted out from beneath her lips, drawn downward into an angry scowl.

As the girl crouched back to break into a run, a pair of arms wrapped around her mouth and middle. Every square inch of her skin tingled as a hand pulled her head to one side. Relief washed over her like a wave when she recognized her accoster. "Stay next to me," Agent Latharo whispered and hugged her to him. "Help should be here soon."

Tears left trails of wet warmth behind on her cheeks, all the while reminding herself Clover Ewing wouldn't *dare* cry. She gritted her teeth, and they came that much faster. With one finger, he lifted her chin to direct her gaze toward his. He shook his head and thumped his chest with his fist.

No crying. Be brave.

Latharo knelt down and peered around the corner of the pallet to where the *Archer* sat at her moorings. She stifled the urge to scream when he swept her feet out from under her and sprinted up the pier, clutching her body tightly to his.

Stuie peeked out from underneath his arm and gasped. The crazy tiger woman sniffed at the air and turned to follow them. She buried her face into his shoulder and shivered. As long as she could remember, she had known

159

about the Affliction's legacy Auntie Alex shared with her two older cousins. After a warm welcome from Jakub and Milda, Stuie had concluded she and her family would also be by Kindred everywhere. Not wanting to believe otherwise, she had chalked up the harrowing tale Grandpa Niko told on the ride up from Białowieża as another of his tall tales. Now, she knew how wrong she had been. Scary wrong.

The woman brandished her spear and launched herself upward out of sight. Her wicked laugh echoed from the darkness above them while Latharo ducked and weaved. Stuie flew from his arms after he lost his balance and landed spread eagle upon the concrete.

She winced and sucked in her breath as she rolled herself onto to her elbows. A strong odor filled her nostrils, like someone mixing cinnamon with drain cleaner. Stuie glanced back over her shoulder to see some kind of red cloud emanating from a canister on the ground in front of Latharo. He coughed and hacked, trying to stand before his eyes rolled up into his head and he collapsed.

A sound like stones skittering down the street after being run over by a car drew Stuie's attention forward. She gasped at the sight of the crazy tiger woman, tapping her foot before her. With a derisive snort, their attacker stepped over top of her to where Latharo lay face down on the pavement. The woman kicked him in the side and shrank back into a defensive stance.

He didn't move. Stuie's teeth began to chatter while the woman glared down at her. "So, kitten, your protector fall do. But why not gas you pass out making?"

The red haze crowded out her normal sight. Stuie felt something lift her chin until she couldn't help but look into the narrow slits in the woman's wild eyes.

"No matter. *Kojaengyi* sage say, 'three keep secret when two dead!'"

With a growl their attacker withdrew the flat of her spear blade from beneath Stuie's chin. When she looked up again, she saw only empty space before her.

Where did she go?

Her answer came as an angry cry from above. The tiger woman plummeted toward them with both hands grasping her spear. Though having only foundation-level training in the Arts, Stuie recognized a killing strike when she saw one.

Her skin prickled painfully all over, like she had fallen face first into a dumpsterful of porcupines. Her head tossed back, guided by instinct. She felt a scream tear from her throat as her world went completely red.

All Stuie heard was a roar.

Lenny groaned and rubbed at one side of his head as he sat up. He remembered being struck from behind but nothing after he dropped the flashbang. The loud ringing in his ears suggested someone must have detonated the device. Moans coming from all around, he sprang to his feet. Four men lay about the pier nearby writhing in pain. Whether longshoremen or gang members, Lenny didn't much care; they had broken the law and threatened him harm either way. SG would deal with them appropriately when they arrived. Surely by now, Latharo had . . .

Oh, shit.

The container handler sat idling nearby, its cab empty. Where the hell did he go? Had his partner taken off after his attacker? Was he trying to rescue the girl? Maybe he had simply gone for help. Regardless, Lenny needed to find him fast. He would secure the scene here first, though, to prevent any rude surprises. His new SG friends would appreciate him bagging up the trash for them to haul away.

He hogtied the first man with several of the thick zipper ties dangling from a karabiner on his web belt. His pat-down revealed a pistol tucked into the top of one of the guy's boots. He ejected the clip and threw both it and the weapon into the harbor. Though he loathed destroying evidence, he was not about to let these guys get the drop on him again.

The next guy was out cold, thankfully. With a grunt, he heaved the big lug into position and secured him. His gun joined his partner's at the bottom in short order.

The third one rolled away while Lenny approached and grabbed the lashing rod eye hook he carried before the blast. He ducked to the side to avoid the clumsy strike with the makeshift weapon, but his assailant popped back up and came at him again. This time, Lenny was ready. He pulled his can of capsaicin spray free from its pouch and gave the man a face full. The guy howled in pain as Lenny barred his arm and took him to the concrete. He bound the man's wrists with the ties, holding him still with a knee jammed into the small of his back. "You really should be more careful—"

A loud *thwack* from behind made Lenny's breath catch in his throat. He glanced over his shoulder in time to see the remaining man's eyes roll up into his head. A wicked-looking knife fell to the deck with a tinny *clank* as he collapsed into a crumpled heap.

"So should you," came a raspy voice.

Lenny whirled around with his spray can held out in front of him. An operative he had never seen before stood there in dark combat fatigues, porting a small wooden staff in one hand while twirling its mate in the other.

His eyes gave his rescuer a glance up and down—clearly a female. What drew his curiosity more was the silver gray fur covering her skin, accented by black stripes along either side of her face. Coarse white hair trailed down the sides of her uniform top like a beard. Long slender ears with black tufts at their ends poked through holes cut into a black bandanna tied around her head. Bits of blonde and red hair stuck out from underneath. Her short muzzle contorted into a lopsided grin. "*Semper Paratus*, right? And mind where you point that thing. I'm on your side."

Lenny lowered his spray can. The woman had a point. If she were indeed an adversary, *he* would be laying on the concrete right now. Not the punk who had just tried to shank him.

The operative chuckled and held a furry fist up under his chin. "It's not polite to stare, you know," she said and pushed his jaw shut.

He couldn't help himself. She appeared so foreign, yet seemed somehow so familiar. "How . . . how can I be sure whose side you're on?"

The woman crossed her arms and focused her gaze far aside them over the black water. "I stood watch over you night after night in a tree outside your room at Bethesda, Lieutenant Lennart Reintz of the United States Coast Guard." She blew out her breath and turned to face him. "I wanted to see you safe. After what went down at Chah Bahar, I . . . I *needed* to see you safe."

Lenny's stomach started doing backflips. From the mere mention of the place where he had witnessed such horrific things? Or his increasingly distressful, increasingly *probable* awareness of the operative's true identity?

"P-Pawly?"

He choked back the urge to vomit. Her mouth drew back along her short muzzle into a shy smile. She didn't say a word. She didn't have to.

Lenny's stupor broke when she grasped his wrist with her hand or paw or whatever the hell it was called. Black claws emerged from the ends of her fingers while she carefully slid his sleeve up past his elbow. She curled their tips into her palm and bore down with their bony parts about halfway up his forearm.

His heartbeat thundered in his ears. A distant memory came unbidden, buried since after the bomb detonated that night. Blinded, bloodied, and scared shitless, the soothing sensation he recalled from that moment gave him hope he might just make it. Just like this one, right now. Had *she* been the one to tend him?

She smiled and released his arm. "That'll help calm your insides when you get the urge to hurl. It's an acupressure trick my grandmother taught me."

Lenny's stomach began to relax after the wave of nausea passed. "Thank you . . . Pawly," he whispered.

"You're welc—"

They both turned up the pier from where the savage roar had come. Her gaze fixed on him while she fumbled at the boom mic stuck into one of her slender ears. She drew in her breath as if spooked by the transmission coming over her tac net and bounded atop a container. "Come on!" she said and waved for him to follow. "Your partner needs our help!"

9

Pawly crouched down and peered over the container's edge. "Tomcat, Polecat. On location," she whispered.

"Roger that, Polecat. Observe and report."

She scanned the area carefully. Leave it to Tommy to work something even remotely useful from the camera feeds after the explosion took out the fiber hub. His work-around, though, was far from ideal. She had sprinted on ahead of Lenny, recognizing her brother still needed her to be their eyes and ears. Sound from the fracas below reverberated off the containers stacked high on either side. Even with her heightened senses, Pawly struggled to identify the fighters. A buzzing noise emanated from the darkened luminary above her head, punctuated by an occasional *pop*.

Hell of a time for the lights to go out.

"I think our Bengal bimbo is down there carrying on about something. Can't get a visual on our lost kitten, though. Will advise when sit-rep changes. Polecat out."

Pawly glanced backward over her shoulder to find Lenny nowhere in sight. He was skilled in surveillance and tracking, so he would catch up soon enough. Though she had become accustomed to operating solo, to extract Stuie safely, she would take all the help she could get.

The faint sound of pawpads thumping on metal drew her attention back to the pier below. She pulled her *tahn bong* from their sleeves stitched into the calves of her trousers and took up her combat stance. Hana was coming.

Her opponent bolted forth from the darkness with a backflip and landed on her stomach atop the container opposite the alleyway. The crazy bitch must have scrambled up here to mix it up, and Pawly wanted to size her up before engaging. To her surprise, Hana ignored her, focused instead on the alley below.

Over several past encounters, Hana's fighting style and technique had earned her Pawly's begrudging respect. Her breath now came in ragged gasps, the child-like glee she often fought with replaced by a crazed, almost feral demeanor. Pawly cocked her head and listened, trying to make out the words the woman mouthed over and over.

"Jigeum jug. Jigeum jug. Jigeum jug!"

Her brow knit. Something wasn't right. What could possibly spook her so? The wind changed direction while Hana recited *"kill it now!"* over and over. The stink of Werecat's Rage wafted up from below, strong and fresh. Into the moonlight stepped a small figure barely five feet tall. Pawly's heart nearly stopped. A Kindred *child* was down there, gripped by their peoples' Affliction.

Which Hana intended to kill.

The blowing wind jostled the luminary above, causing the loose electrical connection inside to repeatedly make and break. Light flickered into the dark alleyway below, affording Pawly a glimpse at the object of Hana's ire. A long, striped tail sprouting forth from the beltline of the creature's pants confirmed her suspicions. But the terror which gripped her when the thing met her gaze caught her completely unawares. Though she didn't want to believe what she was seeing, the girl's clothes and hair were undeniably familiar. Her overcoat was in tatters. Rounded ears poked up through long, black pigtails. Pawly recognized one and only one face beneath the orange and white mask of raw fury.

The creature roared. Hana pounced. Pawly screamed.

"STUIE!"

CHAPTER TWENTY-THREE

MAWRO SLAMMED HIS FIST down on his console. "Hana! Answer me!"
"CIA and ABW troopers are convening on the container," came
Min Soo's grating voice over the speakers. "SG patrol craft are en route. We
will need to move fast if we—"

"I know! I know!" His hacker need not even be in the same room for
Mawro to picture the man's smug sneer. Bad enough the operation was going
all to hell. Worse was neither of them had any clue as to why.

He leaned back in his chair and carded the fur beneath his chin with the
claws sprouting from his fingertips. The console to his right controlled the im-
aging systems on the helidrone hovering near Hana's last known position. He
tapped at the screen with his knuckle to call up the views he wanted, or tried
to. Taking care to not damage the equipment given his hulking form made its
operation awkward and clumsy. It took him several tries and cursing in three
languages to at last pull up the damned screens.

Infrared didn't tell him much he couldn't already tell from the regular
video feed. Turning on the helidrone's spotlights, of course, would give away
its position. Images in the dim light of the object of Hana's fixation weren't
much help either. A long tail, pointed ears and clawed digits, though, told
Mawro everything he needed to know.

Ailuranthrope.

It was a youngling, most probably female, and she was raging. With the
way she carried on, Mawro believed this was likely her first transformation.

He rapped his knuckles against his forehead. So many questions remained.
Who in the hell *was* she? Why was she here? What was her connection to

Hana? His operative's vitals had gone haywire after this other girl appeared, right before Hana ceased responding to his instructions altogether.

Now, here was Hana, running amok. In between her screaming sobs, Mawro heard her mutter again and again how *this* youngling must die. Why had the girl's transformation launched Hana into such a state? Forget about the mission—how was he to extract her safely? Should their enemies exploit their numerical advantage and corner Hana in her current condition, she would surely be shot.

The other girl's resilience and innate fighting ability were as remarkable as they were unexpected. Without them, she would have certainly been ripped to shreds by now. Maybe he would find a way to disable her to let Hana finish her? If it broke Hana out of her catatonic agitation long enough for them to escape, he would gladly write off a potential test subject. Though Pyongyang would not be pleased with him coming back empty handed, losing their breeding stock for their ailuranthropic combatant research program would . . .

Mawro growled and shook his head. This was nonsense. They would prevail. All he had to do was figure out how. Quickly.

With a twirl and click on his trackball, he ordered the helidrone fall in behind Hana a moment before a new combatant appeared. Long, slender ears and exposed fur were dead giveaways of another ailuran, and a lyncean specimen at that. Katczynski had thrown down right bower. "Min Soo! Can you get me a better viewing angle?"

"Of course."

Their drone zoomed up and over Hana's head and stopped with the interloper centered within the camera frame. The unknown fighter parried one blow after another from his operative's staff with a pair of small fighting sticks, one to a hand.

Mawro saw the youngling drop to all fours. He understood the toll a first transformation took on a child's system, and the stress had surely overwhelmed her. She slumped to the concrete beside the prone form of a man, though not anyone he recognized from their ground crew. Maybe this was one of the Americans who had intervened earlier. Well, good riddance.

Their mystery guest, appearing also to have expected the girl to pass out, leapt up to goad Hana into following him. Or rather, *her,* Mawro realized after spying the telltale features of her gender beneath one of the pier's luminaries. One of the on-board cameras managed a clear shot of her face while she cast an icy stare upward toward the drone.

Pawlina?

It stood to reason Katczynski would attempt to implement countermeasures for Hana's unique talents. But how could he justify sending his own granddaughter back in to battle after her disastrous first field command at Chah Bahar?

Then he remembered his Korean underworld contacts in San Francisco telling how their enforcers had been brutally murdered—the claw and bite marks they described made sense now. With nothing but petty crooks and wanna-be gangsters to work her technique on, no wonder Pawlina appeared so out of practice. As if to make his point, she dodged one of Hana's vicious two-handed slashing attacks an instant too late. That seemed to get her attention. With her uniform shirt torn corner to corner across her chest, Pawlina came after Hana with renewed fervor. Fangs gnashed and claws flew back and forth as they fought.

Hana bounded between two stacks of containers to build up speed for her next attack. Mawro cocked an eyebrow, noting Pawlina copy her movements in the opposite direction. Where in the hell would she have learned to do *that*?

Some kind of powder billowed forth from her hand after she changed course in mid-air, forming a cloud around her opponent. Pawing at her eyes, Hana slammed sidelong into a container and tumbled to the concrete below. Pawlina landed next to the child and scooped her up into her arms while his operative hunched over in a coughing jag.

Hana shook off the agent's effects and gave chase, bringing a satisfied grin to Mawro's face. Pawlina's burden slowed her retreat back to the *Archer,* allowing Hana to quickly catch up. A sudden strong gust of wind blew the drone following behind into the pole holding up the flickering luminary. Brilliant light flooded the area below, enabling him a view of the youngling in Pawlina's arms. Her head lolled while long black hair flopped back and forth over her face, revealing her orange and white fur beneath. She was *tigrine*?

Mawro slumped back into his chair. Images of the horrible night years ago he had almost lost Hana flashed through his mind, at the time hardly older than a child herself. Would her emotional wounds ever heal? Gall and venom lurked deep within Hana's psyche, ready to gush forth and poison her entire being when the demons from her tortured past at last caught her up.

Like they did just now.

"Min Soo!" he said, bolting up straight. "Stand ready to max out the Pearls' feedback gain on my signal!"

Lenny panted and leaned forward to rest his hands on his knees. He drew great gulps of air into his lungs while he struggled to accept the bizarre-looking creature dusting him was indeed Pawly. The last time he had been around . . . *them,* he lost control of his bladder. Like any sane person would. He remained under orders not to talk about the now-classified events from Chah Bahar with anyone lacking a need to know. Few things surprised him anymore given the Weird Shit that happened that day, though. Discovering the woman you love morphs into a fucking *cat* would definitely qualify!

Whatever the hell she was, she was fast. Once Pawly bounded atop the containers stacked four and five high the length of the pier, he quickly lost sight of her. Lenny sucked down one more breath before he sprinted over to a container handler parked nearby. On the concrete next to one of its enormous rubber tires, he sat down and pulled a small bottle of water from a pocket on his pantleg. He unscrewed the cap and tipped his head back up against the tire. As he drained the bottle, he glimpsed Pawly dart between the container stacks, pursued by another of her kind. The other fighter's physical features resembled those of a tiger, and her dark battle costume was styled differently.

After a scuffle and heated exchange in some unfamiliar language, Pawly dashed out from around a corner. The long pigtails of the girl she carried in her arms trailed behind while she sprinted toward him, affording Lenny a good look at the colored fur on the girl's face. Just how many of these . . . these . . . *cat people* were walking around out there, anyway?

"Be right back," Pawly said and laid the child on the pavement nearby. The tiger-like woman thrust and feinted with her wicked-looking spear. Pawly took to the air to intercept her opponent, bouncing off containers to gain momentum and altitude. She snapped one wrist and then the other to coax a short saber blade from each of her fighting sticks. Jamming their pommels into one another, she formed a kind of bladed staff. With both hands a blur, she twirled her weapon and landed behind her charge, snarling like a mother cougar protecting her cub.

That appeared to give Pawly's opponent pause. The tiger-looking woman growled and bounded off one of the bollards at the edge of the pier. She reached out toward the steel mooring line from a ship alongside and bellowed out a hideous, gurgling howl. Hands clasped over her ears, she flew headlong into the bow. After impacting with a loud *smack,* her body fell limp into the frigid water below.

Lenny tossed the empty bottle aside and drew his weapon. He scurried over to where Pawly stood scanning the water's murky surface. There was no sign of the tigress save for ripples emanating from where she had fallen in.

The black tip of Pawly's short tail swished back and forth. "Be careful, she's known for her feints," she said without looking up. "She might pop out again when you least expect her . . . " Her voice trailed off as she turned to meet his gaze. The tatters of her uniform top fell away, exposing her bare midriff beneath. She grabbed at their ends, and the few threads holding her sports bra together snapped.

He gawked at her trim yet shapely bosom, covered by fur several shades lighter than that on her face and hands. His eye caught the moonlight glinting off a shiny object on a chain around her neck. He leaned in toward a small silver bead stamped with the image of a lion and griffin above a scrolling banner with two words spelled out in tiny letters—*Semper Paratus!*

168

Pawly had given him the keepsake for his birthday before last. He mourned its loss after Chah Bahar, as it had always made him think of her. And now he realized she must have felt the same way. All along.

The little pendant disappeared from view an instant before she swatted his nose. "Pervert! We're on watch!" she said, scrambling to cover herself with the scraps of her top. "Nothing here you haven't seen before . . . well, except for the fur."

Lenny was about to stammer an apology when a man groaned nearby. He holstered his sidearm and gazed over toward where Pawly had laid the unconscious cat girl. Latharo lay about a dozen yards away, shakily propping himself up with his elbows.

After a dull *thump* and the sound of tearing cloth, he turned to see Pawly's bare back. She had plunged the blade of her staff into a wooden piling and, with her claws, tore a long swatch of fabric from her tattered uniform. "I . . . I have to go," she said over her shoulder while she bound her chest. "I can't let anyone see Stuie in the shape she's in."

"Th-that's Stuie?" Lenny gaped at the girl, lying with her face atop her outstretched arm. Though her bangs were a mess, the thick pigtails confirmed Pawly's assertion. "I trust him," he said and nodded toward his partner. "I believe you can, too."

Pawly shook her head. "No way. If you didn't know too much already, I would have never risked your safety seeing us like this. I won't risk his."

She stepped toward Stuie but stopped cold as Latharo got to his feet. The man stumbled over to the girl's side and knelt down, service piece lost in his trembling hand. "¿Salvación?" he said and pushed the hair away from her face. "¿De veras . . . que eres tu, mi hijita?"

"Oh, shit," he said before he felt the air move beside him. Pawly launched herself skyward, tracing an arc through the night sky toward where Stuie lay. "¡Déjala en paz, la mujer gato malvada!" Latharo said while he raised his arms and took aim.

Lenny drew his weapon and fired.

Chapter Twenty-Four

B RIGHT LIGHT BORE THROUGH her eyelids, flooding her vision with scarlet. Hana opened her eyes and looked to her right toward the rhythmic cadence of the EKG monitor. Next to it on a small table sat a glass vase containing a rhododendron sprig. She remembered sitting on the shore of Lake Chon last summer surrounded by thousands more like it. With a smile, she flexed her fingers to reach over and touch the sprig's brilliant yellow blooms, though her hand hardly moved an inch before a leather strap dug into her wrist. She wriggled her others limbs and discovered each of them were also bound fast to the bed.

"Oh, you're awake, my dear."

She turned toward Mawro after he entered the room. "Where . . . where are we?"

"Back aboard *Pe Gae Bong,* underway for Namp'o."

Hana craned her neck to her left and peeked out at the ocean through a solitary round porthole. "I was raging, wasn't I?"

"Yes," he said in a low voice. "Yes, you were."

"But the mission! What of the mission, Papa?"

"Whoa, whoa, whoa, slooooooow down. There will be plenty of time to debrief and strategize. For now, just let me look at you," he said and smoothed her hair away from her face. "I want to see that you're safe."

Her eyes misted over while the back of Mawro's paw rubbed against her bare cheek. It was only then she realized she had molted. "I must be quite a sight," she said, feeling her shed coat stuck to her skin all over her body.

"One for sore eyes, nonetheless, considering we could have lost you." His voice wavered while he loosened her straps. "I . . . could have lost you."

Her wrists free, Hana sat up and rubbed at the loose fur on her forearms. "What happened?"

"Suk and Park fished you out of the harbor with the semi-submersible after I ordered your Pearls' neurostimulators overloaded and . . . you blacked out."

Tears ran down her cheeks. "Papa, I'm . . . I'm sorry. I failed you. Again."

Mawro undid the straps around Hana's ankles. "You needn't be. Right after extracting you, we put out to sea."

"What about the container?"

"We left it behind."

Hana blinked. "I beg your pardon?"

"You heard me. No one should suspect us since it never reached the drop area. Those buffoons we hired to work with you aren't traceable back to the ship or to us. Besides, I'm sure CIA and ABW were all over it even before we cleared the breakwater."

"You needed that . . . that *thing*, Papa! The morpho . . . morpho-gen—"

"Morphogenetic Synthesizer, yes. I did think it necessary, true enough, but not anymore."

Hana crossed her arms. "And why not?"

Mawro drew his hands behind his head. "Well, it appears the Opoworos are better equipped to research our Affliction than we are."

Her brow knit. "I don't understand. Didn't you say their Kindred family members are too old to use as test subjects?"

"I did, but that was before I knew they had a youngling."

The bottom fell out of her stomach. "Th-they do?"

"You really don't remember, do you?" Mawro sighed and fixed Hana with a sad stare. "Yes, they do. In fact, I believe she was why you raged in the first place."

Emotions volleyed back and forth in Hana's mind. She had attributed her and the girl both being of Korean descent to mere happenstance. "Why? Who is she, then?"

Mawro tugged at the fur below his chin and stared out the porthole. "I'm not sure, but I intend to find out," he said at length. "For the record, I never liked the idea of using you as a test subject. Now I won't need to."

Hana opened her mouth to say something before the sound of bells blared through a loudspeaker outside the cabin door—four groups of two. "I must speak with the ship's master now," Mawro said after he turned to leave. "You stay here and rest. Get up from that rack for anything more than a trip to the head, and I'll put those binders back on you myself."

She grunted her assent before he pulled the door shut behind him. The sound of his sobs permeated the thin metal compartment walls as his footsteps trailed off down the passageway.

Lenny opened his eyes and yawned. The hospital waiting room was deserted save for a handful of people bringing Christmas cheer to their bedridden loved ones. He glanced down at his watch and frowned. Visiting hours would be starting soon.

He hadn't wanted to sleep this long. There was so much he needed to talk to Latharo about. And the fewer people around, the better. Lenny tugged at the growing stubble on his chin and considered his partner may well be still unconscious. Though the attending physician promised to advise him should his partner's condition change, there had been no news since.

Nothing to do now but wait. Any magazines or half-finished newspaper crosswords he might find lying about were bound to be in Polish. He loathed having little to think about besides being grilled by those assholes from the Inspector General. That is, whenever they saw fit to show up. Lenny's orders were to await their arrival here, though no one had said who would be meeting him or when. Being Christmas Day, they would certainly take their time.

He was sure to be the reluctant guest of CGIS once back stateside for quite some while. Would anyone believe he had shot his delusional partner solely in self-defense? Perhaps he would be certain only when his first steps back on American soil required no shackles around his ankles. OIG's final analysis of this incident would be moot anyway in light of what had happened at Chah Bahar. His career as a commissioned Coast Guard officer was as good as over.

He stood and stretched to work out the kinks in his back and neck formed after dozing off on the uncomfortable sofa. Lenny stuck his toes back into his boots and tucked their laces under each tongue rather than tie them. He clomped over to the vending area and stopped in front of a machine with a stylized graphic of a hot beverage above. Fishing a handful of *groszy* from his uniform trousers, he began to drop them into its slot one by one. The digital display counted up by fives, tens, and twenties until the credit amount matched the machine's largest cup price. He scanned the buttons to request a coffee regular and frowned. The writing beside each was in Polish, too.

Lenny stepped over toward the staffers behind the reception desk. Maybe one of them could help him figure out which buttons to—

He turned toward the whirring sound behind him. Pawly pulled a cup from the machine and held it out in front of her. "Fouh sugah 'n fouh cream to a lahge, jes like back in Bahsten deah."

Lenny chuckled and accepted the coffee. "You always know what buttons to press, don't you?" he asked after taking a sip.

Pawly shrugged. "It's a gift. Or a curse. Dunno. Just is." Her face fell. "It's . . . part of who . . . I really am."

She drew several coins from her pocket and fed them into the slot. "My ride doesn't leave until tonight." A moment later, she picked up a hot drink of her own and nodded toward the waiting room. "I thought you might . . . want some company."

Lenny took her hand in his and led her over to the corner farthest from the reception desk. There sat two overstuffed chairs with a small end table wedged between. He took a seat on one and motioned with his hand to the other. "You look . . . different," he said as she sat down and kicked off her shoes.

"Well, I, uhm . . . *changed* about two hours after you left in the ambulance with your partner." She sat down her cup and pulled her knees to her chin.

"No, no, that's not what I meant. I mean . . . your, you know . . . " Lenny rubbed his hands back and forth over his forearms.

Pawly glanced around before she mouthed *Fur?*

"Yeah, that. I . . . I saw you while I was at Bethesda. Sitting in the tree outside, just like you said." He drew a hand to his forehead and took a deep breath. "All this time, I thought I was hallucinating from the drugs they were pumping into me night and day." He laid his hand atop the arm of the chair and met her gaze. "But your, you know, your . . . outsides . . . .were lighter then."

Pawly tapped at her lip. "By the time they took you off your feeding tube, it was, what? March, April? I would have been . . . wearing my, uhm . . . 'spring coat,' yeah! Most people . . . like me . . . wear tawny colored ones all year, but they're always gray in winter."

Just like at Chah Bahar. Last night, too.

"The brass ordered the entire port searched." She reached over for her coffee, never taking her eyes off him. "It was nearly daybreak before they lashed the container down to the deck of the *Archer* and cast off. I, er . . . cleaned myself up and asked one of the ABW men where I might find you. He offered me a ride here."

"Is the rest of your family safely aboard ship?"

Pawly took a swallow and nodded. "We even managed to find the damn cat."

"How . . . " Lenny smacked his lips and tried again. "How is Stuie?"

She stared down at the floor, her cup lost in her hands. "I . . . I'm not sure. No one ever told me or Tommy . . . she was . . . "

He sipped at his coffee for some while, saying nothing.

"I'm tougher than I look, you know," she said at length. "You needn't have risked your career for me like that."

"It's been on borrowed time since our mission failed, Pawly. I . . . I was worried about you."

Her cheeks dimpled. "How ridiculously chivalrous of you. I'm pretty sure if your partner *had* fired, I could have walked off the shot."

Lenny slumped back in his chair and bumped the wall with the top of his

173

head. "He wasn't aiming to disable you. He was aiming to kill you. Lathro was . . . he *is*, I mean, Sally's father."

Pawly gasped and raised a hand to her mouth.

"Guess he mistook Stuie for Sally under the influence of whatever crazy shit that . . . woman . . . hit him with." Lenny reached out and shook her knee, coaxing her into making eye contact with him. "He probably found out about your . . . people . . . after Chah Bahar and thought you were in league with her or something. My partner had a bead drawn on your face, point-blank. The curtain was about to come down on your farewell performance, and you had no idea."

She sat down her cup and turned away. "Neither did you before I left Chicago," she said quietly toward the window, chin in her hand.

"Excuse me?"

She looked at him with misty eyes. "They were setting *you* up to take the fall. Forget about 'Conduct Unbecoming', I'm talking 'Misbehavior Before The Enemy'. That's a capital offense per UCMJ, Lenny!" Pawly hissed through bared teeth. "Would you have rather spent the rest of your life locked up at Leavenworth?"

He sat staring straight ahead for a long moment, too stunned to speak.

"I couldn't bear the thought of being forced to testify against you," she said at last. "Their case was weak at best without me."

"But . . . but how do you—"

"After Chah Bahar, I was sent back stateside to fill a billet on a security detail at Carderock Division HQ." Pawly snorted. "Guess they wanted to keep dibs on the Government's star witness. Your CO and those N2 pukes hatched the whole plan, puffing away outdoors one night at the hospital. They just happened to gather near the trunk of the same tree I liked to sit in while you slept."

"Wait a minute . . . " he said before his eyes went wide. "My room was on the fourth floor!"

"Let's just say I climb really well after I change. I sat outside your window for hours every night once they moved you out of ICU. Sometimes, I made it back to my place with only enough time to shower and jump back into my uniform before reporting for duty. As soon as I had my discharge papers in hand, I left. I . . . I had to."

"Why didn't you wait for me? I'm sure we would have figured out how to—"

"Do I need to draw you a fucking *picture*, Lenny?" Pawly covered her face and rubbed at her temples. "A civilian can be subpoenaed to testify at court martial, duh!" She glared up at him, nostrils flaring. "You would have pointed me out to them like a flashing neon sign."

Pawly cast a furtive glance around the waiting room. "After I was discharged, nothing prevented me from disappearing until after you were too. To subpoena me, they have to first serve me, right? And if they can't *find* me …" Taking his hands in hers, she brought her face in close. "I ran *because* I love you," she whispered in a quavering voice, "not because I don't."

He turned away in time to feel her lips brush the side of his cheek. "Pawly, I…"

Lenny turned to face her, instantly regretting his hesitation. Time slowed for a long, horrible moment while he listened to his heartbeat. She stared down to where her hands grasped his and clicked her tongue on the roof of her mouth. "I can hardly blame you, right?" she asked in a flat voice while she pulled her shoes on. "After all, I'm just a freak."

He got to his feet as Pawly thrust both hands into the pockets of her ski jacket and faced him. "Goodbye, Lenny," she said in a small voice, averting her eyes before she turned and walked away.

Lenny sprang to his feet and set off after her. "W-wait! I … I didn't mean—*whoa!*" Not two steps later, he stumbled in his loose boots, nearly wrenching his ankle. He caught himself on the back of Pawly's chair and dropped to one knee, cursing under his breath. Lenny hastily knotted his boot laces while she stomped through the vending area and disappeared around the corner without once looking behind.

The large sliding doors at the hospital's entrance opened ahead of Pawly as he reached the corridor. He was about to call to her when he heard yelling from behind. Over his shoulder, he saw several people dressed in scrubs racing toward him around an empty gurney. An ambulance squealed to a stop underneath the portico outside. A pair of paramedics threw the doors open and jumped out to meet the hospital staffers. A lump formed in Lenny's throat while he walked to the front of their vehicle and looked around. Pawly was nowhere to be seen.

He turned to continue searching for her but stopped short. "Lieutenant Lennart Reintz, US Coast Guard?"

"Yeah, that's me," he said to a black fellow with graying temples, one of the two men blocking his path.

"I'm Special Agent Samuelson with the Regional Security Office of the State Department in Warsaw." The man flashed his badge holder in Lenny's face. "This is Sergeant Gracia from the Marine Security Detachment," he said and motioned toward the other fellow. "Our orders are to secure you and escort you back to the embassy for debriefing with OIG."

Lenny let out a heavy sigh while trying to peek around Samuelson's shoulder. "Sir, I would like a minute for something very—"

"Son, a phone call at three-thirty this morning woke my family visiting from Alabama. Grandkids only let me leave after promising I'd find Santa before he got too far away and tell him they were all back asleep." The man nodded to his partner. "If you don't mind, I'd like to see what he brought them before our Christmas dinner gets cold."

"I am Sergeant Gracia of the United States Marine Corps." The other man grabbed one of Lenny's wrists in an iron grip and snapped on a handcuff. "I am investigating the attempted aggravated assault of DHS Special Agent Manuel Latharo, a violation of Article 128 Section B(1) of the Uniform Code of Military Justice, of which you are suspected. I advise you that under the provisions of Article 31, UCMJ, you have the right to remain silent . . . "

No time for this! I have to find Pawly!

The Marine cuffed his other wrist.

There's so much I want to say to her. Need to say to her!

His eyes silently pleaded with Samuelson, but to no avail. The man stepped forward and removed Lenny's service piece from its holster.

I . . . I love her!

A loud thumping coming from the back of the ambulance gave Lenny a start. Its crew turned off the flashing lights and drove away while the emergency team rushed their patient on the gurney back inside. Beyond, he spied Pawly as she reached for the door handle of a waiting taxi.

"Hey!"

The mirror image of his own bottled-up pain and longing returned his gaze when she turned to face him. The fateful night they had given themselves over to one another wholly felt like a lifetime ago now.

Pawly blinked and rapped on the taxi's window. After shouting through the glass at the driver, the taxi pulled away from the curb and sped off down the street. The men hustled Lenny toward their car parked opposite the portico at the hospital entrance. She ran up to the chest-high brick wall between the driveway and sidewalk, her eyes fixed upon his.

He laughed to spite himself, considering the surreal nature of their situation while they stuffed him into the back seat. Samuelson settled in up front for the drive back to Warsaw while his partner slammed Lenny's door. There was Pawly, her face separated from his by mere inches while she stared up at him through the back window. Gracia sat down behind the steering wheel and keyed the ignition. Red neon light from the sign above the emergency room entrance glinted off streams of tears running down her cheeks.

Lenny mouthed the words "I'm sorry" as the Marine put the car in gear and drove away.

"Me too," came her silent reply.

Afterword

THERE YOU HAVE IT, FRIENDS. I wanted to give back to the various anime/manga/anthro fandoms that have given me such joy these past three decades, that have enabled me to cultivate some of my closest and most intimate friendships. Writing this book (and working on the next two!) is my way of saying "thanks for the memories." I hope I've left you with some fond ones as well.

Many thanks for reading, each and every one of you.

ABOUT THE AUTHOR

BOYHOOD INTERESTS IN TRAINS and electronics fostered Mark's career as an electrical engineer, designing and commissioning signal and communications systems for railroads and rail transit agencies across the United States. Along the way Mark indulged his writing desire by authoring articles for rail and transit industry trade magazines. Coupled with Mark's long-time membership in anime, manga and anthropomorphic fandoms, he took up writing genre fiction. Growing up in Michigan, never far from his beloved Great Lakes, Mark and his wife today make their home in Wisconsin with their son and a dog who naps beside him as he writes.

Mark is a member of Allied Authors of Wisconsin, one of the state's oldest writing collectives. He also belongs to the Furry Writer's Guild, dedicated to supporting, informing, elevating, and promoting quality anthropomorphic fiction and its creators.

To learn more about Mark and his characters, or to sign up for his mailing list, please visit his web site at:

https://www.mark-engels.com/

He is glad to hear from readers via his site's contact form or via social media.

https://twitter.com/mj_engels
https://www.facebook.com/mark.engels.39
http://mjengels.deviantart.com/

Book reviews at Amazon, Goodreads and other online venues are so very important—and highly appreciated.